SEASON OF MALICE

AN AGE GAP, RUSSIAN BRATVA BILLIONAIRE
ROMANCE

LISA CULLEN

© Copyright 2023, by Author Lisa Cullen .

All Rights Reserved.

No part of this publication may be reproduced, distributed or transmitted in any form or by any means including photocopying, recording, or other electronic or mechanical methods except in the case of brief quotations embodied in critical reviews and certain other non commercial uses permitted by copyright law. Unauthorised reproduction or distribution of this work is illegal.

This book is a work of fiction. Names, characters, businesses, places, events, and incidents are either the products of author's imagination or used in a fictitious manner. Any resemblance to actual persons, living or dead, is purely coincidental.

This book is intended for adult readers only. Any sexual activity portrayed in these pages occurs between consenting adults over the age of 18 who are not related by blood.

DESCRIPTION

**He's old enough to be my father.
He might be the one who killed my boyfriend.
And I can't resist him any longer.**

Not only is my boyfriend dead, he left me with a sizable loan in my name to a mafia boss.
When Dimitri Federov, a handsome, loaded Russian playboy, appears on my doorstep, I panic.

He wants money to repay the debt. Money I don't have.

The prick offers me a solution - pay with my body. I turn him down flat, but the indecent proposal remains in my thoughts, forever reminding me of what could have been...

But when Dimitri turns on his charms, it gets even harder to resist him, and much easier to forget he's a ruthless kingpin... a *killer*.

And once I let him have what he so desperately wants, give into our desires and follow this basic instinct to its heady climax... There will be no stopping Dimitri's dark desires.

One night leaves me with the biggest secret of my life... and I have to make sure Dimitri never finds out he got me *pregnant*.

1

Camille

"No, no that's way too hot!" I shout, snatching the saucepan from the stove as I watch the creamy beurre blanc break before my eyes. Then I burst into tears.

Poor Louis looks like I might as well have slapped him across the face as his eyes widen with fear. "I'm sorry, Chef. I just turned away for a moment…"

He looks utterly crestfallen as my tears come hard and fast, spilling down my cheeks in a torrent. I can't help myself. Normally, I wouldn't cry over something so minor as broken sauce—even in the middle of the dinner rush—not when it's a simple fix of adding water while whisking to re-emulsify the butter. But the last two weeks have been some of the worst of my life. And that's saying something.

"It's f-fine," I stutter, wiping brusquely at my cheeks. "You know how to fix it?"

Louis nods his head vigorously.

Hannah, my best friend and front-of-house manager, steps into the kitchen at the commotion, and when her eyes find mine, her shoulders drop.

"Cami, go home," she insists for what must be the hundredth time.

But I can't. I'm the head chef—the only head chef at my restaurant, Le Fleur—and I have an obligation to see us through the Friday night rush, no matter what state I'm in.

Sniffling, I shake my head and step back up to the grill. "I'm fine," I insist, avoiding Hannah's stern hazel gaze.

She plants her hands on her hips and steps close to speak in a low voice. "You've suffered a major personal loss, honey. Nobody would hold it against you if you closed the restaurant for a few days—hell, even a week—if you need to. And I'm sure we would survive—broken sauces and all—even if you left us to run the restaurant without a head chef."

"I didn't *suffer a loss*, Hannah. Roy was murdered. Why else would the police ask if he had any enemies?" Fresh tears threaten to spill at the memory of that call notifying me that my boyfriend of two years had been found dead in a house fire.

The term 'suspicious circumstances' had been thrown around more than once while I'd bawled my eyes out, but no one had been willing to tell me what those suspicious circumstances were because of the pending investigation. Therefore, I'd been left to speculate and grieve all in one fell swoop.

"I know what you think, Cami. And I totally get it. I just think you're putting yourself under a lot of pressure trying to cook and run a business seven days a week when you haven't even had the time to process."

Sliding the pan-fried sol from the stove and plating it, I keep my hands busy. "I don't need time to process. Cooking helps clear my mind, and right now, the less thinking I do, the better. Besides, Daddy never took a day off, and I don't need to either."

"You're not helping your case with that last statement, hon," Hannah says dryly.

When I shoot her a withering glare, she puts her hands up in surrender. But I suppose she's right. My dad died of a massive heart attack before his forty-fifth birthday—probably due in part to the amount of stress he endured from working so many hours to raise me on his own and put me through college.

But opening this restaurant was Daddy's and my dream, and I won't let it fall apart just because my personal life has.

"I'm fine," I state definitively. "I'll be fine. You just go back out there and win over our customers. I'll get my act together in here."

Hannah releases a heavy sigh, then gives my shoulder a squeeze before heading back through the swinging door to the front of the house, her honey-blond ponytail swishing.

"The beurre blanc is ready, Chef," Louis says apologetically, stepping up beside me.

"Good, good. Thank you, Louis." I take the saucepan from him with a forced smile and finish plating the sol.

It's a long night of grueling work as the rush never seems to end, and after my meltdown, my eyes feel tired, my body heavy with grief. But we make it. At ten o'clock, I glance around the kitchen at my staff. They're cleaning up for the night, hauling dirty dishes toward Marie, our dishwasher, and sanitizing the stainless steel surfaces.

Wiping the sweat from my brow, I turn back to my own station to ensure it's spotless.

"Um, Cami?" Hannah says tentatively from the kitchen doorway.

"Hmm?" I glance up and immediately stop my cleaning from the look of apprehension that scrunches my best friend's face.

"There's a man out front who asked to speak with the owner."

"At this time of night?" I'm baffled. Usually, food critics would alert me to their presence before the kitchen closes, and I can't think of anyone I had an appointment with. "I'll be right out," I add, wiping my hands on my apron.

I scan my station to ensure I've turned everything off—a habit my father drilled into me as a child—then follow Hannah into the dining area.

It's empty and still, the soft jazz music trickling through the speakers sounding almost too loud without the din of customers eating and talking and laughing.

Brushing the stray wisps of auburn hair back from my face, I approach the host stand, and my heart skips a beat. The gentleman waiting there—a businessman from the looks of him in his fine-tailored suit and dark, wavy hair styled to perfection—is gorgeous. He must be over six feet tall with a trim, muscular physique. A healthy amount of facial hair shadows his strong jaw, calling attention to his lips.

Gray eyes meet mine as I approach, and a predatory smile lifts the corners of his mouth as he looks me up and down in a way that leaves me feeling exposed, almost naked. And though he looks nearly old enough to be my father, the appreciative gaze that comes to rest on my face once more makes my stomach quiver.

"Hi, I'm Camille Anderson," I state, my voice sounding more confident than I feel in this stranger's presence. Extending my hand as I close the distance between us, I strive for professionalism, even though he's asking for me at such a late hour.

"Dimitri Federov," he introduces himself, the hint of a Russian accent rolling off his tongue.

He accepts my hand, and rather than shaking it, draws my knuckles to his lips. His gray eyes never leave mine as he brushes a soft kiss over the back of my hand.

Gasping in shock, I pull my hand back quickly, balling my fist in an attempt to subdue the tingles that race up my arm. "How can I help you, Mr. Federov?" This time, my voice wavers slightly.

"Please, call me Dimitri," he insists, his low voice making my stomach quiver. Then the businessman's smile creeps higher as his eyes flash dangerously. "And I've come because your loan payment is overdue. I'm here to collect."

His soft, inviting tone is an utter contradiction to the words that leave his mouth, and for a moment, I stand frozen, not quite sure I heard him right.

"I'm-I'm sorry? You must have the wrong person. I don't have a loan," I state when I finally find my voice.

His dark eyebrows raise as if in mild surprise, but that smile never falters. "No? Then why does my paperwork put your business as collateral for a significant personal loan that is now overdue?"

Is that amusement in his voice? He must be joking. Irritation flares inside me. Whatever stunt he thinks he's pulling, I don't have the time for it. Or the energy. All I want to do is put on my comfiest pair of pajamas, curl up on my couch with my favorite chick flick, and mourn my dead boyfriend. But this jerk thinks tonight's the night to pull one over on me? I don't think so.

"I already told you I haven't put a lien on my business, nor would I ever. So, you need to leave." I force as much authority into my voice as I can muster, though my still-trembling stomach does nothing to help me.

"I have paperwork that would disagree with you, Miss Anderson," the handsome stranger states.

Scoffing, I plant my hands on my hips. "Alright then. Why don't you show me this supposed paperwork?"

"Gladly," Dimitri says. Then he gestures to a nearby booth. "May I?"

"Be my guest." I wave him toward it, though my tone would say he's anything but welcome in my restaurant.

The tall businessman sets his briefcase on the table and pops the clasps before withdrawing a document from inside. I take the opportunity to study his chiseled face, the hint of silver at his temples, looking for any underlying motive he might have. I can find nothing in his expression.

He skims the document as if to ensure it's the right one before flipping it to face me and handing it over. I snatch it from him with unnecessary sass and slowly lower my eyes from his to read the paper's contents.

The document looks official enough. And it outlines a loan for half a million dollars, putting *my* restaurant up as collateral. My blood turns to ice in my veins as I reach the bottom of the page and find a rather adept forgery of my signature. And next to it. Roy's. My boyfriend of two years betrayed me. Used me.

It appears he granted a lien on my business six months ago without telling me. Though what he needed half a million dollars for, I haven't the slightest clue. He never mentioned anything about needing a loan.

"This is my boyfriend, Roy. Not me. And he did this without my knowledge," I state flatly, shoving the condemning paperwork back toward Dimitri Federov.

"Yes, well, your boyfriend stopped making payments a few months ago, and my men have informed me that he was spending a lot of time at the casinos before that, so he probably gambled it away," he explains casually. "The contract states that failure to make payment entitles me to claim this restaurant as collateral. So, seeing as your boyfriend has stopped returning my calls, I've come to collect. You have two options, Miss Anderson."

He steps close to me, invading my personal space and forcing me to look up at him. My heart hammers in my chest. The masculine scent of leather and pine fills my nose as I inhale sharply, and I swallow hard.

A mere foot from me now, the man feels far more intimidating than I had realized upon first meeting him, and a shiver races down my spine. But I refuse to back up.

"Either you can pay me back in full, or I'll take your business," he states softly, his voice almost a caress, even as he threatens to take away my entire life.

"You can't do that," I say firmly, standing my ground. I lick my suddenly dry lips and glare up into Dimitri Federov's penetrating gaze. "I didn't even know about the lien, and besides, my boyfriend is... dead." My voice cracks on the last word.

Dimitri's face maintains the same calm, watchful expression, and I slowly realize with growing horror that he already knows. Cold terror seeps into my bones as a new thought comes to mind. If he already knows Roy is dead, does that mean this is the man who killed him?

As soon as the thought occurs, it solidifies as an undeniable fact inside me. Roy lost the money. He couldn't pay back what he owed, so Dimitri killed him. And now he's here to collect. If I'm not careful, he might just do the same to me.

2

Dimitri

The fear in Camille Anderson's striking features tells me she doesn't have the money. Who would? I'm not surprised that Roy Lochte went behind his girlfriend's back and took out a loan he couldn't afford. He seemed like a slimy git from the start.

But now that we're in this situation, I can't simply rip up the contract and walk away. My brothers and I don't make the kind of money we do by forgiving unpaid debts. We always collect, and that's why they send me.

Still, I have a few alternatives I could suggest for this alluring, voluptuous beauty if she doesn't think she can pay. Though I know my brothers would be pissed, I feel inclined to cut this enticing and fiery young chef a break.

"If you don't think you can pay the debt in full, I might be willing to let you pay it off in installments..." I suggest.

Immediately, the worry lines around her blue eyes soften, telling me her greatest fear is losing her business.

"You could compensate me with sexual favors," I suggest playfully, reaching out to touch a stray lock of auburn hair that falls from her messy bun. I mean it more as a joke. The stunning young woman looks nearly half my age. But still, the idea *does* appeal to me. If she were interested.

"How dare you," she demands, her cheeks turning a delicious shade of red as she takes a step back from me and bumps into the wall behind her. "I would never sell my body to you."

That last statement burrows under my skin in a way comments don't usually, posing a challenge that makes me eager to change her mind. "Not to me?" I press, moving closer once again.

"To anyone," she clarifies forcefully, her eyes snapping with cold fire. "And my business is perfectly capable of paying off the lien if you'll just give me more time."

"Hmm," I hum, considering the offer.

Camille takes a step to the side, moving away from the wall before retreating farther. "I can prove it to you," she offers, her voice growing urgent. "Just... just let me prepare something for you, and you can judge for yourself if my business is worthy of a long-term loan."

Amused by the suggestion, I shrug. "Alright. Impress me."

Camille releases a breath of relief, calling attention to her generous breasts, and I trace my eyes down her body once more. She's on the shorter side, with curves in all the right places, and when she turns to retreat into the kitchen, I can't help but follow the sway of her hips.

Unwilling to let her out of my sight, I join her in the kitchen, stepping through the swinging door a beat after she does. The staff members, dressed in chef's robes, cast curious glances in my direction, but none say anything as they go about cleaning the pristine space.

"How long have you been in business?" I ask, coming to rest beside the stove as Camille turns it on.

A startled squeak bursts from her as she jumps away from me and presses a palm to her ample breasts. "You scared me. What are you doing in here?"

"I want to see you work, watch the magic, know that my investment would be worth my while." My lips tug up into a wicked grin as she throws a thunderous scowl in my direction.

"Fine. Just don't touch anything... please." She seems to second guess her harsh tone and tack on the please at the last minute.

Lifting my hands to show I'll keep them to myself, I lean back against the counter so I can watch her cook. "You didn't answer my question," I state after several moments of silence.

Camille bustles around the kitchen, collecting supplies with a confidence she didn't have when we first met. And the sight of her in her element makes her that much more attractive.

"What question?" she asks, casting me a sidelong glance.

"How long have you been in business?"

"Oh, um, a little over a year."

Impressive. I'm aware of how well her restaurant has been doing in the culinary mecca of San Francisco. I did a bit of digging to learn its value when Roy first took out his loan—to ensure it would make appropriate collateral. But to rise so quickly after just a year in business? That takes talent.

Falling silent once more, I watch with interest as she pounds a piece of meat, her intent expression making me wonder if she's picturing my face beneath her tenderizer. After it's been thoroughly pounded, she seasons the meat before putting it on the grill. Then she moves on to the stove to start a sauce.

As soon as Camille appears to accept my presence, the rest of the staff do as well. I respect that. They seem to trust her as their employer and demonstrate that her opinion is both valued and taken without question. The kitchen staff swiftly finish their work and trickle out the back door, wishing the restaurant owner and chef a tentative good night as they go.

She goes the whole nine yards, cooking me a lamb cutlet drizzled with what looks like a cranberry sauce, adding caramelized carrots and fingerling potatoes as my side. She plates the whole thing like an artist, adding rosemary for garnish.

Then she gestures toward the swinging door, indicating I should lead the way.

I pick a table in the center of the room, one that still has silverware set, waiting for its next customer. Rather than following me directly, Camille stops at the bar, speaking in hushed tones to the bartender, who had been busy restocking a moment before.

He pauses to uncork a bottle of red wine and pours a glass.

With familiar ease, Camille approaches the table with my meal, and the sight of her makes my mouth water. Not just from the fact that my long day at the office delayed my dinner but also the way her blue eyes trap me in a daring gaze.

"Your dinner, Mr. Federov," she says smartly, emphasizing my last name as she sets my plate and glass of wine before me. "Lamb cutlet with a cranberry balsamic drizzle, glazed carrots, fresh from our garden, and roasted fingerling potatoes; paired with a 2016 cabernet sauvignon, for your pleasure."

She takes a step back and clasps her hands behind her, as if waiting for my verdict. And suddenly, I know she's dangerous. Because I find her entirely too appealing. And I'm supposed to be here on business, acquiring another restaurant for my family's considerable empire.

"Come sit," I say, pulling out the chair to my right and refusing to touch my food until she obeys.

After several seconds of hesitation, Camille slides into the seat beside me. Only then do I cut into the impressively tender meat and place a bite in my mouth. The explosion of flavor stuns me momentarily, and my chewing slows as I savor the best bite I think I've ever tasted.

Flicking my eyes toward the heart-shaped face beside me, I find a smile tugging at her bee-stung lips. She knows just how good she is. And that proud smirk might be the sexiest thing I've ever seen.

Following my bite with a sip of wine, I take my time relishing the culinary masterpiece she's put before me. I don't know how she can be so young and so talented all at once, but I would eat here every single day of the week.

"Well?" she asks nervously as I continue to sample my plate without a word.

"How old are you, Miss Anderson?" I ask, and though it's a forward question, I'm dying to know.

Color stains her porcelain cheeks. "Don't you know it's rude to ask women that?" she demands, her eyes flashing.

I chuckle, low and soft, enjoying her consternation. "I only ask because this is some of the best lamb I have ever tasted, and I've never met a chef with this level of skill at such a young age."

Her blush intensifies, and Camille drops her eyes to the table. "Well, thank you."

"You are... I'm going to guess twenty-five." She looks younger, but a man can hope.

Blue eyes snap up to meet mine, and then she narrows them. "I'll be twenty-five in June," she says slowly, her voice laced with suspicion. "How did you know?"

I shrug. "Lucky guess."

Camille purses her lips but doesn't argue. Instead, she watches as I eat another bite.

I swallow deliberately and turn to face her. "And you opened this restaurant by yourself?"

She shrugs one shoulder. "My friend Hannah helps me run it. She hires and manages the restaurant staff while I manage the kitchen. But yes, Le Fleur is *my* restaurant." She says the last almost possessively, reminding me of why I'm here.

Now that I've indulged in what's proven to be one of the best meals of my life, I need to get back to business. But before I do, I have to try something.

Turning to face the young chef, I take her hand and pull her close, moving Camille from her chair to my lap in one swift move. She has time to release a startled yelp before I capture her lips with mine.

Electric attraction sizzles like a live wire between us. She tastes faintly of balsamic glaze, tangy and crisp. And her soft lips yield to mine, molding to my kiss as if made for me. Her rigid body demonstrates her shock, and yet, as I tease her lower lip with the tip of my tongue, she does not pull away.

Instead, she seems to relax, her muscles releasing as I hold her close. Her lips part on a sigh, and I take the opportunity to deepen the kiss, so tempted by her sultry figure and delicious flavor that I have to try more.

We kiss for a long moment, and when Camille finally pulls back, she looks flustered in the best way. Her cheeks are flush with excitement, her lips red and swollen from my exploring touch.

She scrambles back into her seat, her blue eyes wide with confusion and shock. "What was that for?" she gasps, her breaths coming hard, her breasts rising and falling dramatically.

"I've decided to make you a new offer," I say calmly, ignoring her question. My brothers won't like the bold move, but I can't let Camille slip through my fingers. "Rather than taking your restaurant from you or making you pay back the loan in full, I'll buy your restaurant outright. I believe it is worth enough that I can pay you $1.5 million. Cash. We can take the amount of the loan from that. And then you and I will be business partners."

Her look of utter horror tells me her answer long before she manages to regain her voice. Her lips move silently for several seconds, opening and closing as if trying to formulate a sentence.

Finally, she gasps, "How is that in any way a business partnership? That sounds like you're just taking my business from me!"

"Only you would be a million dollars richer," I counter logically. "And you would stay on as head chef, managing your restaurant exactly as you have been for the last year. I would be a silent investor of sorts."

Camille's expression brews with a storm of fury, her eyes flashing like lightning, and her beauty in that moment is breathtaking.

3

Camille

"Absolutely not!" I object.

I take a deep breath and close my eyes for a moment, trying to calm myself because I know losing my temper won't help anything. My life could very well be on the line, and Dimitri Federov has already proven that boundaries mean little to him. Not to mention, he's clearly dangerous.

I picture poor Roy's final moments, probably as terrified as I am now, before he died at Dimitri's command. Whether it was by Dimitri's own hand or one of those men he sent to follow Roy, I have no doubt the loan shark before me is capable of murder.

My sympathy for Roy mingles with a newfound resentment, the emotions conflicting inside me as I think about how my dead boyfriend is the reason I'm in this position in the first place.

I can't believe he would do something so reckless with my restaurant. A business he knew meant so much to me. I trusted Roy, poured my heart out to him about my father and how much I wanted to open this restaurant in his honor. Roy knew this place was my dream, so the betrayal feels that much deeper. Roy used me, then abandoned me.

And now I'm stuck dealing with a man who's treating me like he owns the world. Like he can do anything he pleases—even kiss me. That it was practically in the same breath as him trying to intimidate me only furthers my angst.

Just the thought of that kiss brings it vividly back to me. I can feel his lips lingering against mine like a ghost. The way he boldly claimed me. An involuntary shiver runs down my spine. Terrified as I am to be in this situation, I couldn't help responding to his strong, confident touch. I lost myself for a moment in the overwhelming heat of his mouth on mine. The way his tongue stroked between my teeth.

Warmth pools in my belly once more at the memory.

"No?" Dimitri presses, bringing me out of my reverie, his lips curving into that devilish grin once more. His eyes tell me I'll change my mind before he's done with me. "Is the thought of working with me so unappealing?"

On the contrary, I find this man far more appealing than I should. But I can't lose my restaurant. Not because of some stupid loan Roy took out without telling me. *What did he even need the money for anyway? Is Dimitri right? Did Roy just gamble it away?*

My gut twists at the notion. It also makes me feel far less guilty for the undeniable attraction I have toward this dark, menacing stranger.

"This is *my business*, Mr. Federov," I state, intentionally using his last name to try and get my brain back on track.

"Not for much longer, it would seem to me." Dimitri's eyes dance playfully.

Is he toying with me?

I get the sense that it's not just money he's after. If it were, wouldn't he be willing to accept my payments as willingly as he did Roy's? Then again, he knows just what to say to make me squirm. No, this man is skilled at putting on the pressure to ensure he receives the money he's owed. And he's come to take everything from me.

I'd heard about the Russian crime families around San Francisco before; the men willing to play high-stakes games when it comes to lending because they could always take what they're owed in pounds of flesh if needed.

And I've unwittingly fallen into one of their snares.

"Please, this restaurant is everything to me," I beg, feeling the walls closing in around me.

I can't lose Le Fleur. It's everything I've worked so hard for. It's all I have left to uphold my father's legacy, to honor his memory. Leaving it in the hands of some greedy mob boss would go against everything my father believed in. He was about hard work and honest pay, about having a passion for what we do and changing the world through our love of cooking.

How could I possibly maintain that under the ownership of a man willing to kill my boyfriend over an unpaid debt? Yes, I'm furious with Roy for putting me in this position. It hurts to know how deeply he betrayed me. But I can't just hand over my life's passion. Or my integrity.

There has to be another way.

"Let me make payments," I plead, coming back around to my original offer. That was the whole point of me cooking Dimitri a meal anyway, and now he's refusing to give me an answer. "Even though I haven't spent a dime of the money you loaned Roy, and frankly, I don't consider it my debt to repay, I'll do it."

I hold Dimitri's intense gray gaze as I make my case, placing my hand flat on the table to steady my resolve.

"If you give me the time, I can pay back the loan. I will."

Dimitri's eyebrow raises in speculative amusement, and he studies me silently.

"Honestly, I feel like it's the least you can do," I press when I can't take his silence any longer, "considering you're the one who made a bad bet on the loan in the first place."

"And how was it a bad bet?" he asks, his amusement growing visibly.

"Well, because apparently, Roy didn't plan to pay it back," I snap, then rein in my temper before it gets me into deeper trouble.

Dimitri releases a rich, melodic chuckle that makes my skin tingle.

"From where I sit, I think I placed an even better bet than I had anticipated," he says, his eyes bright with laughter.

"But..." I don't even know how to complete my question. My body's doing strange things, leaving my brain muddled and my stomach in knots. This is all just too much.

"You see, Miss Anderson, when I signed off on the loan entitling me to this restaurant should Roy Lochte fail to pay me back"—his eyes scan the room, taking in all that he intends to claim—"I had no idea *you* were here. That is why I've offered to buy you out of the contract. I can see you're quite... talented. And I rather like the thought of having you beneath me."

Fire licks up my belly, and I gasp at the complete lack of propriety.

"As manager of my restaurant, of course," Dimitri tacks on. His gaze brims with suppressed mirth.

"Of course," I grit through my teeth.

"But if you're sure you don't want to sell..." He leaves the sentence unfinished, dangling the carrot expertly before me.

"Le Fleur is not for sale," I state adamantly, slapping my hand on the table.

"Well, then, I don't see why I shouldn't consider your offer. I'll tell you what, I'll think about it and get back to you. In the meantime, promise me you'll reconsider *my* offer. It's more than generous, considering the predicament you're in."

Speechless, I watch as Dimitri finishes his glass of wine, wipes his mouth, and sets his napkin beside his empty plate. Then he rises from his seat, buttoning his designer suit jacket as he goes.

"Deal?" he asks as I rise with him.

I intend to lock the door firmly behind him.

"Yes, fine," I agree, though I already know I won't change my mind. Not after years of dreaming this restaurant into existence.

"Good."

Then the tall, muscular loan shark closes the distance between us. One strong hand glides around my waist to find the small of my back. The other cups the back of my head as he pulls me firmly against his broad, solid chest.

I don't have time to think. Time to breathe. As Dimitri leans in to steal another kiss, all I can do is freeze. His lips find mine, their warmth sending fireworks of excitement racing across my skin.

The passion with which he kisses takes my breath away, and my knees feel suddenly weak, my strength vanishing in his iron grip. Despite myself, a soft whimper escapes my lips, and Dimitri's curl into a wicked smile as his fingers comb up into my hair. At the same time, his tongue dances out to tease the crease of my mouth.

Stroking between my teeth, he tastes me deeply, and I shiver violently at the fire that erupts deep in my core. Mafia boss he may be, but this man can kiss better than anyone I've ever known.

I shouldn't want this. I *can't* want this. He's toying with me, showing me that he can take what he wants when he wants it, and I can't do anything about it.

Flattening my palms against his ridiculously muscular chest, I push purposefully against him. He doesn't resist, allowing me to force space between us and break our kiss, though he keeps his hand solidly on the flat of my back.

Probably a good thing, considering my knees are shaking so hard I don't know that I can hold myself upright.

"What do you think you're doing?" I hiss, my fury evident in my tone.

Dimitri chuckles, slowly releasing me to take a step back. Gripping the back of the chair beside me, I try to ground myself. Because I am far more attracted to this man than I should be. His kisses set my soul on fire, and I hate it.

"That's how I like to close deals," he says playfully, his accent growing more pronounced in his distraction as his eyes rake appreciatively down my body once more.

"I highly doubt you kissed my boyfriend before signing the contract for that loan," I counter, crossing my arms over my chest as I attempt to throw him off balance the same way he keeps destabilizing me.

Warm, spine-tingling laughter rises from deep in his chest, the sound filling the room like music. Dimitri's chiseled features soften with his broad smile, revealing straight white teeth. "You're right. Generally, I save kisses for the beautiful women who sign their souls over to me," he says as his laughter dies down.

Anxiety turns my stomach into knots as my heart hammers in my chest. Those words hit all too close to home. Because I've offered to make a deal with the devil himself, all but selling him my soul in a bargain to keep my restaurant.

With a polite nod, Dimitri straightens his elegant red tie and turns toward the door. The bell tinkles lightly as he vanishes into the night. And for a moment, all I can do is stand and stare.

Goosebumps erupt across my arms as I realize how much danger I just put myself in. Not only did I most likely come face-to-face with Roy's murderer, but I also dared to challenge him to defend my restaurant. And now, I'm promising to pay him money I don't have over God only knows what kind of time frame.

What have I done?

4

Dimitri

"In other words, you have nothing?" Maksim demands, his voice gruff and unforgiving.

"Relax, big brother. I've got everything under control," I insist, leaning against the corner of his desk as I attempt to wriggle my way out of an argument in the middle of our weekly family meeting.

Alexei tosses a stress ball from hand to hand as he watches silently from the modern leather couch in the office's corner. A mischievous grin parts his lips, and I roll my eyes at him. Leave it to my baby brother to find my tongue-lashing amusing.

"That contract is well overdue. And unless you plan on bringing Roy Lochte back to life, I don't see your angle on this. Please explain why we don't currently hold the deed to Le Fleur." Maksim demands, steepling his fingers as he plants his elbows on his desk.

"You look like a villain when you sit like that," I tease, smirking.

Maksim growls, dropping his palms onto the mahogany surface and rising from his chair. "You have a weak spot for the chef, is that it?"

My smile falters ever so slightly before I force it back into place. Leave it to my brother to see right to the heart of the matter. Maksim's too perceptive for his own good—or for my good, at least. I only wished that keen insight might extend to his money-grubbing model of a fiancée. But so far, no luck.

"Whether I find Camille Anderson attractive or not has nothing to do with the offer I made," I insist, not being entirely truthful. If she were a sixty-year-old man with a receding hairline and a ruddy face, the odds would have been a lot slimmer. But I didn't make the offer *just* because I find her incredibly beautiful and enticing.

Alexei snorts, and both Maksim and I shoot him death glares. Our baby brother holds his hands up in surrender, always willing to concede business matters when it comes to the family empire. He could care less about which restaurants we own or who we lend money to. Alexei's interests are more security driven, which is why he's in charge of our company's surveillance and security team. We only insist he joins these meetings so we can keep him in the loop.

Shaking his head with a sigh, Maxim studies me. "Perhaps you're too close to this one," he suggests. "Maybe I should take over the restaurant acquisition and let you focus on a different project if you can't handle this one professionally."

Grinding my teeth, I fight to rein in my irritation. Snapping at Maksim will only support his suggestion that I'm too involved. "If you think it's best," I state casually once I have my temper under control. "But I assure you, my offer is in the best interest of our company. This chef is exceptional, and I can tell she won't give up her restaurant easily. Taking it from her could make her walk, and that's the last thing we want for business."

It's a convincing argument, and while it's not the whole truth, Camille is a rare chef. It would hurt our acquisition considerably to lose her.

Alexei raises an eyebrow in silent applause, seeming to appreciate my new angle of defense. I turn my eyes from him pointedly, not really interested in how well he thinks I'm supporting my argument.

I want this, and frankly, I rarely push for business decisions because I trust Maksim's eye for profit. But this time, I know I'm right. And even if I weren't, this is *our* company. I have earned my place in it, same as my brothers.

"She's that good, hmm?" Maksim asks, watching me closely.

"She received high praises in *San Francisco Flavors*, and she's been open for less than two years. Yes, she's that good. Consider it an investment to woo her into selling rather than taking the restaurant from her." Sensing weakness, I push off my brother's desk to face him directly.

Maksim chews the inside of his cheek and looks down at the paperwork on the desk beneath his palms. "How much did you offer?"

"One point five."

His gaze snaps back up to mine, his gray eyes holding that same familiar look of disapproval we all inherited from our father.

I shrug. "She's worth more than the debt Roy owed us. And I couldn't very well offer to buy it from her for a blank slate. That's essentially taking the business as the collateral we're due. A million to keep a chef I guarantee will earn that back in profits within a year or two."

"I don't like betting profits on the success or failure of a chef's talent. Restaurants, we can make successful or turn a profit by selling the real estate. You're asking me to put a million down on a bet that one girl is going to make waves in an industry that's already strangling itself with new restaurants popping up every other week. Most of them fail." Maksim's flat, entirely logic-based delivery grates against my nerves.

"Her counteroffer was to pay us back in installments." I don't like the thought of taking money from Camille. Not after it became clear that she didn't even know Roy took out a loan in her name. But more than that, it frustrates me that Maksim is so rigidly against my offer.

And whether he wants to back it or not, I intend on sticking by the investment. If I can get Camille to sell, I'll do it with my own money. Because I want her. Even if I shouldn't.

"How much did she offer to pay?" Maksim asks, intrigued.

"She didn't say, but she seems confident her profits could afford it. I want her to accept the sale, though. In the end, I promise it will be a better business call. And I have ways of putting on the pressure. I can get her to sell."

No one's ever turned me down when push came to shove, and I could see it in her eyes the other night. I was getting to her. It's only a matter of time before I wear her down.

From the corner of my eye, I can see that smirk return to Alexei's face as he shakes his head. The sound of the stress ball snapping back and forth between his hands only winds me up, and I turn to glare at him once again.

A light tap on the door cuts our meeting short.

"Come in," Maksim commands, standing upright and combing his dark hair back off his forehead.

A moment later, Symphony struts in, her long legs showing off the golden brown of her fake tan. Dressed in bedazzled heels and a black bodycon dress that only covers the bare essentials, my brother's fiancée flaunts her stuff without shame.

Blond hair coifed to perfection, and wearing enough makeup for a photo shoot, Symphony looks more like a Barbie doll than a model. But I guess that's what some guys are into. Not me. I like natural curves and porcelain skin that glows without all the creams and powders. Like Camille. That girl has natural beauty in abundance.

"Hey, boys." She greets me and Alexei with a casual flick of her fake nails on her way to Maksim's desk.

Alexei rises from his seat on the couch, mimicking my thoughts exactly. *Meeting adjourned.*

"We're not done talking about this, Dimitri," Maksim states as Symphony wraps her arms around his neck, leaning into him with an affectionate purr.

"Yeah, yeah." I give him a half wave over my shoulder and shut the door behind me. In the meantime, I intend to take that as a silent agreement.

"So, a chef, eh?" Alexei asks, nudging my elbow with his ribs.

"Why do you insist on annoying me like a child?" I gripe, giving him an affectionate shove.

"Well, I am the baby."

"You're thirty-eight."

"Yeah, but Maksim acts enough like a stick in the mud for both of us, so I don't see why I have to."

I snort, rolling my eyes at Alexei. My younger brother's always been the wild one of us. He may be lethal, but it's nearly impossible to get him to take life seriously. He would rather party with girls on yachts and fly to Ibiza for the weekend than think about growing the company.

Not that I blame him. He throws one hell of a party. And when it comes to personal security, he's the best there is.

"You like her?" Alexei presses, refusing to be deterred.

"She's beautiful, intelligent, and knows how to stand up for herself," I admit as we make our way toward the elevator. "But that doesn't mean I have feelings for her. This is about the business she's sitting on and our best strategy for acquiring it."

I seem to be doing a bad job of even convincing myself. I want Camille. From the moment I laid eyes on her, she hooked me with her curves, her sharp blue eyes. And once I got a taste of her, I wanted so much more.

I shouldn't have. One kiss was all it took to lead me down this path. And as much as I want to argue the point with my brothers, my interests are anything but professional.

Still, I can't get her out of my head, and taking Camille's restaurant from her will slam the door on any potential we might have.

"You've got it bad," Alexei observes with a smirk.

I give him another shove as the elevator doors open with a ding, and Alexei stumbles inside.

"Aren't you coming?" he asks as I turn to continue down the hall.

"I'm taking the stairs," I state, flipping him the bird over my shoulder.

Laughter follows me through the hall until the doors close, carrying my brother down the fifty floors to the lobby. I love my brothers. But some days, I want to knock their heads together. Both for different reasons.

Maksim because he feels the need to control everything and Alexei because he prefers chaos to any world order. But mostly because they can read me like a book. Try as I might, I didn't manage to convince either of them that my reasons for buying Le Fleur are legitimate.

And maybe my judgment is clouded when it comes to Camille.

But I don't intend to let that stop me.

5

Camille

"This is where the tickets print," I state, pointing to the simple machine that sits just over my head at the start of the line. "We take the yellow copy. White copy goes through the window to the food runner, and you're the last line of defense when it comes to ensuring everything is plated and ready to go. Only pass the yellow copy through when you're certain everything is good to go."

"Yes, Chef." My chef-in-training, Hank, seems smart enough.

I've already walked him through the layout of the kitchen and grilled him on how he cooks meat and manages the staff around him. It may have taken me weeks to give in to Hannah's nagging, but I've finally caved and hired a second head chef—just for a few slow nights during the week.

After losing Roy and not having someone to step in for me, I've come to terms with the fact that I need help. And the restaurant can afford it. We're making good money, so it's time to relax my grip on the reins. Just enough to prevent burnout should another situation arise.

Now that the decision is made and Hank's here, training, I can't say that I hate my decision. It'll be nice to have the time to catch up on things. Maybe even spend some time cooking creatively so I can change up the menu some. However, the thought of handing over my prized possession, even for a few nights a week, is rather nerve-racking.

I'm trying not to be one of those hovering mother hens who pick at every little detail. And so far, Hank hasn't disappointed. But this is only his third day.

"Um, Cami?" Hannah pops her head through the swinging door, a cheeky grin on her face. "That hunky businessman is back and asking for you."

My stomach drops. I know exactly who she's talking about. That's how she's been referring to Dimitri for the past week. I couldn't bring myself to tell her all that had happened. I'm still trying to process that it's real.

"Thanks, Hannah. Hank, why don't you take a lunch break?" I suggest.

"Sure thing, boss." He flashes me an easy smile, and I'm grateful that, on top of what has proven to be a solid set of executive chef skills, Hank seems like a go-with-the-flow type of guy.

Unlike the man waiting for me out front.

Removing my apron, I straighten my dress and take a deep breath, bracing myself for another round with Mr. I-Get-What-I-Want-When-I-Want-It. Shoving down the nervous anticipation that bubbles deep inside me, I remind myself that this is the man who killed Roy. And now he's here to take my restaurant from me. But I won't let him.

Following Hannah through the swinging doors, I follow her fingers as she gestures toward the bar and the immaculately dressed Dimitri Federov.

"I'll be up front rolling silverware if you need me," she says, giving me a quick wink.

Tension coils in my chest as I approach the large and rather intimidating Russian. He leans against the bar, a mug of fresh-brewed black coffee from Le Fleur cupped in his hand.

"Miss Anderson," he greets, flashing a dangerous smile as soon as he sees me approach. "Good morning."

I glance at the clock above the bar and note that it's eleven o'clock. Hardly morning anymore in my book, but I keep my thoughts to myself. And my hands. I'm not about to make the same mistake twice and go for a handshake.

"Mr. Federov. What brings you in today?"

Dimitri runs a long finger around the rim of his steaming mug. Then his gray gaze shifts playfully back to mine. "I'm here to take you to brunch."

I scoff, crossing my arms over my chest. "And what makes you think I have time for brunch? I need to prepare for the dinner rush tonight."

"And you're the only one who can do that?" he counters, glancing around the restaurant.

I shoot him a withering glare, maintaining several chairs' worth of distance between us so I can keep my head on straight. "My staff is well-trained, if that's what you're asking."

"Well then, I'm sure they can chop a few vegetables without your supervision." Dimitri stands tall as if it's decided and sets his half-empty mug toward the inside edge of the bar. "Thank you for the coffee, Trent."

Our Friday-night bartender gives a polite nod and flashes a friendly smile as he continues to set up his workstation. He seems completely at ease with the loan shark gangster he just served coffee to. Not a care in the world. Oh, to be naive of what's really happening here.

"Come," Dimitri commands, closing the distance between us.

I swallow a gasp as his hand finds the small of my back, and he guides me toward the front door with an air of confidence that turns my insides to Jell-O.

"Everything alright?" Hannah asks, pausing her work.

No. I'm being carted from my restaurant by a murderous loan shark who's threatening to take my business from me unless I accept his ridiculous bribe. "Yes, it's fine. Um, I'll be back before we open. Will you keep an eye on things; make sure all the prep work is finished in time? And maybe send Hank home? I'm not sure how long this meeting might take."

I glance up at Dimitri, but his silent amusement tells me nothing.

"Sure thing," Hannah agrees, her smile bright and knowing, like she thinks I'm ditching work for a date or something. "Have fun!" she calls as the bell rings above us, announcing our departure.

She definitely thinks I'm going on a date. I, on the other hand, wonder just how smart it is to allow this treacherous man to take me somewhere unfamiliar. At least he knows he has to have me back before the restaurant opens if he wants to avoid suspicion. Though I don't get the sense that this 'brunch' is a ploy to take me somewhere secluded and kill me, I hope.

Right out front, next to the curb, sits a sleek black Lamborghini with paint that glitters like starlight in the bright California sunshine. My jaw drops as Dimitri reaches for the passenger-side door and opens it for me.

"Shall we?" he suggests, holding his hand out as if to help me into the car. But his steely eyes tell me this is anything but a request.

Swallowing nervously, I pull my mouth shut and slide into the front seat, clinging to the hem of my skirt to avoid flashing him and purposefully ignoring his offered hand. Dimitri releases a low chuckle before closing the door behind me and making his way around the front of the car.

"You're coming after my restaurant when you drive around San Francisco in a car like *this*?" I demand as soon as he slides into the driver's seat.

The masculine scent of his cologne fills the small space as he closes the door behind him, making my mouth water as it brings back the memory of his lips on mine in a flash.

"People don't get rich by being soft and letting others walk all over them. Whether you like it or not, the deal was agreed upon, the terms set before we gave your boyfriend a dime. And he chose to offer up your restaurant for the loan," Dimitri says rationally, his tone smooth and even, seemingly unbothered by having to explain the situation to me yet again.

Then he puts his car in gear and glides out into the bustling city traffic. I gasp as he weaves his way toward the left lane and floors it, launching us forward. Gripping my knees tightly together, I swallow my heart and try not to show my fear.

"Where are you taking me?" I demand as we fly down the street toward the Golden Gate Bridge. My palms start to sweat as I picture some abandoned location with a shallow pre-dug grave.

"I told you, brunch." Dimitri flashes me a cheeky grin.

"We've already passed five perfectly decent brunch places," I point out, my voice quivering. I don't like the fact that he's taking me outside the city. Everything in me screams that I should run. This man is dangerous. I was an idiot to get in his car.

As we leave San Francisco, the city vanishing behind us along with the iconic bridge that serves as my best landmark of home, the car starts to slow. We pull off the highway, and I'm still debating whether we're rolling slowly enough that I could jump. Maybe if I make a run for it, he won't be able to stop the car or turn around to follow me before I find somewhere to hide.

Hand twitching toward the door handle, I peer out the passenger-side window, and my heart skips a beat. I know where we are. A moment later, Dimitri pulls into the parking lot of the Galley, an upscale restaurant that serves the best brunch in Sausalito, if not San Francisco itself.

Daddy and I used to come here for special occasions—like when I graduated from high school or got my acceptance letter into the hospitality program at USF. Caught off guard by Dimitri's choice, I pause, and suddenly, it's too late. He pulls into a parking spot right near the door and kills the engine.

"Hungry?" he asks.

My stomach answers for me, releasing a resounding rumble that makes Dimitri's lips curl into a smile. In my line of work, grazing is the standard meal of the day. So I haven't eaten anything yet. I prefer to taste things here and there, allowing for quality control without overindulging.

But the Galley?

I don't know how to resist. My fury over being taken from my restaurant against my will dims slightly as Dimitri leads me inside the fine dining establishment. And I remind myself that Hannah is more than capable of ensuring that the kitchen is fully prepped and the restaurant ready for me to walk in the door. She's done it before.

Dimitri gives his name to the host, and though a slew of patrons occupies the waiting area, we're escorted directly to a table looking out over the bay. Someone had to pull major strings for this. Even when Daddy booked reservations a month in advance, we weren't guaranteed such prime real estate.

"Two mimosas, and keep them coming," he says to the host before they depart, unconcerned with the fact that she didn't ask for our drink order.

She gives a nervous nod and scampers off toward the kitchen.

"I have to work tonight," I point out dryly.

Dimitri levels me with a daring gaze. "Is it tonight?"

I flush. "No."

"Is your boss going to fire you?"

"I don't have a boss," I snap. Only then do I see the pitfall he guided me into so easily.

Dimitri smirks, his perfect lips curling across his chiseled face. "That would be just as true if you sold your restaurant to me, you know. I don't see the harm in a few mimosas before work."

I'm half tempted to show him just how dangerous day drinking could be for a chef. But I don't want to hurt my own business just trying to prove a point. Instead, I lift my menu pointedly, blocking him from view.

"Your mimosas," our server says a moment later, setting the champagne flutes before us. "Are you ready to order?"

"I'll take the Galley benedict," I state promptly, giving the young server my menu. It's what I order every time I come here.

"Very good. And for you, sir?" the server says, turning to Dimitri.

"I'll have the same," he says, cocking an eyebrow at me as he hands over his menu as well.

"Right away." Our server strides briskly away.

From the look on his face, I half expect Dimitri to ask if I've been here before. My answer hovers on my lips, a snarky reply ready to be fired. Instead, his gray eyes study my face for several long seconds, then skim down my body to the red dress that fits me like a glove.

I prefer to wear business attire during the day, when I might have to meet with other industry professionals, then change into my chef's robes before work. Still, I like the stretchy fabrics that make movement easy because my job requires constant physical labor. And though the long sleeves and high neck keep me modest, I suddenly feel exposed, as though the thin fabric is far sheerer than I had realized when I left my house this morning.

"Sell Le Fleur to me," Dimitri demands, his tone insistent and yet playful, as if he knows just what I'll say next.

"No." The rejection leaves my lips before I even know I'm saying it.

Dimitri chuckles, low and dark. "Have you even considered my offer?"

I scoff. "Have you considered mine?" I counter, leaning back and crossing my arms.

"Of course," he says, his eyes dancing.

"And?"

"I would still prefer to buy your restaurant. It's a good deal, one you would benefit from greatly," he states.

"And if I don't want to sell?" I challenge him because I sense that the choice he's offering me isn't much of a choice at all. If I don't sell, he'll take Le Fleur from me without a second thought. The possibility sends my heart hammering against my chest, and a trickle of sweat runs down the nape of my neck.

"Then your payment is overdue," he states calmly.

My pulse flutters. Does that mean he'll accept payments over time? I can't get a read on Dimitri. Everything he says sounds like a cryptic message I have to translate before understanding the full ramifications.

"What kind of payment do you expect?" I ask, holding my breath as I pray he doesn't say a number over ten thousand. While that would be a stretch, I could dip into my savings to make it happen.

"Sex in the bathroom would satisfy me." He tilts his head casually in the direction of the Galley's restroom hallway.

My blood turns to ice in my veins.

I swallow down a wave of panic.

"Excuse me?" I ask, my voice breathy with anxiety.

The low chuckle that rumbles from deep in Dimitri's chest is all the answer I get. Heat pools in my stomach at the dangerous sound.

"That is not... I *will* not..." Words sputter from me as I struggle to find how to tell him no, even as my body lights on fire at the thought of it. "I can give you five thousand dollars as my initial payment," I state finally, redirecting the conversation before I lose my last shred of dignity.

"I'll accept that," Dimitri says simply, his lips twitching with amusement. "Though I must say, I would prefer to get a taste of you."

Leaning forward to rest his elbows casually on the table, Dimitri levels me with a smoldering gaze, and suddenly, I can't breathe. I can't think.

What did he just say?

6

Dimitri

"Excuse me?" Camille gasps, her blue eyes widening in shock.

I love the color that stains her cheeks. A delicate red over her creamy complexion. I can't get enough of teasing her. Normally, I don't have to work for girls, but I like this game. Camille's pride and determination to keep me at arm's length makes her all the more attractive.

Because I like the chase.

"You can't just go around saying that kind of stuff to people," she hisses, leaning in closer, as if afraid the restaurant staff might overhear.

A smile tugs at my lips. "And why not?"

"Well, let's start with the fact that you're trying to take my business from me. You can't possibly think I would accept your advances when you're practically blackmailing me for my restaurant." Her eyes narrow into an accusatory glare.

The word blackmail sounds ugly as it leaves her lips, and though technically I'm well within my rights to take her business, I don't want to argue about the contract her boyfriend signed. "Maybe not. But I do find the challenge you present rather... diverting."

Camille's fiery defiance gives her an almost regal pride as she draws back from the table once again. "Challenge?" she repeats, shock evident in her tone.

"Women don't usually turn me down," I state matter-of-factly.

Her perfectly shaped eyebrows press together in a frown, and Camille stays silent long enough that I start to wonder just what's on her mind.

Finally, when she speaks, her tone rings with resentment. "Is this just some game to you?"

"On the contrary, I take my business very seriously. But like I said, your resistance is very distracting."

Her lips part as if to argue, but before she can respond our food arrives.

Camille leans back to give the server plenty of room, and he sets our plates on the table before us.

"Anything else I can get for you?" he asks, glancing between us.

"No, thank you. This looks delicious," I state, never taking my eyes off Camille.

Her cheeks turn scarlet, and the server departs with a polite bow. As soon as he's gone, Camille snatches her mimosa off the table and downs the whole thing in three large gulps.

I'm getting to her.

And I like it because she gets under my skin without even trying. Those sultry blue eyes and kissable lips, her ample curves. I really would like to taste her again, the sweet honey flavor of her mouth. I want to sample more of her.

As she cuts into her benedict and takes her first bite, I find I'm jealous of the fork that glides between her lips to deliver her food.

"You've been here before?" I ask as I turn to my own plate. But I already know the answer. I could read it in her face the moment we pulled into the parking lot.

Camille clears her throat. "My father and I used to come here."

"Used to?" I press.

"He died. A few years ago." I can hear the pain in her voice, and she keeps her eyes focused pointedly on her food.

"I'm sorry." And to my surprise, I genuinely mean it.

Her sadness strikes a chord with me, and though I have no clue how her father died, I feel an intense urge to comfort her.

"You were close?" I observe, posing it as a question to see if she'll open up.

She nods, setting down her silverware though she's hardly touched her food. A moment later, the server places a fresh mimosa beside her empty champagne flute and clears the spent glass from the table. She gives him a grateful smile and swallows a generous amount of juice-flavored bubbly as soon as he leaves.

"Do I make you nervous?" I ask, watching her closely.

Camille stills, her fingers lingering on the stem of her champagne glass. Then she quickly busies herself by cutting another bite of benedict. "Well, we haven't exactly started on the best of terms," she hedges before placing her fork between her lips.

She chews delicately, truly savoring each bite in a way few know how.

I consider her for several seconds, finding her candor both interesting and something to appreciate. "You don't need to fear me, Camille," I state. The sensual feel of her given name rolling over my tongue for the first time awakens my senses.

I don't offer that luxury to just anyone. My business thrives on people's fear of what I might do to them if they don't pay their debts. But for some reason, I dislike the thought of scaring Camille. Maybe it's because she's so clearly been a victim of her deadbeat boyfriend. Still, I want her to trust me, to let down her guard so we might explore this intense magnetic pull I have toward her.

A visible tremor ripples through her body, and Camille swallows hard. She gives a nod of acknowledgment before returning her eyes to her plate.

Though I intend to continue wearing Camille down on the sale of her restaurant, I let her eat her brunch in peace. Instead, I keep the conversation light, asking casual questions about her life—where she grew up, what she enjoys doing with her free time, who she spends that time with.

It quickly becomes apparent to me that cooking isn't just what Camille does. It's integral to who she is. And she spares little time for relaxation or hobbies. No wonder she didn't know about Roy Lochte's gambling addiction. The girl works constantly. She probably didn't even know he vanished into the casinos for days at a time.

When our meal is over, I drive Camille back to Le Fleur, and whether it's because of the two mimosas she downed in that time or the casual conversation, she seems to lose some of the tension in her body.

"Thank you for brunch," she says as I help her out of my car and onto the sidewalk in front of her restaurant.

"My pleasure." I flash her a smile and gesture that she should lead the way inside.

She does, seeming relieved as she turns and makes a beeline for the front door. I follow her through the restaurant and down a back hall painted a rich blue and lined with elegant sconces. Reaching a door halfway down the hallway, Camille opens it and slips inside.

Amusement tugs at the corners of my lips. She didn't expect me to follow her.

My suspicion is confirmed a moment later as I join her in the tiny office space and close the door gently behind me. "Cozy," I observe, eyeing the cluttered desk that occupies the middle of the room, the filing cabinets tucked snugly into the far corner.

Camille releases a terrified shriek and whirls to face me. "What are you doing here?" she demands. "You shouldn't be back here. Get out!"

I chuckle as she closes the distance between us to try and herd me from the room.

"Just what do you think you're doing anyway? Why did you follow me in here?"

"I didn't get a proper goodbye," I tease, my eyes flicking down to her lips as I recall our first encounter. I know it's wrong—mixing business with pleasure, tempting myself with someone so much younger, pursuing Camille when she only just lost her boyfriend—but she's just too alluring.

Her breath catches in a quiet gasp as her insistent shoves slow to a stop, and Camille swallows hard. Her blue eyes find mine, emotion churning in them, though I can't quite decipher what it is she feels.

"Let me take you on a real date," I insist.

Her eyes widen in speechless surprise as she takes a slow step back.

"Just because you don't want to pay off the loan with sex doesn't mean we can't have fun together," I coax, closing the distance between us to gently cup her chin.

Her lips part as if to say something, and I give in to temptation, slowly tracing the enticing line of her lower lip with the pad of my thumb.

"I'll be a complete gentleman," I murmur, tipping her chin as I slowly close the distance between our mouths. But I don't kiss her. Not yet.

Wanting to draw out the delicious tension humming between us, I peer deep into her eyes, silently promising her a level of pleasure she's never known before.

For a moment, I hover there, mere inches from her lips, our eyes locked in a silent battle of wills. I can see the conflict and indecision in her gaze, the war between her pride and her attraction to me. Because she has to feel it too. This connection between us is molten and electric.

Guilt flits through me as I admire the youthful vibrance of her face. She's old enough to make her own decisions, but still considerably younger than me. Perhaps I'm taking advantage of her vulnerability.

I hesitate, torn between my need for her and the instinct to keep her safe. From the world. From me. But before I have the chance to rein myself in, to stop myself from pursuing my carnal desire, she kisses me.

Rising onto her toes, Camille closes the distance between our lips. Heat rockets through my chest as our mouths collide in a scintillating kiss. Her talented chef's hands press against my chest, this time curling around the lapels of my suit to pull me closer.

I groan like a starved man taking his first bite of food in days as her tongue traces between my teeth, deepening our kiss. Combing my fingers into her auburn locks, I cradle the back of Camille's head with one hand, my other finding her hip.

Slowly exploring the curve of her waist, I encircle her with my arm, pinning her against my chest. Camille gasps into my mouth as our bodies meet firmly, and my cock hardens in an instant.

Tongues twining as we explore each other hungrily, Camille and I kiss with newfound passion. All her hesitation and resistance seem to have vanished, replaced by a seductive need that lights my blood on fire and sends it pounding through my veins.

"I fucking *want* you," I growl, my hands moving to explore her body as I walk her backward until her hips find the edge of her desk.

Breath heaving from her lungs, Camille guides my hand from her hair, down the curve of her neck and collarbone to cup her full breasts. I knead the supple flesh, a ravenous groan ripping up through my chest as she releases a sexy moan.

Finding her lips once more, I consume the fiery chef with an eager need. For as much resistance as she's given me, I know without a shadow of a doubt that she wants this too. Because she's kissing me with just as much passion, her back arching as she presses adamantly into my palm.

And when I grind forward, pressing my erection against her soft flesh, she releases another soft groan. Her arms snake up around my neck, pulling me closer still, and I take the opportunity to explore her curves, running both hands over her hips to grab her round ass.

Then I lift her, spreading her legs as I wrap them around my waist, and set her gently onto her desk. The stretchy fabric of her dress slides up her thighs to accommodate me, stopping at the bend of her hips. The sight of her exposed flesh drives me wild, and I can't help myself.

Finding her knee, I slowly run my hand up her silky leg until my fingers slide beneath the hem of her dress.

Releasing a growl of appreciation when I realize she's wearing a thong, I palm her bare ass, and Camille gasps into my mouth.

"You're so perfect," I rasp against her lips. "I want to be inside you."

And to my utter astonishment, Camille nods.

7

Camille

Fire sizzles through my veins as Dimitri's strong hands explore every inch of me. The feel of his large palm cupping my breast, the urgency with which he grips my ass, the iron rod of his arousal pressing against me. I've never felt so alive.

And as he wraps my legs around his hips, lifting me onto my desk as if I weigh nothing, wet excitement soaks the thin lace of my panties. Because as terrifying as Dimitri might be, he's also intoxicatingly sexy.

I can't stop thinking about Dimitri's words at lunch, the acknowledgment that when I reject his advances it almost fuels his persistence. *I find the challenge you present rather... diverting. Your resistance is very distracting...*

It gave me an idea.

What if I can use his interest in me to my advantage?

I refuse to be his whore, to pay off a debt I don't owe by selling my body to Dimitri. Though he clearly isn't backing down from the idea of buying my restaurant—or wanting to have sex with me. But maybe if I give him what he wants, he'll be more willing to let me pay off the loan over time.

It could also help me get close to Dimitri—close enough to learn how Roy really died. And if I can find evidence that Dimitri killed my boyfriend, I can take it to the police. If Dimitri gets arrested, I might just be free of Roy's debt entirely. Because surely Dimitri wouldn't be able to enforce the contract from jail.

Spurred by the liquid courage of two mimosas over brunch, I acted on my momentary boldness when I saw my window of opportunity. And now, as I lose myself in the overwhelming electricity of Dimitri's touch, I think my half-cooked plan might just work.

The thought of it lights a fire inside me, and suddenly, I don't feel bad about giving in to the desire pounding through my veins. I can't deny that Dimitri excites me in a way I've never known before. His hands explore me with an expertise that promises the deepest sense of satisfaction. *So, what's the harm in taking a bit of pleasure while I dig myself out of this monstrous debt Roy left me?*

"I want you to say it, Camille," Dimitri rasps as he grinds more adamantly between my thighs.

God, he says my name like a caress, the soft curve of his Russian accent making it sound beautifully exotic, and I shiver as warm arousal pools deep in my core.

"Say what?" I gasp before kissing him deeply once more.

His tongue strokes between my lips in a tantalizing imitation of how I want him to penetrate me—demanding and greedy, just like I feel.

Then his fingers wind into my hair. They curl around the roots, making my core throb. And when he gives a slight tug, forcing my head back so I have to meet his eyes, an involuntary gasp of pleasure parts my lips.

"Tell me you want me to fuck you," he commands. Then, keeping a tight grip on my hair, he leans in to trail a scintillating line of kisses down my throat to my collarbone.

"I want you inside me so badly," I whimper, my pussy throbbing with anticipation.

Tingling relief races across my scalp as Dimitri releases my hair, intensifying the pleasure as his hand slowly works its way down my body, touching and kneading, stroking and teasing every inch of me as it goes.

His other hand keeps a strong grip on my ass cheek, holding me steady on the edge of the desk as my legs turn to jelly. As he reaches the hem of my dress, his fingers tease the flesh of my inner thigh, tickling the soft skin with his feather touch.

I suck in a shuddering breath, my arousal consuming my mind as I suddenly forget my plan. All my thoughts focus on my sudden and intense need for him to bring me relief, to ease the pressure building deep inside me like a volcano.

His hand moves beneath my dress, finding the peak of my thighs, and I gasp as his fingers hook around the skimpy fabric of my panties. Then two thick digits stroke between my folds.

"Like this?" he teases, tracing my wet slit before pressing his fingers inside me.

It's not nearly enough, and yet a wave of pleasure ripples through me as my walls clamp greedily around him.

"More," I beg, gripping the back of his neck and pulling his lips to mine.

He kisses me with a fierce demand, his tongue claiming my mouth with the same provocative rhythm as his fingers penetrating me. I whimper as he finds that hidden spot inside me, the one that makes me want to cry out every time he hits it.

Using his thumb to circle my clit, Dimitri sends electric pleasure crackling through my body. Tingling excitement numbs my fingers and toes as I barrel toward an orgasm with alarming speed.

"Tell me what you want, Camille," he breathes, his deep baritone vibrating through me like an earthquake.

"I want to come," I whimper, clinging to him as my body hums with the intense need for release.

"Then ask me nicely."

"Please—fuck—let me come!" I plead, shuddering violently

against his palm. My hips buck with urgency, nearly lifting me off my desk.

"Come for me, *kotenok*," he purrs, his thumb crushing my clit.

Like that, I explode around him.

Pussy throbbing, I grip his fingers like a vise, pulsing with an intense orgasm as my clit twitches euphorically. Biting down hard on my lower lip, I stop myself from screaming. Because I only just manage to remember where I am and that I'm not the only one at the restaurant right now.

Dimitri continues to punish my clit, his fingers stroking deep inside me until every drop of ecstasy has been milked from my body. Physically spent, my muscles relax as an overwhelming sense of contentment seeps through me.

"You are so sexy," Dimitri rasps, his voice hoarse with the effort to show restraint.

My eyes flutter open to find his gray ones smoldering with unsatiated hunger. And in an instant, my desire flickers back to life. I'm in trouble. Because this man is dangerously good at what he does. He knows just how to touch me, and those eyes undress me with an insatiable need that tells me we're only getting started.

Slowly, he eases his fingers out of my dripping pussy, and arousal coats the inside of my thighs.

"You still want more, *kotenok*?" he teases, his eyes dancing.

But two can play this game, and now that I've placed a wager, I'm not about to back down. Taking the hand he just fingered me with, I slowly guide it to my mouth, keeping my eyes trained on his all the while.

Air hisses between his teeth as I part my lips to press his slick fingers into my mouth. My own tangy juices coat my tongue as I lick his fingers, sucking my excitement from them.

"*Chertov*," he growls in Russian, sending a fresh spike of adrenaline coursing through my veins.

I don't know what he just said, but I find the sound of it entirely too delicious.

Then he's leaning behind me to sweep the mess of documents

and office supplies from my desk. Pencils ping off the walls and papers flutter to the floor in a jumbled heap. But I don't care. The movement brought his strong chest forcefully against mine, and in the same movement, he laid me back across my desk.

"Tell me what you want," he demands again.

And this time, I won't play coy. Because I've never wanted sex so desperately in my life. "I want to come on your cock," I murmur, biting my lip as my skin ignites with fresh need.

Dimitri releases a snarl, his strong, beautiful face intense with desire. Leaning on top of me, he presses my body against the firm surface of my desk as he kisses me deeply. I can still feel my slick arousal on my lips, and knowing that he must taste it lingering on my tongue sends my body into overdrive.

He groans appreciatively, consuming my lips with spine-tingling fervor, and his hips grind forward, spreading my thighs until I feel his erection like an iron rod against my lace-clad clit.

Then his hands are sliding beneath the elastic fabric of my dress. Pushing it up over my hips, he exposes my lacy thong, red to match my color of the day. His fingers hook around the waist of my panties, and he guides them down over my hips and fleshy thunder thighs, as Roy used to call them.

I don't have time to feel self-conscious as Dimitri works the lace down past my shoes. My fingers are too busy working to undo the belt and zipper of his pants. As soon as I'm done, he's shoving the fine fabric down over his hips, taking his boxers at the same time.

His cock springs free, and I gasp, breaking our kiss to stare down at the impressive girth of him. I've never seen someone that large before. A flicker of nerves flutters to life in my belly as I wonder if he might be too big.

Long fingers comb into my hair, and Dimitri's thumb aligns with my jaw as he tips my head so I meet his eyes. The intensity of his gray gaze silently asks the same question he's demanded from me twice now. *Is this what I want?*

And though it wasn't initially my motive for starting down this sinful track, I find that I want it far more than I should. I want to feel just how good sex can be. Because already, Dimitri has proven a skillful lover. He knows exactly how to turn me on and excite me.

"Fuck me," I plead. "Please," I add, when his eyes flash dangerously.

"I don't have a condom," he states like the last line of defense before we take this past the point of no return.

"I'm on the pill."

Leaning me back onto my desk once more, Dimitri trails kisses down my throat to the collar of my dress. Then, as he stands tall. His hands travel down my body, tracing the curve of my waist and out over my wide hips. He grips each thigh before hooking my legs around his waist. Then he grasps my hips and jerks me forcefully to the edge of the desk.

A startled squeak bursts from me at the unexpected movement. But as my ass hovers just on the precipice, I feel his hard cock, the silken head brushing against my slit. The thick tip parts my folds, and I shudder with anticipation as he finds my entrance.

Then he presses inside of me.

I gasp at the intensity of the way he stretches me, filling me like I've never known before. It's almost painful, and yet every inch deeper seems to awaken a new tingling arousal. And when he finally comes to a stop, I can hardly believe I can fit all of him. My pussy throbs with the erotic sensation of being almost too full.

"You feel so good," he rasps, his fingers digging into my hips with urgency.

"So good," I whimper in agreement.

And then he starts to rock.

Slowly at first, he eases in and out of me as if to give me time to acclimate. And I need it. Brilliant bursts of tingling pleasure crackle up my spine and out to my extremities every time he presses deep. And as his pace increases, so do the jolts of pleasure.

"You like that?" Dimitri rumbles, his voice teasing.

But I'm so far gone, I don't even care. "Yes!" I gasp, my head tipping back as my eyes roll up into my head.

"Are you ready to come, *kotenok*?"

"Yes. Oh God, please," I moan, trying to keep my voice low through my lust-addled thoughts.

Dimitri's thumb finds my clit a moment later, and he starts to circle the sensitive bundle at the same time as he fucks me. His penetration steadily grows more adamant with each thrust. And as his cockhead finds my G-spot, I feel myself climbing quickly toward a second orgasm. Something no boyfriend has ever taken the time to make me achieve.

As if sensing my quickly approaching climax, Dimitri softly pinches my clit between his thumb and finger. Rolling it lightly, he elicits a shocking combination of pleasure and pain that releases my orgasm before I even know it's time.

A silent cry parts my lips as I arch off the desk forcefully. The air vanishes from my lungs as I convulse with the intensity of my pleasure, and I shudder as heady euphoria sends stars exploding across the backs of my eyelids.

Walls throbbing around his cock, I milk him hungrily, my body begging him to go deeper, to stretch me and fill me until I scream with pleasure.

Dimitri groans, the sound laced with agony. And when I finally reclaim my senses enough to open my eyes, I find his muscular neck taut with strain, the veins bulging.

"Does it hurt?" I ask, confusion rising in the fog of my ecstasy.

He shakes his head, and a thin smile curves his lips. "On the contrary, you're making it very hard not to come."

I frown as fragmented thoughts flash through my brain before I can follow through to voice them. Finally, I latch onto one. "You don't want to come?"

A deep chuckle rumbles from Dimitri's chest, reverberating through me and causing a ripple of aftershocks that make my clit throb. Air rushes between his teeth as he inhales sharply, and the smile vanishes from his face. Fiery lust takes its place, making my core shiver.

"Then why..." I start to ask, still trying to understand.

"I like watching you come," he rasps. "To feel your tight little pussy gushing over me."

He rocks his hips forward to emphasize his point. And though he's still almost too big for me, he glides easily inside me from how wet I've become.

"Are you ready to come with me this time?" he teases playfully.

"Yes," I whimper as he pushes inside me to the hilt, leaning forward to wrap his arms around my waist.

"Good," he murmurs. Then he lifts me from the desk.

In one fluid motion, his cock slides out of me. My feet barely touch the ground before he spins me to face away from him, and I gasp as he bends me over the desk. He flicks the hem of my dress up over my curves, exposing my full ass. One strong hand kneads my cheek as the other pins me to the flat surface.

"You have the best ass," he praises, showering it with affection.

Then he gives it a sharp slap.

I yelp, shocked by the unexpected strike. As my skin flames beneath his palm, a deep, dirty desire turns molten in my core. I've never been spanked before, and I never knew how much I wanted it until this very moment. But as Dimitri holds me captive, claiming my body for his own, I find myself craving his punishment as much as I do his praise.

Terrifyingly vulnerable, I breathe heavily, my sensitive nipples pressing painfully against the wood. I flatten my palms against the cool surface and relish the feel of it under my burning face. Then his cockhead, still slick with my juices, finds my entrance once again.

8

Dimitri

The sight of Camille's full, round ass bare and waiting before me makes my balls throb with painful need. It's taken all my self-restraint not to claim her hard and fast, to fuck her as forcefully as I want.

But I could feel it as soon as I entered her.

Camille has never taken anyone as large as me. And in truth, I don't think she's had cock in some time. Because, fuck, she's tight. Almost too tight, but most definitely tight enough that I just about lost my mind with the need to be inside her.

Still, I want her to enjoy every second of this. I want to make her scream my name and keep begging me for more. I've never seen such a sexy woman. Never felt someone unravel so completely around me. And I'm ready to make her do it again and again.

If we weren't on something of a time crunch, what with Camille having to get back to work, I might be tempted to see just how many times I can make her come. But I suspect she wouldn't like it if one of her staff members walked in to find me fucking her across her desk.

Keeping her pinned to its surface with one hand, I knead her other bare ass cheek, then deliver a second spank to even out the pink handprints that mark her flesh. This time, Camille moans, and a trickle of fresh arousal coats her slick folds.

"You like that, dirty little *kotenok*?" I tease, relishing the way she shivers every time I call her a kitten in my native tongue.

Camille bites her kiss-swollen lower lip and nods against the desk's surface.

"You want more?" I tempt, letting my cockhead stroke between her folds to spread her increasing wetness.

"Yes," she moans.

I give her a third spank, and she gasps.

"Yes, what?" I demand, kneading the quickly reddening flesh.

"Please," she mewls.

"Good girl." Stepping between her feet, I force her to spread her legs farther apart, fully exposing her pussy to me. Then I run my fingers up and down her glistening folds, using her own arousal to tease her clit.

Camille sobs, her legs vibrating as I edge her closer to a third orgasm. But I stop just shy, relishing her devastated whimper when my touch disappears. I won't make her wait long though. I'm so close to coming, I don't know that I can last much longer, and I want to come with her this time.

Guiding my cock to her tight entrance, I ease just the tip inside. Then, shifting to grip her hip with one hand and keeping her bent over the desk with the other, I thrust inside her balls deep. This time, she can't seem to contain herself.

Crying out, Camille trembles as her pussy tightens around me. I reach around her hips to tease her clit with my fingers, coaxing her toward another release. Simultaneously, I move inside her, and this time, I can't hold back.

I fill her with each thrust, my cock swollen and almost painfully hard with how good she feels. Her tight, wet pussy clenches around me with each relentless penetration, as if begging me to come inside her.

"Oh God, I'm gonna come!" she gasps as the pressure builds at the base of my spine.

My balls tighten, and her breathy words nearly undo me.

"Say my name," I command, driving into her hard and fast.

"Dimitri," she moans, and her lips part in a beautiful O as her pussy explodes around me.

The sound of my name on those tantalizing lips is all it takes. Like pulling a trigger, I shoot inside her, shoving into her depths as I come hard. Burst after burst of hot cum fills her. Camille throbs around me, her pussy fluttering with her own release as her clit pulses against my fingers.

Heavy breaths gasp from us as we twitch together, and I fill her so full that cum oozes out around the base of my cock and drips down her sexy slit. I can hardly believe the intensity of my orgasm.

Our first time together was hot and fast, but just from this small taste, I know I want more.

I want all of Camille.

I want to take my time.

And I want to make her come all night long. To touch her in ways she never imagined and make her darkest desires come true.

Because now that I know just how delicious she is, I don't think I'll ever get enough of her.

But this is not the time or place. I didn't even check to see if her office door has a lock, and I know we're not the only people here. Still, I couldn't help myself. As soon as she kissed me, I had to have her. And when she said she wanted me too, no one on God's green earth was going to stop me.

As our breathing calms, I slowly ease out of her. Taking a step back, I release her from my grip, and she rises shakily to her feet. Our eyes meet, and a wicked smile stretches across my lips. Her breathy laugh makes my cock twitch with fresh desire, even though I've only just had her. I can't wait to do it again.

But not now. Reaching down, I tuck myself back into my pants and zip them, then deftly buckle my belt. Not a moment too soon, either, as a knock comes at the door.

"Fuck," Camille hisses, quickly trying to straighten her dress by smoothing it over her hips. She kicks her panties beneath her desk—no time to put them back on.

"Cami?" someone asks, turning the handle before peeking her head inside.

It's the same blond hostess who greeted me the first night I spoke to Camille.

The affectionate nickname surprises me somehow, and as I swiftly comb my hair back into place, I sneak a glance at the voluptuous chef standing beside her desk. Camille suits her better—full, soft, and sexy, just like her.

"Hey, Hannah, what's up?" she asks, surreptitiously trying to straighten her mussed hair. Fortunately, it was up in a messy bun to begin with, so it doesn't look too suspicious.

"Everything alright?" Hannah asks, her hazel eyes narrowing in concern as her gaze flicks toward me.

"Fine, fine," Camille assures her, smoothing her dress down nervously, once again.

"Okay," Hannah says hesitantly, though she drops it. "Is this a bad time?"

"No, not at all. Dimitri, er, Mr. Federov was just leaving." Camille flashes me a smile.

"Right," I say, a grin tugging at my lips at her obvious dismissal.

"Oh. Great." Hannah steps more confidently into the room now, leaving it open for me.

"I'll see you again soon, then," I say, raising an eyebrow playfully at Camille but willing to keep her secret.

"Yeah, absolutely," she agrees, an adorable blush coloring her round cheeks.

"Ladies." With a slight incline of the head, I exit the room, closing the door behind me.

That may be the first time a girl has ever excused me after sex, and while I could consider it demeaning, somehow, I only find

Camille's feisty side that much more appealing. She doesn't shy away from saying what she wants. And I'm left with no doubts that she prefers to keep her image professional at work.

I can respect that.

Especially after seeing just how naughty she can be.

Better to let her staff think she's as disciplined as she had me believing after my first impression of her. I can keep her dirty little secret all for myself.

Making my way back down the hallway and into the restaurant, I see myself out. All the while, plans for the next time I'm with Camille float through my brain. Because sex with her has only made me want her more. So when I see her again, I intend to make it a proper date. A lavish one where she can experience everything I have to offer.

And to top it off, we can finish the night at my penthouse. Seeing just how wild she can get between the sheets.

The bell jingles over my head as I open the door and step out into the San Francisco sunshine. Though it's the middle of June, a brisk coastal breeze still cuts through the air, bringing with it the salty smell of the bay.

I inhale deeply, taking a moment to appreciate the perfection of this day. I knew I would enjoy brunch at the Galley—seeing as my family owns it, and we only buy the best restaurants in town. But I didn't go into the day expecting to have sex with Camille.

On the contrary, I was only hoping to take a small step forward in our potential relationship. But she surprised me when my teasing flirtation turned into something real. She kissed me. She wanted to have sex. That was the last thing I had anticipated. And definitely not sex of that caliber.

Releasing my breath of fresh air, I glance across the street as movement catches my eye. And the smile that had stretched across my face moments before falls away.

The glass door of the designer clothing store swings open, and I immediately recognize the slender, middle-aged man who steps outside. Dark hair slicked back from his face, Aleksandr Volkov looks as oily as he is.

Flanked by two burly henchmen who wear twin scowls, Aleksandr looks less like the Bratva *pakhan* I know him to be and more like a business tycoon who's scared of his own success. Not that I can blame him. Owner of San Francisco's two best-known casinos, the man is not afraid to step on toes.

He's put himself firmly on my shit list over the last year with the purchase of not one, not two, but three of the restaurants I've had my eyes on. Whether he's doing it intentionally or has simply developed a taste for the profitable business of acquiring fine-dining establishments, I don't know.

My hands ball into fists as our eyes meet across several lanes of traffic, and I get the sudden, overwhelming sense that he gets a kick out of pissing me off. Because, as his dark gaze lingers on mine, a slow smile spreads across his face.

I bristle instinctually, suddenly territorial as his gaze flicks up toward the fancy cursive script that reveals Le Fleur's name. Embossed across the red brick below are the golden words 'Fine French Cuisine.' They all but mark a bull's eye on the business I'm so eager to acquire.

The smirk that follows turns my stomach to lead as Aleksandr gives a mocking nod. Then he turns to walk down the street without a care in the world. It takes no time for his slight frame to disappear behind the looming figures of his two bodyguards.

But as I watch his swiftly retreating figure, I get an ugly sense of foreboding.

And just like that, my perfect day is shattered.

9

Camille

"That looks great, Hank. Excellent." Standing back and letting my fully trained executive chef run the kitchen is harder than I thought, but tonight, I'm testing if he can manage on his own.

So far so good.

Hank, a man in his early sixties and born in New Orleans, knows a good amount about French cuisine—albeit with a definitive Cajun twist. But he was a good hire. A fast learner and a well-organized mind, he runs my kitchen like a tidy ship, and the staff seem to like him as much as I do.

And now, he's proven he can handle a busier-than-normal Sunday rush without needing me to step in.

"Thanks, Chef." Hank takes the time to flash me a brilliant white smile as he plates the bouillabaisse.

"Cami?" Hannah asks, stepping into the kitchen.

I know what she's going to say as soon as I look up. Taking a second to glance at the clock, I note that it's nearly nine o'clock—past the worst of our dinner rush. Good timing.

"He's ba-ack," Hannah singsongs, a grin stretching across her face.

I roll my eyes. Dimitri has stopped by every night for over a week now to ask when our real date might be, and I keep putting him off. It seems sex with him worked better than I had intended, at least as far as bringing him closer is concerned. He's persistent. I'll give him that. And has a silver tongue.

"You're good on your own for a few?" I ask Hank.

"Yes, ma'am." He gives me another bright smile. That combined with his southern accent makes him feel so familiar and friendly. He reminds me of my father in a way, and it makes my heart twinge with loss.

"Sexy Russian Businessman has been here to see you every night this week," Hannah whispers conspiratorially as she stays close to my side, joining me on my way toward the host stand. "Are you finally going to go on another date with him?"

"That was not a date," I insist, thinking back to the brunch he forced me to join him for... then the passionate sex in my office that followed.

As soon as Dimitri left, Hannah was on me, asking what had happened and if we'd kissed. Apparently, it was evident on my face. Thank God she didn't ask if we had sex that day. Because I can't keep a secret from my best friend. She knows when I'm lying.

"Come on. He clearly likes you. You deserve to take a night off. Let him wine and dine you. Roy never did."

"That's because I work nights, Hannah. And Roy and I did stuff..." Though not in a while.

In the past month, since learning of Roy's death and then following it up with the knowledge that he went behind my back to put my restaurant up as collateral, I've done a lot of reflecting on that relationship.

Roy and I had some good times. Especially in the beginning. But our relationship wasn't exactly the healthiest toward the end. Not when I worked all the time and Roy hardly seemed to notice. Before he died, it'd been over a month since we'd even had sex. Being with

Dimitri had brought that knowledge to the front of my mind. Because Roy and I had *never* had sex like *that*.

"Yeah, okay," Hannah teases sarcastically as if picking the thoughts right from my brain. "All I'm saying is you deserve to have a little fun. And that man looks like a very good time."

Laughing, I give my best friend a playful bump with my shoulder.

Hannah walks me to the table where Dimitri's sitting for the evening. He's tried something new each time he visits, awakening my creativity by asking me to cook whatever I'm inspired to make.

"Camille," he greets me from his booth, his eyes flashing appreciatively when I meet his gaze.

"Back again?" I tease, easing onto the bench across from him.

Hannah keeps walking, casting a quick wink over her shoulder as she leaves us alone.

"You still haven't told me when I can take you on a proper date," Dimitri points out.

"I'm working on it," I hedge. Though with Hank fully trained and seeming completely comfortable in the kitchen, I suppose it's about time I let my new chef try a night on his own.

"Well, in the meantime, I don't see the harm in sampling all Le Fleur has to offer," Dimitri says, his eyes skimming down my body to remind me that he's sampled *me* as well as the food. "After all, I'm still holding out hope that you'll change your mind and agree to sell the restaurant to me."

And there it is. The persistence that I can't seem to get away from. The constant reminder I am in debt to this gorgeous Russian mobster and my best way out of it is to play his game by turning it to my advantage.

Get in, get close, learn what I can about how Roy *really* died, then turn Dimitri over to the police so I can get out from under the loan. My nerves tingle as I think about just what my plan entails.

Though we haven't had sex since that first time, I can't get that day in the office out of my brain. And my body, at least, seems fully on board with the concept of sleeping with Dimitri again. Hopefully, that will deter his relentless offers until I can be rid of him completely.

"It's not gonna happen," I insist. "So you can stop hoping."

Dimitri leans conspiratorially toward me in his seat, making my pulse quicken. Lowering his voice to a whisper, he says, "I always get my way in the end."

I swallow hard, my skin lighting on fire as he gives my body another bold appraisal. But I refuse to fall for his flirtatious banter. "Well, not this time," I state, pressing my palms to the table and rising to lean over it. "Because Le Fleur will never be for sale."

Dimitri grins wickedly. "Perhaps."

Turning the topic to his food order, I ask, "Surprise you?"

"Please," he agrees, allowing me to escape.

Heading back to the kitchen, I find everything in perfect working order. Hank leans over the stove, his tight iron-gray curls, russet complexion, and healthy figure quickly becoming a familiar sight on the line.

"Mind taking a break while I test out a new recipe?" I ask.

"Be my guest," he says as he plates his latest order.

I've been considering coq au vin as a new menu item, and since I have a perfect test subject, I might as well see how it's received. But this won't be the traditional slow-cooked version. Rather, I want to try marinating the chicken before panfrying it. Then I plan to reduce the sauce to drizzle over it more like a glaze and strain the sauteed vegetables to keep as the side.

My staff works around me, completing dishes for the patrons still waiting on their dinner. I keep the grill fired up, attending to the orders that come in while I cook Dimitri's meal. This is my element, where I feel most at home. Slowly, I calm down, regaining control of my body as I work with the food before me.

I don't know why Dimitri flusters me, but I can't seem to be in his presence for long without losing my mind. Perhaps it's the way he looks at me. His intense gray gaze seems to see straight through me. It leaves me feeling naked and exposed, both physically and mentally.

And every time he undresses me with his eyes, it feels as though he sees exactly what he wants. It both flatters and unnerves me. Growing up on the heavier side, I learned from a young age that I don't have the figure society might deem the most beautiful. I got teased about it considerably all through high school.

As I was one of the first girls to develop curves, boys never missed an opportunity to call attention to my cleavage or make lewd jokes about the junk in my trunk. And while they never brought me to tears over my body image, I've developed a sense of self-consciousness that's hard to shake.

So when Dimitri gives me those looks, it completely destabilizes me. Because he looks at my body as if I'm the finest dessert he's ever seen, like he wants to devour me. And he would savor every bite.

Fighting to keep my body under control, I force myself to focus on my plan. I've been postponing my date with Dimitri for too long, scared of how easily he flusters me. But as I plate his dinner, I know I'll have to move forward with it if I'm going to succeed.

"Are you ready to try a night without me?" I ask Frank as I turn the stove over to him once more.

"Yes, Chef," he says, beaming as if I've given him the highest of honors.

"Tomorrow?"

"I won't let you down," he assures me.

"Great. I'll let Hannah know. If you need anything..."

"I'll be sure to ask her," he promises, seeming to know just how challenging I find relinquishing control of my kitchen.

I release the breath I hadn't realized I was holding and return Hank's toothy grin. "Great."

Then I collect Dimitri's coq au vin and carry it out into the restaurant.

"I'm free tomorrow night," I state, setting Dimitri's plate in front of him.

He looks up from his phone, taking in the sight of his meal, then follows the curves of my body up to my face. "Is this you asking me on a date tomorrow?" he teases, his eyes dancing.

I plop onto the bench across from him once again, trying to

ignore the quiver of excitement that blossoms in my belly. "I think, technically, this is me answering your question of when you can take me on a date," I qualify cheekily.

"Well then, tomorrow it is," he agrees.

Internally, I breathe a sigh of relief. Though my work's only just begun, I've taken the first step to finding out what happened to Roy so I can dig myself out of this debt. And hopefully, buy myself more time.

"And what am I eating tonight?" Dimitri asks, turning his attention to the beautifully plated chicken set on a bed of mashed potatoes and garnished with mushrooms, carrots, and pearl onions.

"Coq au vin, Camille style. I want your honest opinion because I haven't added this to the menu yet. It takes too long to cook the traditional way, so I adjusted the recipe, but I want to make sure it still has enough flavor."

Dimitri chuckles as I fold my hands and place them on the table, looking at him pointedly.

"Alright," he agrees, taking up his silverware and cutting into the chicken breast.

He chews silently for several moments, taking me back to the first meal I cooked him and how nerve-racking waiting had been then. Now, though I'm still trying to win him over to save my business, the stakes feel far less high. Because his approval doesn't hold the fate of my restaurant in the balance.

"It's wonderful," he confesses after swallowing.

I grin.

"Did your new chef cook this?" he asks. "The one you've been training?"

"This was all me. But he's doing well. It's thanks to him I'll finally have a night off tomorrow," I admit.

"How long has it been?" Dimitri asks, one strong brow arching.

I blow a breath between my lips as I try to recall my last full day off. "Three... years..." I say doubtfully.

"You're overdue," he observes, cutting into his meat once more.

I laugh, turning on the charm to make my ploy more convincing.

"Yes, I can't wait for our date. I wouldn't want to spend my first night off in years with anyone but you."

Mild surprise flits across his face, and Dimitri pauses momentarily, making me wonder if I laid it on too thick. His gray eyes study me intently, and heat warms my cheeks as I worry that I might have blown my chance by being too obvious.

But then a smile curves his handsome lips. "Well then, I'll have to make sure you enjoy it thoroughly."

The suggestive undertone to his statement sends a shiver of anticipation down my spine, and I swallow hard as I try to regain my balance once again. I need to get past this effect Dimitri has on me if my plan is going to work the way I want it to.

10

Camille

"You're sure you don't want me to stay?" Hannah asks, leaning against the doorframe of my office, coat slung over her arm.

It's been a long night. After sending Dimitri on his way, I took the rest of the time to make sure Hank would have everything he needs to run the restaurant without me tomorrow. And now it's nearly midnight as I try to finish entering payroll before I go home.

"No really. I'm fine," I promise. "You've been here longer than you need to be already." I smile at her from behind my laptop.

"Alright," she says doubtfully. "Hey, I'm proud of you for actually taking a night off."

I laugh. "Thanks. But seriously. If you need me, I'll be here in a flash. Call if anything goes wrong, okay?"

"First off, nothing is going to go wrong," she states, holding up a finger. "And second, even if it does, I'm sure I can handle it. This may be your brainchild, but I've been here from the start, Cami. I know how this place runs, and I promise to take care of our baby."

"*Our* baby?" I tease.

"Yeah. You might be the mother, but I'm definitely Le Fleur's honorary aunt, at the very least. So stop worrying. Go have fun with Sexy Russian Businessman, and I want to hear all about it when you come in on Tuesday."

"Why do you keep calling him that?" I ask.

"Because I'm worried if I use his real name you might swoon on me. *Dimitri*," she trills, then falls back against the doorframe with the back of her hand to her forehead. "Seriously, even his name is sexy. I can't believe your luck."

"How do you mean?" I frown.

"You lose one boyfriend—who I'll admit had his charms, even if Roy was a bit of a deadbeat riding your coattails—and then, like, two weeks later, a hunky, charismatic sugar daddy with a sexy accent and a body that could kill comes walking through the front door, asking for you by name? I mean, come on."

My heart stutters at her apt wording, and I swallow hard as I wonder if Dimitri killed Roy with his bare hands. He's certainly strong enough to do so. He picked me up like I weighed nothing.

"And he's clearly into you," she continues, oblivious to my inner conflict. "He's practically been stalking you for the last two weeks, coming in here to see you since you refuse to take time off."

She laughs, and I join her, though her assessment troubles me more than I would like to admit. I haven't told her about what's really going on. I can't bring myself to vocalize everything that's happened since Dimitri walked into my life. And while she's right, Dimitri Federov is dangerously sexy, that's not why I agreed to go on a date with him.

Still, I suppose it would be smart to tell *somebody* about my plan in case something goes terribly wrong on our date tomorrow. It would be better if someone knew to call the police if I don't show up for work on Tuesday.

But before I can get up the courage to tell her my plan, Hannah pushes off the doorframe once again. "Alright, alright. I know that look. I'll stop bothering you so you can finish up and get home. But seriously, enjoy your day off, okay?"

"Okay," I agree, my stomach dropping at her departure.

"Love you!" she calls as she disappears around the corner.

And then I'm left alone to consider just how stupid my plan might really be. Sleeping with a Russian gangster in the hopes of postponing him from taking my restaurant while I try to unearth his deep, dark secrets? I better not screw this up.

If it were anything less important, I might think twice about my plan. But I can't lose Le Fleur. It means too much to me.

Sighing, I turn back to my computer screen.

An hour later, I finally close my laptop and rub my sleepy eyes. It'll be nice to sleep in a little tomorrow morning. Rising from my chair, I collect my jacket and purse and head to the office door.

Before turning off the light, I take a final look around the room. My eyes land on the surface of the desk that Dimitri had bent me over, and warmth pools in my belly at the memory. In truth, I'm looking forward to tomorrow night for more than one reason. Because, while I'm eager to find out what happened to Roy and regain my freedom, I'm also quite certain Dimitri has an encore planned for us.

My pulse quickens at the thought of his hands on me once again.

I flick the office light, dousing the room in darkness, and lock the door. Then I make my way down the dim hallway to the main dining area.

Performing my final sweep, I check the kitchen and back door to ensure everything is turned off and locked up for the night. Then I head to the front room.

The open dining room with all the empty chairs feels eerily quiet without the background music pouring from the speakers in the ceiling. I've never enjoyed closing by myself, though I've gotten used to it over the past year because I hate asking anyone to stay behind with me.

Turning off the last of the lights and flipping the sign to *closed*, I open the front door. The bell tinkles a cheery farewell as I close the door behind me. Digging into my purse, I search blindly for my keys as I turn to lock the deadbolt.

As I slide the lock home and remove my key, sudden, inexplicable icy fear races down my neck. The hair on my arms stands on end as I get the creepy feeling that someone's watching me. Whirling to face the street, I scan it for the source of my reaction.

The street's practically empty aside from a few cars parked along the far curb and my little mint-green VW Bug half a block away. For a moment, I'm sure I must be imagining things because nothing moves beneath the steady glow of the streetlamps.

All the stores across the street look dark and closed, their windows vacant except for the promotional displays.

"You just need to calm down, Cami. You're letting your imagination run wild," I tell myself, the sound of my own voice somehow easing my nerves slightly.

I've spent so much time thinking about all the terrible possibilities that might happen if I get close to Dimitri Federov. It must be starting to get to me.

Then, just as I turn toward my car, my eyes land on a tiny black sedan parked on the corner. My heart stops as I realize someone's in the driver's seat. It's too dark to make out their face or any distinguishing features. But as soon as I spot them, I'm sure they're watching me.

Cold sweat breaks out across my brow as I debate going back inside and locking myself in the restaurant. I could call the police. I doubt I would make it to my car before they come for me. I stand frozen with indecision, terror gripping my chest.

My hands tremble violently as the black car's motor rumbles to life, and before I have time to flee, its headlights flash brilliantly across the road. Then it pulls away from the curb and drives off, rounding the corner.

Shaking from head to toe, I stand frozen for a moment longer. I get the strangest feeling that whoever it was had been waiting for me. Watching to see me leave. Why they would decide to take off right now, I'm not sure. Maybe it's because I spotted them and they were worried I might see their face.

I don't know. But I can't get to my car fast enough in my panic.

And I don't dare breathe until I've clambered into my front seat and securely locked my door behind me. On the brink of hyperventilating, I start my car shakily and pull out onto the street.

But I can't seem to stop trembling. I need to tell someone what just happened to me. Though I know it's late, I dial Hannah and wait impatiently as the phone rings.

"Hello?" she answers on the fifth ring, her voice hoarse, as though I've woken her.

"Sorry. Were you asleep?" I bite my lip, suddenly regretting my panic-driven call.

"Mmm. It's fine. What's up? Everything okay?" she asks groggily.

"I just locked up for the night, and I'm pretty sure someone was watching me." I describe what happened—the creepy feeling I got, the dark figure in the car, and how the person drove away as soon as I spotted them.

"Oh my God, Cami. That's terrifying. Are you okay? Do you want me to call the police?"

"No, no. I'm fine. I'm on my way home now, and he didn't stick around. I just... needed to talk to somebody."

"You don't think this has anything to do with your Russian guy, do you? I mean, I was just joking earlier about him stalking you, but..."

"But what?" I ask.

"I don't know. He has come around a lot lately, and the timing seems a bit suspicious. Maybe."

I consider whether Dimitri might be capable of following me. It's not completely out of the realm of possibilities. Especially considering he most likely murdered Roy. He's clearly dangerous. And he does seem to have a certain disregard for rules—and personal space.

But I didn't recognize the car tonight. It definitely wasn't the Lamborghini he took me to brunch in the other day. Then again, with the kind of money he has, he can probably afford more than one car —or perhaps to hire someone to stalk me for him.

Still, the timing seems odd to me. If he wanted to keep an eye on me, wouldn't he have done that before I agreed to go on a date with him? Although, who's to say this person hasn't been watching me all along? Maybe tonight's just the first time I noticed. God, I hope not.

"I'm sure it's a coincidence," I say lightly. "Probably just someone who was waiting to sober up before they drove home or something. Right? I bet I'm making a big deal out of nothing." That possibility gives me an intense sense of relief, and suddenly, I feel like I can breathe. "Go to bed, Hannah. Sorry for waking you."

"Girl, you can call me anytime. Are you sure you're okay?"

"I'm fine. Really. Now that we're talking about it, I think I just gave myself the creeps while I was locking up. Sometimes, I let my imagination get the best of me." And the thought that someone might actually be watching me is entirely too unsettling.

"Alright. I'll see you Tuesday."

"Sweet dreams," I say.

"You too," Hannah murmurs sleepily before ending the call.

It helped to talk it through with her. Now, I'm sure it was just a coincidence. The person was probably sleeping off one too many drinks in their car, and I woke them up as I came out of the restaurant. I bet that's why they drove off so quickly.

Still, I can't help but glance in my rearview mirror more than once during my drive to reassure myself that no one is following me home.

11

Dimitri

"Where are you taking me?" Camille asks from the passenger seat of my Lamborghini, her tone somewhere between excited and nervous as she watches me.

"Dinner," I tease as I weave my way down the busy San Francisco streets.

Food is our first stop, but I'll need to take her to the roof of my penthouse so we can exchange the car for appropriate transportation. Because what I haven't told her is that the restaurant where we'll be eating is in Carmel. And we'll need my helicopter to get there before the sun goes down.

"That's all you're going to give me?" she demands, crossing her arms over her chest. The gesture intensifies the tantalizing cleavage over the sweetheart neckline of her low-cut dress.

She looks ravishing in a royal-blue satin gown that makes her eyes pop. When I told her to dress for a fancy evening, I hadn't imagined she would have an outfit quite so stunning. I suppose because I'm used to seeing her in chef's robes or aprons.

But tonight, she seems to be enjoying the opportunity to dress up. Her hair is down for once, styled into loose auburn curls cascading down one shoulder, exposing part of her long neck. And she's wearing a hint more makeup tonight, just enough to accentuate the beautiful, almost feline shape of her eyes.

"I don't want to ruin the surprise," I insist, flicking my eyes over to meet hers. A smile tugs at my lips before I turn my attention back to the road.

Camille huffs. "Fine."

It's a short drive to the tall skyscraper with my penthouse at the top. I leave my car with the valet, helping Camille out of her seat before guiding her into the lobby and taking her to the elevators.

The cinched waist leading into the flowing skirt of her blue dress makes the fabric move like water around her. And as her heels tap against the marble floor, I catch sight of the high slit that reveals one voluptuous thigh.

"You look beautiful tonight," I state, taking a moment to appreciate every inch of her as we stop to wait for the elevator to arrive.

Camille blushes a delicate pink. "Thanks."

The doors ding open, and we step inside the small space. Using my fob, I gain access to the topmost buttons and choose the one that will take us to the rooftop.

"I didn't know this building had a restaurant on the roof," Camille observes, noting the button that lights up.

"It doesn't," I state coyly. I love the way she squirms with the new mystery, her blue eyes trying to unravel my secrets.

Tension builds between us in the silence that follows, and the thought of touching Camille, of pushing her up against the elevator wall and kissing her has my pulse quickening. But tonight, I plan on thoroughly spoiling her before we get to that. Because I want her first night off in three years to be one she won't forget.

The doors open onto the roof, and Camille steps out, her face revealing her nervousness. Momentarily, I wonder if she might be scared of heights. Resting a stabilizing palm on the small of her back, I gesture toward the open-air stairs leading up to the helipad. It's then that she sees the helicopter waiting for us above.

A gasp parts her lips, and her head jerks in my direction as she gives me a look of utter disbelief. "We're taking a helicopter to dinner?" she demands.

"I figured you might prefer it to the hour-and-a-half drive to Carmel."

"I've never been in a helicopter before," she confesses as she allows me to guide her toward the aircraft.

"Well then, tonight is a good night to be your first." I give her a wink.

Climbing into the chopper, we buckle up as the pilot starts the rotor blades. Camille seems riveted by the experience, looking this way and that, trying to take in every view as we smoothly rise from the landing pad.

She shouts something over the noisy machine, and I hand her a headset before donning my own.

"This is amazing!" she repeats, her voice clear as it carries through the headpiece.

"I'm glad you think so."

The sky is a brilliant pinkish gold with the setting sun, and as we fly over San Francisco Bay, the water seems to reflect the bright colors, intensifying the beauty of the sunset. Buildings glitter along the city skyline, their lights like stars against the quickly darkening horizon.

Camille glues herself to the window, her palm pressed firmly along the metal frame as she watches the world far below.

"Why Carmel?" she asks once the city's a distant glimmer of light behind us.

At this point, I don't see the harm in telling her. "That's where my favorite Japanese restaurant is."

Camille's eyes widen as she considers the information. "Do you fly down often, then?"

I give a casual shrug. "When I'm in the mood for sushi."

Her face lights with enthusiasm, and suddenly, I'm glad I picked the place I did.

It's a relatively short flight to the coastal town and an even shorter drive from the heliport to the seaside restaurant called Oishī. A full Japanese garden leads up to the front doors, with an idyllic pedestrian bridge over a koi pond just before the building's covered entrance.

"Good evening, Mr. Federov," the hostess says as soon as we enter.

Camille seems taken aback by the empty dining room. The only person aside from us and the host is a piano player who sits in the far corner of the room, tickling the keys with finesse.

"Right this way," the hostess instructs, giving Camille a broad smile before turning to walk us to the best seats in the house.

"Where are all the people?" Camille murmurs so only I can hear.

Amused by her seeming need for secrecy, I release a low chuckle and whisper back, "I booked the entire restaurant for the evening."

Stopping dead in her tracks, Camille gapes at me. Pausing with her, I turn and quirk an eyebrow.

"You booked the whole restaurant?" she repeats, slightly louder this time.

"Why not?" I smile wickedly.

"Well, for starters, I don't see how the owner could be okay with losing that kind of revenue. Unless you paid an arm and a leg for the space."

"I'm sure he won't mind," I tease, gesturing for Camille to take her seat.

And though she looks doubtful, she finishes walking to the table beside the window and slides into the bamboo seat. "Thank you," she says to the hostess before the woman departs.

Then she turns her eyes back to me.

"And what makes you so sure the owner wouldn't mind?" she challenges looking around at the impressive ocean view before taking in the authentic Japanese decor. "This place looks expensive. They probably rake in a fortune each night."

My smile intensifies as I lean over the table, whispering conspiratorially. "Because I am the owner."

Her eyes snap to mine, assessing me sharply.

"Well, my family owns it anyway."

Camille scowls. "Another business acquisition when someone fell behind on loan payments?" she accuses, crossing her arms over her chest in that sassy posture that I'm *really* starting to appreciate while she's in that dress.

"No, more like an angel investor for a family who dreamed of opening a place like this. They had just immigrated to America and wanted to open a restaurant, but they could only afford a small cart. So, we fronted them the money and built this business together. Think of it more like a partnership—even if we technically own the restaurant."

"Hmm." Camille pursed her lips skeptically.

"May I interest you in some plum wine this evening, miss?" a server offers, showing off the bottle so she can see the label.

"Oh, um, yes please."

I give the server a nod when he turns to my glass, and once we both have a drink, he departs once more.

"*Za zdaróvye,*" I say, raising my glass of wine.

Color tinges Camille's cheeks as she raises her glass and clinks it delicately against mine. "Cheers," she echoes.

Then we sip. As she sets down her glass, her eyes turn to the open space around us, her gaze both interested and impressed.

"I can see why you would want to invest in this place. The details are so perfect, the atmosphere tranquil. Someone really knew what they were doing," she says with admiration.

"I may not be a talented chef, but I have an eye for those who are," I say playfully, looking at her pointedly.

Camille glances back at me and freezes as she seems to realize my statement was directed at her. "As flattering as that might be, I don't need your help. Le Fleur is already a successful business, and I don't need rescuing."

"Let's not talk business tonight, hmm? It's your first night off in three years. Why don't you just relax and enjoy it?"

The statement was meant to be teasing, but I can see the relief that eases her shoulders down, releasing tension I hadn't known she was carrying. And even though she agreed to this date and has demonstrated a clear interest in being with me, it seems she hasn't yet let her guard down completely.

Though I can't say I blame her, considering the foot we started off on, I had hoped she might start to feel more comfortable around me over the past week.

"Your dinner," the server says, bringing out our food in record time.

It arrives on a grand wood-carved sushi tray fashioned in the shape of a detailed ship. Bright slices of raw fish, avocado, and mango cover seaweed-wrapped bites with brilliant orange tobiko and crispy tempura garnishes.

Camille gasps, her blue eyes round as she takes in the countless varieties.

"I wasn't sure what you might like, so I ordered one of each," I state.

"You're not kidding. I hope you don't expect me to finish half of this." She sounds breathless with astonishment.

"I expect you to eat to your heart's content," I say.

We each prepare a bowl of soy sauce, spiced with traditional wasabi. And I wait for Camille to select her first piece of sushi. She handles her chopsticks like an expert, delicately placing a mango roll onto her tongue and chewing slowly.

A groan of appreciation hums from her lips as her eyes sink closed.

"Good?" I guess before selecting a piece for myself.

"Better than good. That might be the best piece of sushi I've ever tasted," she says, covering her mouth to speak around her bite.

Something about how completely Camille appreciates food, I find entirely sexy. Though she doesn't say anything explicitly sexual, I get the sense that her enjoyment is beyond that of good flavor and food that satiates her hunger. She experiences the value of exceptional taste with her entire body, relishing each bite as she savors it slowly.

And I find the way she guides her bites between her full lips to be almost sensual, as are the quiet sounds of pleasure that coincide with each new taste. By the time we start to slow down, my cock is already throbbing with need, my body ready to see just how much I can make her enjoy this meal.

"Dessert?" I offer when she finally sets down her chopsticks, admitting defeat.

She leans back in her chair, a look of intense satisfaction on her face. "Mmm, I don't know where I'll put it, but after that exquisite meal, I'm more than a little curious about what this place can make."

I wave our server over, and he's there in an instant.

"The lady would like to know what you have for dessert."

"We have matcha ice cream, green tea macarons, and a honey hibiscus crème brûlée, all made in-house today," he says warmly.

Camille releases a groan of longing, her shoulder slumping as if to say the choice is an impossible one to make.

"We'll take one of each," I state confidently without taking my eyes from the delicious woman before me.

"Very good, sir."

As the server departs, Camille leans forward to whisper, "We can't possibly eat all that! What are you doing?"

"I assure you, it won't go to waste," I say playfully.

Camille shakes her head, but a slow smile spreads across her face as she lifts her plum wine to take another sip. Then her eyes shift to the window and the last brilliant colors painted across the darkening sky.

"I can't believe this place. The food, the music, the view? It's unreal."

"I'm glad you like it." I take the opportunity to admire Camille's profile, the soft curves of her cheek, her tiny button nose, the gentle point of her chin.

Her hair falls down her back in a thick cascade of waves, the color as unusual as it is enticing. I'm mildly surprised by its impressive length. At the restaurant, she always wears it up, and I had assumed it might fall just below her shoulders, but it's long enough to reach the middle of her voluptuous waist.

Everything about her is inviting. And I find my desire to touch her nearly impossible to contain.

"Your desserts," our server says, placing them in the center of the table and providing a spoon for each of us.

"I can't believe you ordered all three," Camille states, but that doesn't stop her from tasting each. And her whimper of appreciation is entirely worth the choice.

I watch her with unbridled interest as she slowly draws her spoon from between her lips, enjoying her bite of matcha ice cream with entirely sinful joy. Her eyes flutter open a moment later to find me staring openly.

"Don't you want any?" she asks, her blush adorable as she glances down to see I haven't taken a bite.

I shake my head, and her blush intensifies as she sets her spoon gently on the plate.

"What I really want is to watch you play with yourself," I state boldly to make it clear my lack of appetite has nothing to do with her sugar craving. It has everything to do with how ready I am to move on to the next chapter of our date.

Seeing how many times I can make her come in one night.

My blunt honesty seems to do the trick, completely wiping away her momentary self-consciousness as her jaw drops open in disbelief.

"Right now," I add.

"What, here?" she asks, her head whipping from side to side as she looks around the empty restaurant as if expecting to find a slew of patrons gawking at us.

Her eyes land on the piano player, whose back is turned as he remains intently focused on the piano keys.

"What about the staff?" she whispers, her blush intensifying impossibly.

"They wouldn't dare to look at what's mine," I growl, my hunger growing.

Camille bites her lip nervously, her eyes uncertain. But when I stand and offer her my hand, she places her fingers willingly against my palm.

I pull her to a stand, and her breaths quicken as I wrap my arm around her so she might feel my growing need pressing against her abdomen. Guiding her slowly backward, I lead her to a long table, one large enough to accommodate a good-sized party.

Removing the end chair, I set it aside before gripping Camille's hips firmly and lifting her onto the table. She gasps as I set her down and step between her knees, spreading her thick, sexy thighs.

"Masturbate for me, Camille," I murmur, leaning close to her lips.

She releases a shuddering breath and nods slowly. Then her eyes sink closed as I lean in to kiss her softly parted lips. Keeping her distracted with my tongue, I move my hands down her hips to find the high slit of her cocktail dress.

And when I find the warm, silky skin beneath it, I separate the layers of fabric, exposing her creamy legs. Camille gasps into my mouth as my palms roam higher once more, moving beneath the dress until I find the soft lace of her panties.

I ease them down an inch at a time, prepared to fully enjoy every second of this evening with her, and she squirms as the fabric tickles across her skin, slowly slipping down the insides of her thighs.

With her back to the kitchen, her bare thighs facing the restaurant's wall of windows, I'm sure Camille can see herself reflected there, the night sky darkening the view beyond the glass. She seems to notice herself as her eyes flick over my shoulder momentarily, then she focuses pointedly on my face.

Sliding her panties into my pocket, I give her a wicked grin. "I might just keep these as a souvenir," I purr. Then gripping her hips once more, I guide Camille back onto the table until her high heels find the flat surface.

Bracing with her palms behind her, Camille seems momentarily lost, and I don't mind telling her exactly what I expect of her.

"Bend your knees and spread your legs," I command, guiding one high-heeled foot into position as she does the other.

The motion allows her flowing skirt to fall open once more, revealing her bare pussy in all its perfection. Stepping to the side of her, I lean close to whisper in her ear.

"Now, play with your pussy. I want to watch you make yourself come, *kotenok*."

Camille shudders as I nip lightly at the lobe of her ear. And hesitantly, she shifts to lean on one palm as her other hand reaches forward between her legs. I can see everything in the window's reflection—Camille's fingers as they start to stroke between her folds, the gentle tremble of her thighs, the way her eyes find mine and burn with molten excitement.

"That's it," I praise, keeping my eyes on her a moment longer before I bend to press my lips to the soft curve of her throat.

Camille moans, her head falling to the side, granting me access to the tender flesh. I explore her with my mouth, my tongue, moving slowly down to her exposed collarbone and then her full chest. Her breasts swell with each quickening breath, fighting to burst free from their cage, and I want to see them in their full glory.

But not yet.

Shifting my attention to the real show as Camille's sensual gasps grow more adamant, I walk around to the end of the table once more. Her tiny feet, clad in strappy black stilettos, brace against the table, making her beautiful calves flex and bulge.

Unable to resist, I take one shoe in hand and raising her foot, I start at her ankle and slowly kiss my way up the inside line of her leg.

"Oh God!" Camille breathes, her leg trembling in my grasp, and I can hear her growing excitement.

Propping her ankle on my shoulder, I lean in to nip and kiss the inside of her silky thigh. Her fingers work above me, stroking her slit and then circling her clit as she plays with herself in a tantalizing display.

My cock throbs at the sight of her pleasure, the arousal that slicks her sexy slit. Breathing in her heavenly scent, I knead her thighs with my hands as I watch her now, not wanting to miss a second of the provocative show she's putting on.

Because now that she's consumed by her growing excitement, Camille's inhibitions have completely fallen away. Her eyes burn deep into my soul as she dares me to watch her without partaking. And it takes every ounce of self-restraint to stop myself from joining in.

Her lips form a perfect O as her back arches and her cleavage spills over the low-cut neckline of her dress. The image of a siren, dressed in the rich blue of the ocean, Camille releases the sweetest sounds I've ever heard. And just like the immortal creatures of Greek myths, she draws me to her.

I'm captivated by her song, bewitched by her beauty, ensnared by her alluring body.

And just as I think I can't hold off any longer, Camille releases a heavenly gasp.

Her legs jerk as her fingers tremble over her wet pussy, and from the look of intense relief that washes over her face, she's come right here, in the middle of my restaurant for me to see. Muscles relaxing as her orgasm recedes, Camille stills slowly.

"Hmm," I hum appreciatively.

Then I step back around the table, settling behind Camille as she sinks contentedly against my chest.

"My turn," I murmur in her ear, and she shivers deliciously against me.

Her head rests softly on my shoulder as I wrap one arm around her waist and pull her closer to me. Knees still bent, thighs spread tantalizingly, Camille looks entirely too sexy as I find her reflection in the window again.

And holding her firmly with one arm, I reach forward with my other to find her fingers resting delicately on the inside of her thigh.

Then I palm her warm, wet pussy.

Camille moans, her body coming back to life as she inhales deeply. And I stroke my fingers between her slick fold. She's so wet and swollen with need that it makes my balls ache with the need to be inside her. But we have more than enough time for that.

First, I want to watch her come on my fingers.

A whimper issues from her lips as I gently pinch and roll her clit, and it twitches under my touch.

"You like that, *kotenok*?" I tease. "You like it when I touch you in the middle of my restaurant?"

"Yes!" she gasps, her breaths quickening as her breasts start to swell once again.

"You want me to make you come again all over this table?"

"*Mmmm please,*" she moans.

Plunging two fingers into her depths, I relish the sensation of her pussy tightening around me, greedy for the penetration she so eagerly wants. And at the same time, I shift my other hand, wrapping it around her shoulder so I can slide my fingers beneath the satin fabric of her dress.

Supple flesh spills from her dress, falling out of her bra and into my palm. And the taut nub of her nipple presses adamantly against my palm. A rumbling growl issues from my throat at the sexy way the soft flesh oozes between my fingers.

"Oh God," Camille moans, arching into my palm as her hips grind forward onto my fingers.

"You say *my* name, *kotenok*, when you want me to let you come. God has no part in what we do here," I growl possessively.

"Dimitri," she breathes like a supplication.

"Good girl," I praise, kneading her breast as I circle her clit with the pad of my thumb.

Her walls tighten around my fingers, demanding more as I stroke into her depths to find her G-spot. Camille bites her lip fiercely in an effort to muffle the cry of pleasure.

Not that it helps.

But the pianist continues on with his song, not missing a beat. And the waitstaff know better than to bother us right now.

"Come for me, Camille," I command, intensifying my pressure.

And as her head tips back, her lips parting with her release, I claim her succulent mouth.

Swallowing her cry of pleasure, I consume her lips.

I relish the feel of her pussy as it explodes around my fingers.

The throb of her clit against my thumb.

Warm juices coat my palm as Camille orgasms with shuddering force. And she trembles against me, her body utterly undone as she comes hard.

Continuing my attention until the last of her fluttering contractions fades, I soak up the feel of her pleasure. I can't wait to make her do it again.

But Camille releases a deeply satisfied moan as she slumps limply against me. I chuckle as I hold her to me, allowing her a moment of euphoria.

I press my lips to her temple before I even think about what I'm doing, and the unusual display of affection catches me by surprise. Though fortunately, Camille seems too lost in her own contentment to think much of it. But her eyes meet mine in the window's reflection.

Slowly, I withdraw my fingers from her pussy. And playfully, I lick them clean, my eyes never leaving hers as her expression shifts from shock to something far hungrier.

"Yes, that was exactly the dessert I wanted," I say.

Camille shivers against me as she bites down on her lower lip once more.

"What do you say to a nightcap at my place?" I offer. Though I intend to extend this evening far longer.

She swallows audibly. "That sounds nice," she agrees, her voice breathy.

Then she sits up as if suddenly remembering we're not alone. In a flash, she covers her bare legs with the folds of her dress and scoots modestly off the table. A low rumble of amusement rises from me as she self-consciously shimmies her breast back into her dress, putting herself back together.

She glances sidelong toward the piano player and seems relieved to find him exactly as he was before. Then her eyes dart toward the kitchen to confirm no one had been watching. Only then do her shoulders relax once more.

"I told you. No one would dare look at what's mine," I tease.

Her radiant blush is the only response I get. And it's all I need.

"Come," I state, offering her my hand.

And it fills me with intense satisfaction when she takes it without question.

12

Camille

The helicopter ride back to San Francisco is filled with sexual tension as my gaze meets Dimitri's numerous times. But I *refuse* to do something with a pilot not fifteen feet away. It doesn't matter how hot I found the experience of Dimitri fingering me in the middle of his restaurant.

The way he took command of the situation so completely.

It was intoxicatingly sexy.

And now, as I keep my legs firmly crossed for the flight across the bay, I'm intensely aware of my panties still tucked away in his pocket.

The chopper lands on top of the same tall, grand building where we rode up the elevator before dinner. I follow Dimitri inside and to the single elevator that reaches this high.

It only takes a few moments for the elevator to arrive and an even shorter time before they ding open once more, opening up onto the luxurious penthouse on the top floor.

"You're joking," I state flatly as I gape at the massive, open-style apartment.

White marble covers the floors, and a glass staircase climbs one side of the immense vaulted living room, leading up to a second level. The kitchen to the left is large enough to fit my entire apartment. It's separated from the living area only by a massive island counter containing the sink and stove with cabinets beneath.

Two full walls are made up entirely of glass that reaches high enough for two stories. They look out across the city and bay, including the Golden Gate Bridge, Alcatraz, and as far east as Pier 39.

"Is something funny?" Dimitri asks, his rich tone almost innocent.

"If you're about to tell me that this is where you live," I state, twirling to take in every detail.

A glass table holding a beautiful vase of fresh flowers decorates the open entry. Stunning pieces of colorful, abstract modern art cover the walls.

"Well then, what should I tell you?" Dimitri teases, his gray eyes dancing when I finally turn to meet them.

"You live here?"

"This is my apartment, yes," he agrees, his lips twitching at my disbelief.

"I didn't even know places like this exist," I admit, turning to take in the fine gray couches and the chic coffee table sitting on a plush white rug that looks soft enough to sleep on.

"Perhaps you should spend more time with me then," Dimitri says, his smooth accent making the suggestion that much more enticing. "These are the kinds of places my world is made of. Wine?" he offers, leaving my side as he heads toward the wet bar lining the back wall of the kitchen.

"Please," I agree, making my way toward the couch.

The night hasn't gone at all as I intended so far. I had meant to get Dimitri talking, perhaps open the door to the debt hanging over my head and work my way toward what happened to Roy.

But the luxury of that wonderful Japanese restaurant and its breathtaking views got me off track, and the stuff following dessert... completely derailed me. That's why I accepted the nightcap.

Maybe now I'll find the opening to dig further into what

happened. See if I can get Dimitri to open up and trust me with his secret. Or at least set some good groundwork.

"So tell me, Camille," Dimitri says, stealing my line as he joins me on the couch and hands me a glass of red wine. "How did you get into cooking in the first place?"

"Oh, um, my dad actually. He was a chef, and I grew up in the kitchen with him. He taught me almost everything I know." I smile warmly at the fond memories that flood through me at the mention of it. Mornings spent making crepes and waffles, evenings rushing around his workplace, filling orders. I sip my wine as I get lost in those wonderful moments.

"You spent a lot of time with him at work?" Dimitri asks.

I nod. "He was a single parent and couldn't really afford childcare. But restaurants are like a big family, in a way. So as long as I didn't get underfoot, no one seemed to mind keeping an eye on me too much. And they all loved it once I was old enough to be put to good use." I laugh affectionately at the fresh wave of memories that come to mind.

Dimitri mirrors my amusement, his gorgeous smile softening his strong, chiseled features. "So you started your first cooking job when you were how old?"

"Thirteen?" I'm not entirely sure since I wasn't technically allowed to work in the kitchen until my sixteenth birthday. But Daddy always let me get away with practice here and there. "Though if child protective services ever come knocking, my official answer is sixteen."

Dimitri laughs, the low, rumbling sound making my heart flutter. "No wonder you are such a good chef."

I beam with pride, knowing so much of my education comes straight from a chef with such a deep passion for good food.

"And your mother was not in the picture?" he asks, one eyebrow raising.

I shake my head. "She died in childbirth."

"I'm sorry to hear it." His tone is genuine, his face shifting from amused to serious as the conversation takes a sad turn.

I give a shrug. "It's okay. My dad never left me wanting for love or attention. We were as thick as thieves, and I had a wonderful childhood because of him."

"And he inspired you to open your own restaurant?" Dimitri suggests, his observation impressively insightful.

"Actually, Daddy and I had envisioned running Le Fleur together. We talked about opening a restaurant with French-themed cuisine, sharing duties as head chef. Coming up with fresh menu items together." My smile falters as I think about how different my reality is without my dad.

I'd never really taken the time to acknowledge how much of a team we were and how it impacted my business strategy when he died. Hannah's been a lifesaver, taking up responsibilities without hesitation, never failing to have my back. She helps in a very different way than my dad would have, but I honestly don't think I could have made my dream a reality without her. Not after Daddy passed away.

"That is why owning your restaurant is so important to you," Dimitri observes, his gaze intense as he peers deep into my soul.

I nod, lost in his captivating gaze, and suddenly, I realize how easily I find it to open up to Dimitri. Maybe it's the alcohol talking, but I'm strangely at ease with this tall, dark, dangerous man.

Taking my wine glass from my hand, Dimitri sets both of our drinks on the coffee table. Then he moves closer, removing the distance between us as his knee brushes against mine.

"You are exceptional, Camille. Do you know that?" he asks, his voice husky as his hand cups my chin so he can study my face closely.

Nerves flutter in my belly, and I lick my suddenly dry lips.

His eyes shift down, catching the quick movement, and heat races through my body as he leans in. Kissing me with shocking tenderness, Dimitri covers my mouth with his. Excitement uncurls low in my stomach as the air vanishes from my lungs.

Tongue tracing the seam of my lips, Dimitri requests access in a tantalizingly intimate way. My mouth opens on a gasp, and before I can overthink it, I lean into the kiss, my fingers combing into his thick black hair.

A low groan of appreciation rumbles up his throat as he deepens our connection, his tongue stroking between my teeth to tangle with mine. And though things are escalating once again and I still haven't asked about Roy, I find I'm intensely grateful that Dimitri hasn't once asked to buy my restaurant tonight. He even touched on the subject without pushing it further. So in a way, at least my plan to stall is working.

That's what I have to tell myself because my body's ready to completely throw those thoughts out the window.

Strong hands find my hips as Dimitri and I start to make out passionately. And then I'm lifted up off the couch as he pulls me on top of him. Placing one thigh on either side of his lap, he makes me straddle him.

I'm intensely aware of the way my flowing skirt creates a nearly nonexistent barrier between us.

And I'm still not wearing any underwear.

My dress falls open along the line of its slit, revealing one of my thighs completely. Dimitri's large palm takes advantage of it in an instant, his hand shifting from my hip to knead the exposed flesh of my thigh.

"I could eat you up," he breathes against my lips, and my core tightens deliciously.

Wrapping my arms more firmly around the back of his neck, I find that sounds like a surprisingly spectacular idea. Strong arms wrap around my waist, pulling me tightly against his broad chest, and I can feel the urgent press of his erection fighting to be free of his dress pants.

The thought of Dimitri filling me, his hard cock buried inside my pussy, makes me throb eagerly. And suddenly, it's not about my plan to buy time for the loan or getting information about Roy. I'm consumed with fiery need.

"Take me," I plead, kissing him passionately as I roll my hips to show him exactly what I mean.

A low snarl rumbles from his chest, vibrating against my breasts, and he hoists me off the couch, standing in one fluid movement.

No one's ever carried me like this before. I wrap my legs around his hips and he walks blindly, holding me like it's nothing. Anticipation pounds through my veins at all the things that Dimitri could do to me.

His gait shifts, and I break our kiss momentarily to glance sideways at our surroundings. A gasp bursts from me as I see the floor far below, a thin sheet of glass holding us up as he climbs the stairs effortlessly.

Dimitri chuckles darkly as I cling more tightly to him, turning my face into his neck as my stomach drops. Not that I have a major thing against heights, but I'm not exactly a fan of them either.

"Are you worried I will drop you, *malen'kiy kotenok*?" Dimitri teases, his low voice close to my ear.

"Not when I hold onto you like this," I murmur, tightening my thighs around his waist.

A rumbling growl vibrates from his chest into mine, raising goosebumps along my arms and back. Then we're at the top of the stairs, and relief floods me.

Taking a quick left, Dimitri steps into a massive master bedroom. Decorated in dark grays and blacks, the space looks just as chic and modern as the rest of his apartment. And along the far wall, glass stretches from floor to ceiling once more as it looks out over the bay.

Carrying me to the bed, Dimitri lays me gently across it. His hands roam down my body, exploring my curves as he straightens, leaving me sprawled across his sheets as he undresses me with his eyes.

"I want to play with you all night," he promises, making butterflies erupt in my belly.

Stretching across the soft mattress, I smile at him languidly, tempting him to do his worst.

Dimitri shrugs out of his fine steel-gray suit jacket that calls attention to the silver of his eyes. Then he works slowly on his red silk tie.

"Take off your dress," he commands, his eyes sparking. "Slowly."

Sitting up, I look at him through my lashes as I reach behind me for the zipper of my dress. Sucking part of my lower lip between my teeth, I bite it as I obey, letting him watch me as he pulls his tie out from the collar of his shirt at a tantalizing pace.

The heat of his gaze intensifies as I rise off the bed and turn around to reveal my back. After the hot, rough passionate sex in which we didn't take the time to undress before, this slower, teasing buildup is driving me wild.

My skin tingles as I drag my sleeves down off my shoulders and glance over one at Dimitri. His fingers work the buttons of his shirt, though his eyes never leave me. And as his shirt falls open, my mouth goes dry instantly.

Dimitri might be older than me, but his body is unlike anything I've ever seen. Strong muscles ripple across his chest and down his stomach, forming washboard abs that make my heart race.

Ink colors his chest, though I can't quite make out the pattern with his shirt still on. I hold my breath, dying to see the full package of his body.

Pausing, Dimitri arches an eyebrow, and heat pools in my cheeks as I realize I only get a show if he does. I got so wrapped up in my own tempting display that I stopped undressing myself.

I pull my dress the rest of the way down my arms, and as soon as it's free, fluttering to the floor pooling around my feet. Clad in nothing but my bustier and high heels, I feel intensely exposed. Because Dimitri never gave me back my panties.

A wicked grin curls across his face as Dimitri's eyes rake down my bare back and waist to my exposed ass. Then silently, he shrugs out of his shirt, letting it fall to the floor behind him.

I gasp at the sheer perfection of his body. Strong, corded muscles ripple beneath his skin. His broad shoulders and bulging biceps look large enough to pick me up and snap me in half.

The tattoo I couldn't distinguish before is an intricately curling design that licks its way up one side of his ribs like fire, swirling out over his pec, spilling across his shoulder, and snaking down his arm. It's a riot of patterns that are sharp and dangerous, yet at the same time, curve sensually over his glorious physique like a caress.

"You like what you see?" he teases darkly, his dangerous tone matching the inferno of his gaze. His hands reach down to his belt, unbuckling it at a casual pace.

"Yes," I murmur breathlessly and nod.

Lifting a finger, Dimitri twirls it, indicating I should turn to show him more of me. Suddenly shy about my body in comparison to his godlike figure, I step slowly, my arms covering as much of me as I can.

A hint of irritation flits across his masculine face. Snapping his belt the rest of the way out of his loops, Dimitri strides forward purposefully. My breath catches as he stops right in front of me, towering over me in all his physical glory.

"You think you can hide from me?" he asks flatly, his tone suddenly deadly.

My heart skips a beat, as I think for an instant that he might know why I'm sleeping with him. He's found out, and now I'm dead.

Reaching out with lightning speed, Dimitri snatches my wrists and forces them behind me. I gasp, too shocked to respond quickly, and thick leather wraps around my arms, confining me. I feel the belt buckle as he cinches it tightly, trapping my hands so I'm helpless.

Fear grips my throat, silencing the scream that nearly bursts from me.

Then Dimitri's fingers are combing into my hair, cradling my head as he forces me to look up at him. "Your body is perfect, and I want to see it, to worship every inch. You do not get to cover it. Not tonight."

Heat erupts through me like a volcano at his words, and suddenly, my fear melts into something far more thrilling.

Closing the space between us, Dimitri kisses me fiercely, his tongue claiming my mouth as it opens in astonishment. I moan at the possessive way he touches me, consumes me. One hand trails slowly down my body as the other fingers curl in my hair, gripping it firmly as he holds me captive against him.

His fingers find the eye loops of my bustier, and hook by hook, he frees me from my lingerie. I gasp as the strapless support falls to the ground behind me, exposing every inch of my flesh to him.

Arms tied firmly behind me, my breasts press forward eagerly, my nipples hardening against the firm planes of his chest.

Pulling away, Dimitri breaks our kiss and takes a step back to truly see me. The hunger in his gaze blasts away any self-doubt lingering in me, and my skin heats as I suddenly feel sexier than I've ever felt before.

"*Krasivyy,*" he purrs. "You are perfect."

Slowly leaning close, Dimitri's molten gaze meets mine. His hands reach behind me to gently undo the belt, and he releases me. Heady relief washes through me knowing he doesn't intend to tie me up for whatever he has planned, though the hint of disappointment that mingles inside me I find surprising.

"Don't worry, *kotenok*. We will have plenty of time for bondage play before I'm done with you," he promises as if reading the conflict in my mind.

I swallow hard, trying to dislodge my heart from my throat. Then Dimitri smiles wickedly.

"Lie on the bed," he commands.

But when I reach down to remove my strappy heels and obey, he snatches my wrist.

"On. The. Bed," he states pointedly.

Scarcely daring to breathe, I do exactly as he says. Leaving on my stiletto shoes, I slide into the center of the silky sheets and watch him as I wait.

"Good girl," he praises, sending a ripple of excitement through my body. Then Dimitri steps out of his shoes, undoing the button and zipper of his pants all in one.

He pushes them down his hips, letting them fall to the floor, and once again, I'm captivated by the sheer size of him. Thick cock standing fully erect, Dimitri's massive. Deep lines form a V down from his abs to his groin like an arrow. Not that anyone could miss the impressive specimen glaring at me.

His swollen red tip glistens with precum, and my core tightens at the thought of having him inside me once again.

"Bend your knees and spread your legs for me," he commands, just like he did at the restaurant.

Running my hands up my thighs, my waist, my breasts, I do as he says, putting on a show at the same time. Dimitri releases a low groan, his eyes drinking in the sight of me. Then he prowls toward me.

Strong hands grip my knees, keeping my legs spread wide even as my natural instinct is to close them at his sudden proximity. His lips find the tender flesh along the inside of my leg, and just like he did at the restaurant, Dimitri slowly trails kisses up my thigh.

Only this time, my fingers aren't covering my clit as it starts to throb.

He's dangerously close to my pussy, his lips caressing, his teeth nipping, the soft scrape of his facial hair tickling my skin. And just when I think he's going to press his fingers inside me, his tongue strokes out to press between my folds.

Eyes flying wide, I arch up off the bed in shock. Because no one's ever gone down on me before. Roy always thought it was gross, and I never had much time for boys or the typical wild college experience. And I never knew it could feel *that* good.

Dimitri slowly traces my slit, his tongue flicking as he reaches the sensitive bundle of nerves at its peak. I whimper as intoxicating pleasure thrums through me, pulsing up my body in waves.

And when he hums appreciatively against me, I nearly come undone.

"Oh God, Dimitri," I moan, shocked at how close I am to an orgasm already.

Strong fingers press into my thighs, locking my legs in place as Dimitri strokes more adamantly between my folds, his tongue lapping up my juices before rolling the warm, wet surface over my intensely sensitive clit.

All thoughts of why I'm here or what I'm supposed to be doing are long gone as I fall into heavenly bliss, enjoying my time with Dimitri far more than I ever thought possible. Because no one's ever made me feel this good before.

He's unlocked something in me, a sensuality I didn't know I possessed, a confidence that allows me to relax completely and enjoy just how good he makes me feel. A hunger that I'm not sure I'll ever be able to satiate.

Not with anyone but him.

Dimitri licks and sucks my pussy lips, lavishing them with attention that makes my body tremble. And then, he closes his mouth around my clit and starts to suck.

"Oh, fuck!" I scream as I come violently, my orgasm slamming through me like a freight train. Breasts heaving, I buck beneath Dimitri as he pins me down with his strong arms, his hands gripping my hips with bruising force.

My fingers curl around his silky sheets, balling the fabric as my pussy throbs, my clit pulsing indefinitely. And when Dimitri's lips finally release me, I collapse onto the bed in a gasping heap.

"I think you like it when I eat your pussy," Dimitri teases, wiping my juices from his chin with his palm. His gray eyes dance dangerously.

"Mm-hmm," I whimper, scared that I won't actually have the ability to speak. Because my heart's lodged somewhere in my esophagus.

He shifts then, stalking forward to lean between my hips as he brings his face level with my breasts. "These beauties have been taunting me all night," he murmurs.

Cupping my breast, he guides my nipple between his lips and sucks, making it pucker as excitement pools deep in my core. Then he moves over to my other nipple, awakening my arousal as he teases it into a hard nub as well.

"Put your hands above your head, Camille," he murmurs as his lips work their way up my cleavage toward my throat.

Nerves blossom in my belly, but I find it easier to trust Dimitri now. At least with my pleasure. Because he knows how to make my body sing. With a hooded gaze, I watch his face, holding his eyes as I guide my arms up over my head until my fingers brush the headboard.

Dimitri's hands follow mine as he shifts to align our bodies, his fingers twining with mine until our palms kiss.

"Tell me what you want," he murmurs, his lips brushing lightly across mine.

"I want you to come inside of me," I breathe, and giddy excitement coils in my belly. I don't usually talk dirty, but Dimitri draws it out of me, making me feel bold as he demands to know my desires.

He hums with anticipation as his cockhead lines up with my wet folds, and he glides between them to find my entrance. My clit twitches as my core pulses with need.

Then he pushes slowly into my depths, his cock stretching and filling me deliciously.

13

Dimitri

Camille's hot, wet pussy tightens around my cock as I ease inside of her, intent on taking my time. Milking every ounce of pleasure from her. Her soft, curvaceous body arches beneath me, her breasts pressing firmly against my chest as I penetrate her deeply.

Pushing until I'm buried inside her to the hilt, I relish the way her walls throb. After a night of watching Camille come from her own fingers, from my fingers, from my tongue... I ache with the need to make her come on my cock.

Again. And again.

As I rock slowly in and out of her, Camille releases a luxurious moan.

I want to taste the pleasure leaving her lips.

Slanting my mouth over hers, I kiss her deeply. And she kisses me back, her head rising up off the bed to keep our lips locked.

Her fingers tighten around mine as I pin her hands above her head, holding her captive as I claim her body for my own. Nipples brushing against my chest, their taut excitement spurs me on.

I love the friction between our bodies. It lights my veins on fire and makes me want to drive her wild. Thrusting with increasing speed, I roll my hips with every forward movement, grazing her clit and stimulating her G-spot at the same time.

Mewling, Camille rocks greedily against me. Then her legs wrap around my hips. Feet still clad in those sexy high heels, she digs the points adamantly into my flesh, spurring me on.

Cock wrapped in her tight folds, her pussy gripping me firmly, I fuck her deliberately, driving her toward release. And as her legs start to tremble, I know she's close.

Cries of pleasure burst from her as I start to pound more forcefully into her depths. And then her head tips back, her eyes rolling into her head as she screams silently.

A moment later, she explodes around me, her pussy pulsing and gripping my cock as she falls apart beneath me.

My ears ring as all the blood rushes into my cock, hardening and engorging it further until I'm panting to hold back my impending orgasm.

Camille shudders beneath me, her body going limp momentarily, and I release her hands.

Reaching down, I scoop her legs up one at a time, hooking her knees with my elbows.

And as I continue to slide in and out of her slick hole, I ease her legs up, spreading her thighs wide. Moaning, she braces against the headboard as I trap her knees beside her breasts, her sexy heels in the air.

Her pussy's fully exposed now and at my mercy as I penetrate her deeply.

"Oh, ffffuck," she hisses, her walls tightening around my cock.

"You like that?" I rasp, circling my hips to stimulate her more.

"Yes, yes!" she gasps, and her eyes fly open.

Deep in their blue depths, I can see the intensity of her desire. She wants this as much as I do. And I want to give it to her until she begs me to stop. Any doubts or hesitations about our age difference are long gone. Because Camille wants me. I can see the craving in her eyes.

It leaves me ravenous, intent on drawing every drop of pleasure from her. She breathes heavily as I pick up a punishing pace, gliding into her wet pussy and easing out as I revel in the agonizing pleasure of her perfect body.

So bendable and supple, Camille yields completely beneath me, her body rocking with my thrusts, her eyes fathomless pools of ecstasy.

I don't have to ask if she's about to come. It's written across her face, the glassy lust in her gaze, the tantalizing way her lips part in anticipation. And I can't hold on much longer. I'm so close I feel as though I might implode.

"Come for me, *kotenok*," I groan, moments away from my own release.

She does, her body trembling violently as her legs jerk softly against my iron grip. Her pussy spasms, tightening like a vise around my hard length.

Shoving inside her, I come hard, my balls emptying as I pour my seed deep into her depths.

Breathing hard, I slow, gradually coming to a stop, relishing her aftershocks that throb around my cock. Every time my erection twitches in response, it makes her clit flutter. I love the way her body responds to me, the intensity of her pleasure.

It only heightens my own to see her young, beautiful body so eager to take all of me.

We still, our chests heaving in sync as we gasp for air together. Camille's muscles unwind, relaxing in my grip. And I slowly ease out of her, allowing her to settle comfortably onto the bed.

Rolling onto my back next to her, I stare up at the ceiling and consider whether that might be the best sex I've ever had. I can't quite put my finger on it, but something about Camille drives me absolutely insane.

And though I'm slowly coming down from the high of my release,

I'm already thinking about how I want to take her next, what positions I want to see her in.

Camille shifts beside me, rolling onto her side and scooting closer to rest her cheek on my shoulder, her thigh across my abdomen. Warmth radiates from her, seeping through my skin as she snuggles against me.

I wrap an arm around her shoulders, grazing my thumb up and down her silky soft skin. I don't usually hold women after I fuck them. I don't go for cute cuddles and pillow talk.

But Camille is so soft and inviting. I love the sight of her curves, the way her supple breasts press against me. And her fingers trace a delicate pattern up the side of my ribs and over my pecs. My eyes sink closed as I soak up the feather-light touch, somewhere between a tickle and a caress that makes the hair prickle on my arms.

"Your tattoo. It's beautiful," she murmurs, her breath whispering across my flesh.

I hum but don't say anything else, content to experience her dexterous fingers tracing the outline of my ink.

"Tell me about your family," she says as I come dangerously close to dozing off.

"What do you want to know?" I murmur, opening my eyes to look down at her thick head of auburn curls.

"Well, at dinner, you mentioned that your family owned Oishī and it got me thinking that we've talked about my dad and how I grew up, but I know nothing about you. Do you have siblings? Where do your parents live? Where are you even from?" Camille releases a soft laugh as if realizing how little she knows.

Talking about my personal life is usually another no-no. Either girls know exactly who I am and who I'm related to, or I prefer to keep them in the dark. But hearing Camille's story makes me want to open up somehow, to share a small part of me like she did.

"Well, I have an older brother, Maksim, and a younger brother, Alexei. We run a company together, Federov Brothers Investments, and the bank our father opened shortly after bringing us to America," I explain.

"And when was that?" she asks, tipping her head to look up at me.

"A long time ago now. I was about thirteen I think."

"And you've lived in San Francisco since then?" Camille presses.

"*Da.*" Just thinking about my past has memories of our life in Moscow flooding through my brain. I rarely think about my childhood there. It seems like a lifetime ago.

"And your parents?"

"My mother's still alive. She lives on our family estate south of here."

She gives a gentle nod, her arms giving me a gentle squeeze as if she picked up on the fact that my father's dead but doesn't want to bring the mood down.

"So, a family business, eh?" she asks playfully.

I glance down to meet her teasing gaze. "Yes, we've done well and turned my father's vision into a decent empire. We own quite a few restaurants and clubs in San Francisco and the surrounding areas."

"Sounds to me like a perfect front for some elicit Bratva activity," she jokes lightly, though her words dig deeper, raising my suspicion immediately.

"Yes, well, all of us Russian bastards who come to America must be Bratva criminals, mustn't we?" I sidestep, confessing to the truth but adopting a wicked grin that would say I'm obviously joking.

But I think that's enough of my personal history for the evening. Better to stop while we're ahead because we're treading on dangerous territory.

I roll on top of Camille, pinning her beneath my body and exacting a surprised giggle from her lips.

"What are you doing?" she squeals, wiggling under me and bringing my body to life.

"I think it's time for round two," I state, finding the curve of Camille's neck and sucking the soft flesh between my lips.

She gasps, goosebumps rising on her flesh, and I growl appreciatively as her nipples harden against my chest.

I suck harder, knowing it's going to leave a mark. But I like the thought of leaving something on Camille's body. Marking my territory.

She moans, arching into me, and her hands travel down the muscles of my back as she explores my body. I trail kisses down her neck to her collarbone and across her chest, licking and tasting every inch of her as I slowly worship her body.

She smells floral and citrusy and tastes as sweet as honey. As I work my way over her body, taking my time, her fingers comb into my hair. They curl, tugging lightly at the roots and making my cock stiffen with anticipation.

"Dimitri," she whimpers when I continue my delicious path over her body and down to the round, pert mountains of her breasts.

"Hmm?" I murmur against her flesh, too distracted by the feel of her soft skin on my lips to fully pay attention.

"I want you," she pleads.

I glance up at her from where my lips close around the hard nub of her nipple. Heat radiates from her gaze, consuming me.

"Impatient, are we?" I tease, releasing her breast with my lips and replacing them with my palm as I knead her supple flesh.

She moans, her hips rolling beneath me, calling attention to just where she needs me to be. Sliding my hand slowly down over her belly, I make my way to the peak of her thighs. I'm curious just how wet she'll be.

Gasping as my fingers brush across her clit, Camille jerks up off the bed with her hips. I find her slick folds in an instant and groan as my cock throbs with anticipation.

"You're so wet for me already."

Camille bites her lip in coy innocence, then nods, the picture of a fallen angel. And suddenly, I can't take my time. I need to bury my cock inside her and know just how many times I can make her beg me for release.

This girl is insatiable, and she brings to life a craving in me that is entirely too intoxicating.

Gripping the base of my cock, I glide my tip between her wet slit, collecting her juices and making her squirm. Then I line up with her entrance and push inside her once more.

14

Camille

I moan as I slowly wake, rising from sleep to find my body aching. It takes a moment to recall just what happened last night. And then excitement trickles down my spine as I recall vividly all the hot ways Dimitri took my body.

No wonder I'm sore.

And after such a long, sex-filled night, it's no surprise that my pussy is throbbing. The hollow ache deep in my core reminds me of just how intensely Dimitri fills me. Like going to yoga after too many months between sessions, I feel as though I've been stretched almost to the point of breaking.

Muscles I didn't even know I had twinge with my slightest movement, on the verge of cramping from such a thorough workout. Intense satisfaction seeps through me as flashes of our night together run through my mind.

It's almost too good to want to wake up. But I have to go to work eventually.

Opening my eyes, for a moment, I'm confused about what time it is. The room is still very dark, though I feel as though I got a decent amount of sleep. Then I spot the blackout curtains covering the wall of windows. They block out the bright day, allowing only the faintest slivers of bright sunlight to filter around the edges.

Glancing toward the side table next to me, I'm shocked to find it's nearly nine o'clock in the morning.

I didn't mean to spend the night with Dimitri, but here I am. I must have drifted off to sleep after our last round of sex in the early hours of the morning. I can hardly blame myself, honestly. I've never had so much sex in my life. So much good, intensely erotic, deeply satisfying sex.

Dimitri wrung every drop of pleasure from me, sapping my strength and energy with his insatiable appetite.

Rolling over to see if he's awake, I find his side of the bed empty. My heart skips a beat. Sitting up abruptly, I pull the covers around me, covering my breasts as I turn my attention toward the en suite bathroom. Maybe he went to take a shower or something.

But it looks empty.

Does this mean he's done with me? We had our date, now he's ready to move on?

Disappointment knots my stomach, and I realize with sinking remorse that my plan has failed completely. I tried a few times last night to dig for details about Dimitri's life and business, but I'm nowhere near finding out what happened to Roy. Dimitri's talented fingers and sinfully skillful lips distracted me every time I thought I might have found a window into broaching the subject.

Tears sting the back of my eyes as I realize how easily Dimitri used me. Because while I thought I was being smart and using his persistent pursuit of me to earn my freedom, he just wanted one night. One very passionate, steamy night.

He certainly got his fill.

I'm so stupid.

What was I thinking? Fighting the urge to cry, I climb slowly out of Dimitri's king-size bed. Searching the floor in the dim light trickling between the blackout curtains, I find my bustier and put it back on. Then I don my dress.

Collecting my heels, which got taken off at some point in our wild night, I hook my fingers through the straps to carry them. I'm not ready to put them back on my sore feet.

Embarrassment pools in my belly as I realize my walk of shame is going to require an Uber. Because Dimitri insisted on picking me up for our date last night, and I'd stupidly compromised by letting him get me from Le Fleur. I find it more than a little insulting that he wouldn't think about that beforehand. He could have at least let me bring my own car.

Then again, I suppose I got an amazing meal and a free helicopter ride out of the deal. Still, no one wants to sit in the back of an Uber, smelling like sex and wearing the same cocktail dress as the night before—sans panties because mine never reappeared.

Opening the bedroom door, I slowly make my way to the stairs, padding on quiet feet as I start to descend them. The cool glass feels wonderful on my blistered soles, the consequence of wearing those strappy new heels.

The heavenly scent of coffee lingers in the air, and my mouth waters at the thought of a hot cup of joe. He must have made some for himself before he took off. I'm sure it's too much to hope that he left a bit in the pot for me. I could use some caffeine right about now after such a late night.

The sound of sizzling catches my ear, and as I reach the bottom stair, my eyes snap toward the kitchen.

"Morning," Dimitri says as he pours a second dollop of pancake batter into a frying pan.

He must have been standing in the recessed corner of the kitchen when I first looked over the stair railing. I hadn't seen him at all.

Dressed in black joggers and a soft-looking designer T-shirt that molds to his sculpted body, he looks perfectly at ease. His dark hair, flecked with silver at his temples, is tousled in the best way; screaming sex and not yet styled after a night of sleep.

"I hope you're hungry," he states, glancing at me from the corner of his eye. A wicked grin tugs at the corner of his lips.

He's cooking breakfast for me?

Warmth floods my body at the thought, and butterflies come to life in my belly. As a chef, I never get the pleasure of people cooking for me. Roy always insisted my food was so much better than his, so whenever we ate together, it was a meal I made. And most nights I spend working at Le Fleur anyway. I think it's been since Daddy died that anyone's made a meal for me.

"Not that I'm complaining, but you look a bit overdressed for breakfast," Dimitri teases lightly as I continue to stand frozen, searching for words.

Still, I'm speechless as I try to wrap my mind around the reality of my situation. Not only is Dimitri here, cooking me breakfast, but the fact that he stayed fills me with intense relief and happiness that I'm not prepared to feel.

I shouldn't want to spend time with him. He's a murderer for Christ's sake. But just knowing he came down to prepare a meal for me while he let me sleep… that means everything.

"You look suspiciously ready to sneak off without saying goodbye," he observes as he sprinkles fresh blueberries onto each pancake and then flips them.

A nervous giggle bubbles up from me. "Sorry. I, um, assumed you'd left for work."

Dimitri's intense gray gaze assesses me as he considers my statement, and he seems to find my explanation unconvincing. In one smooth motion, he slides the finished pancakes onto a plate beside the stove. Then he sets aside the frying pan and slowly approaches me.

His face is predatory, his eyes tracking me like I'm his cornered prey. As he rounds the kitchen counter, I take an automatic step back, my nerves tingling as my instincts warn me of impending danger.

But before I can turn to flee, Dimitri closes the distance between us in three long strides.

Bending swiftly, he scoops me up fluidly, tossing me over his shoulder in the same motion as his strong arms close around my thighs.

"What are you doing?" I squeal, my heart jumping into my throat as he carries me like a sack of potatoes back toward the stairs.

A strong hand connects with my ass as he delivers a sharp spank, and I squeal again as my core tightens with anticipation. The warmth that radiates out across my skin reminds me of the day he bent me over my desk at work and spanked my ass thoroughly.

I shouldn't like the punishment, but something about his playful dominance turns my insides to mush.

My stomach turns upside down as we climb back up to his bedroom. The ground sinks away from me, growing more distant with each step he takes. Dangling helplessly over his shoulder, I brace against his muscular back.

And then he carries me through the door of his bedroom, flicking on the lights as he goes.

I shriek as he deposits me unceremoniously on the bed, leaving me weightless for a moment before my back finds the mattress. I bounce there, gasping for breath as I wonder at how easily he tosses me about—like I'm little more than a rag doll compared to his immense strength.

Reaching for his side table, Dimitri picks up a small remote, and the blinds whisper open behind me, revealing the San Francisco skyline, the pier, and the bay.

"Take off your clothes," he commands, turning his attention back to me. His eyes crackle with unbridled lust.

Biting my lip, I hesitate as I look up at him.

He watches me closely, the heat of his gaze turning impatient when I don't move to do as he says right away.

"You want me to help?" he offers.

Reaching forward, he grasps the folds of my skirt. I gasp as his hands find the high slit of my dress.

And with a sharp yank, he rips it.

My brain tells me I should feel offended by the desecration of such a beautiful dress. But carnal lust clouds my thinking, unfurling in my belly as he gives another forceful tug, opening my dress completely to expose my bare pussy and lingerie.

Breath shuddering between my lips, I rise slowly from the bed as I lock my gaze with Dimitri's molten one. And I let him ease the fabric gently down my arms.

The contrast of his violence toward the beautiful blue dress and his tender touch as his fingers push the soft fabric over my shoulders makes my skin prickle with goosebumps.

The ruined garment falls to the floor, and a wicked smile lights Dimitri's eyes.

"Would you like help with this one too?" he offers devilishly.

My hands fly up to the clasps of my bustier, and I work the hooks loose deftly.

A low rumble of appreciation vibrates from his chest as Dimitri's gaze rakes down my naked body. But he doesn't touch me. "Now, get back on the bed," he commands.

I do, scooting to its center as I watch him closely, my muscles tense and trembling with excitement.

"Stay," he warns, his eyes brilliant with lust as his joggers tent, revealing his quickly swelling cock. "I have plans for you," he promises darkly.

I shiver at the hungry look in his eyes.

And then, without another word, he turns and leaves.

15

Dimitri

I never let girls stay the night, but I couldn't keep my hands off Camille once I brought her up to my room. And by the time I finished my fifth round of deeply pleasurable sex with her, it was late enough that I couldn't even think about driving her back to Le Fleur.

Not to mention, the feel of her body curled against mine, her curves molding to my side, filled me with intense satisfaction—a contentment that made it all too easy to fall asleep.

I rose around eight o'clock in the morning, the floral scent of her shampoo filling my nose as she used my chest for a pillow. I'd slept solidly through the night, my arms wrapped around her as I held her close.

Waking with a raging hard-on, I was sorely tempted to rouse her by going down on her. But she looked so peaceful, and the thought of dressing her up in whipped cream before eating it off her sounded too tempting.

So instead, I rolled her to her other side, gently spooning her until she settled back into sleep. Then I slipped down to the kitchen.

And now, as I trek back downstairs to finish cooking, I can't wait to finish what I started. Camille looked so deliciously enticing. Her wide blue eyes looked up at me expectantly, her legs curled beneath her like a docile pet just waiting for her treat.

I know she's anything but meek. The girl's a firecracker, ready to take me head-on when most people would concede out of self-preservation. Not Camille. She challenges me in the sexiest ways, putting her foot down and taking control of the situation when it's something she's passionate about. Like her restaurant.

And yet, the more vulnerable side of her that I caught glimpses of last night—and again this morning—calls upon my instinctual need to protect her. I don't want her to fear me, and I find I'm physically repelled by the idea of doing anything to hurt her.

Cooking a fresh set of pancakes, I think about the sight of her creeping down the steps from my bedroom. I could see the rejection written clearly across her face. And though she brushed it off, saying she thought I'd left for work, I could see her sadness.

It bothers me more than a little that she would think I'm capable of bringing her to my apartment, spending that kind of night with her, and simply walking out the door without even offering her a ride. I might be a prick when it comes to girls, but even I'm not that heartless.

I focus on my cooking, finishing the one breakfast I've made an art of preparing. Then, with a tray loaded up with plates of pancakes, a bowl of fresh fruit, a bottle of whipped cream, syrup, and two cups of coffee, I make my way back upstairs to the provocative woman waiting in my bedroom.

Camille's exactly where I left her, a pillow tucked behind her back, her legs curled beneath her as she holds another pillow against her chest.

Her lips part in awe at the decadent tray I set in the middle of the bed.

"You went all out," she observes appreciatively, carefully sitting up without disrupting the coffee.

"I thought breakfast in bed sounded nice," I state. Though, in truth, my thoughts had started in a far less innocent place. This is only the start. I plan on taking full advantage of Camille's naked state.

"Thank you," she says, her smile warm as she gets to work spreading the butter over her blueberry pancakes, then smothering them in syrup.

I follow suit, cutting into my pancakes but waiting for her reaction before I take a bite.

"Mmm," Camille groans, her shoulders slumping as her eyes close in a gesture I'm quickly learning means approval. "Okay, how come you never mentioned being a breakfast master before?" she demands. "These are cooked perfectly, and those blueberries just burst across the tongue."

I chuckle, my eyebrow quirking at the suggestive sound of her words. A gentle blush colors Camille's cheeks as she seems to realize it as well.

"This is about my only forte in the kitchen, but I find pancakes are just the right level of challenge for my skill set."

She laughs, the soft sound warm and syrupy. "Well, I grew up cooking crepes, so anyone who can cook a pancake all the way through without burning it has considerable talent in my book."

Popping a strawberry into her mouth, Camille chews enthusiastically. Her love of food comes out in every bite she takes, the way she savors each flavor before swallowing. It's how I want to savor her.

She keeps her pillow tucked neatly over her lap, covering her breasts as she eats, and I fight the temptation to take it from her. I want to let her enjoy her breakfast before I get down to properly eating my meal.

She sips coffee politely, seeming content with the moderate amount of cream and sugar I put in. Next time I make breakfast for her, I'll know just how she likes it.

After eating the majority of her food, Camille releases a satisfied sigh and sets down her fork. "That's the best breakfast I've had in a long time," she states.

"Well, don't be too impressed. This is entirely for me," I tease.

Camille's head tips questioningly to the side, her eyes flicking to the two cups of coffee and her nearly empty plate. Confusion flits across her face.

I chuckle darkly and reach across the tray to take the pillow clutched against her chest, setting it aside pointedly. "I misspoke. What I meant to say was this is entirely for my benefit."

Picking up the tray, I move it to a side table. Then, turning, I grip Camille's ankles and pull her down the bed until she's stretched out before me like a sexy, voluptuous table.

Her breasts swell, as she takes a sharp breath, her nipples puckering like two beautiful mountain peaks.

"Dimitri!" she gasps as I quickly strip my shirt.

Selecting a raspberry still remaining in the bowl of fruit, I hold it before her lips.

Excitement flickers in Camille's blue eyes, and her exasperation shifts into silent anticipation as she takes the berry delicately from my fingers with her lips and chews it slowly.

Reaching for the whipped cream next, I pop the top off and shake the aerosol can.

Camille giggles, the light sound pouring from her like a fountain, as I squirt a dollop of the sugary treat onto each of her nipples. Next, I slowly draw a line down the center of her, tracking between her breasts and all the way down her stomach to her navel. Then lower, adding a generous amount to the peak of her thighs.

I finish by holding the nozzle over her mouth, offering Camille a taste. She parts her lips seductively, accepting the offer, and I squirt a burst of white cream onto her tongue. She moans appreciatively, and the sight of her swallowing the sweet cream makes my cock ache.

I want to have those juicy lips wrapped around my girth, to watch her swallow *my* cream and moan like it's as good as Reddi-wip.

Leaning in, I kiss the sugar from her lips, my tongue delving into her mouth to share the suggestive treat. I swallow her soft whimper as Camille's fingers comb into my hair, her nails scraping lightly along my scalp.

Her hand, tangled firmly in my locks, follows as I shift my focus to the whipped cream swirled into peaks around her nipples.

My pulse quickens as her breaths turn fast and shallow, her breasts rising and falling dramatically. Sucking the sugary cream from her taut nubs, I relish the way she moans, squirming beneath me. Once the hard pebbles of her fine tits are pristine, I move on to the line of white frosting that tracks down the length of her body.

"Oh God, that feels so good," she breathes as I suck the cream from her body, inch by inch, and then lick her clean.

"Mmm, it tastes even better, I assure you," I tease.

Camille's fingers tighten convulsively in my hair, tugging at the roots as I shift my body, moving between her legs. Gripping her knees firmly, I guide her thighs apart, exposing her delicious pussy already glistening with her arousal.

A small mountain of whipped cream still waits for me on her clit, and I lean forward, my shoulders spreading her thighs further so I can slurp the sugary goodness from her body.

Camille groans, her head falling back and her shoulders lifting from the bed at the sudden contact of my lips on the sensitive bundle.

The tang of her juices mingles with the sweet sugar on my tongue as I trace her sexy slit. Sucking in a sharp breath, Camille shivers deliciously beneath my hands as I transition from eating things off of her to eating her pussy.

I love that even though I fucked her within an inch of her life last night, she's still eager for more this morning. Wet and ready for me just from letting me eat whipped cream off her.

Circling her clit with my tongue, I tease Camille, and my balls tighten at the sound of her mewling pleas. She's the sexiest kind of greedy, hungry for my touch and ravenous for release.

Reaching around her thighs, I run my hands up her sides to find her breasts. And as I penetrate her with my tongue, I palm her full tits.

"Fuck!" she gasps, her walls constricting as I stroke into her core and suck gently on her pussy lips.

I find the taut nubs of her nipples, and this time, I pinch them and roll them between my fingers, drawing a pain-laced cry of ecstasy from her lips. She finds her release a moment later, a fresh wave of juices coating my tongue and chin as her clit twitches against my mouth.

Her pussy throbs, clenching again and again as if begging for the cock I intend to fill her with momentarily.

Leaning back onto my knees, I strip my joggers, tossing them aside haphazardly. Then I return to the sweet peak of her enticingly spread legs.

Licking and sucking my way back up the line of her body, I find Camille's lips. She kisses me fiercely, her tongue stroking into my mouth with a demanding hunger that makes me crave her even more.

Snaking my arms beneath her body, I roll beneath her until Camille's on top, and she looks absolutely scintillating as she leans back to sit astride me. Scooping her thick curls to the side with one arm, she peers down at me with a smoldering gaze.

Her palms rest on my chest, her fingers splayed across my pecs as she rolls her hips on top of me. The slick wetness of her folds stroke my hard length as she rides my cock, pinning it between my abdomen and her warm, tantalizing pussy.

Fire dances in her gaze as I grip her hips firmly, crushing her to my erection as I nearly come from the sexy way she humps me—as if teasing me with the true pleasure to come.

"Tell me what you want," she breathes, turning my words on me. And I think she might just be the most glorious creature I've ever seen.

"I want to watch you use my cock like your personal dildo, *kotenok*," I growl. "I want you to ride me into oblivion."

Camille takes her full lower lip between her teeth and raises up onto her knees to reach between us. Her eyes trap mine with a lusty gaze as she lines my cockhead up with her entrance.

And then she eases down onto my hard length. I feel every slick, torturous inch of her as she slowly sits on me. She doesn't stop until I'm buried balls deep. My muscles vibrate with tension at the heavenly feel of her pussy wrapped around me, her curvaceous body on full display.

Her thick thighs spread wide to accommodate me, her full ass so grabbable I can't resist. Running my hands back around her hips, I grab a handful of her booty that's large enough to swallow my cock.

Camille arches her back as she combs her fingers into her thick locks, a picture of erotic pleasure as she starts to roll her hips. A moan parts her lips as my hard cock slides in and out of her tight core, and a rumbling snarl echoes from me in response.

This girl is Aphrodite in the flesh, come to tempt me in a way I never knew I needed until now. But every second I'm with Camille, I grow more and more addicted. Like a drug addict in desperate need of a fix, I can't seem to stop craving her.

And only when I'm buried deep inside her pussy do I feel the heady relief I need.

"You are so fucking sexy," I rasp, kneading her ass, and when she leans forward to press her breasts against my chest, I give her a hard spank.

Camille's pussy tightens deliciously around me as she groans.

And then she grips the back of my neck as she leans in to kiss me.

"Again," she pleads against my lips.

And I spank her other round cheek.

Kissing me deeply, Camille grips the back of my neck and guides me into a sitting position. And as I wrap my arms around her waist, she starts to rock against me forcefully.

Grinding her clit against my body, she rolls her hips to take my cock deep inside her and then eases it back out. The way she rides me is confident and provocative, her breasts pressing firmly against me with each forward thrust, her hips undulating, showing off her flexibility and strength.

Where has this girl been all my life? I don't know, but I'm consumed by her now. Her tight pussy takes every inch of me as she fucks me slow yet hard. I shift my arm, wrapping one around her hips as I pull her more firmly to me. I thrust upward, driving my cock deeper inside with every roll of her hips.

"I'm coming," Camille groans, her hips rocking harder as her pussy tightens around me.

Leaning in, I capture her nipple between my teeth, and like

pressing a button, she explodes around me. I suck hard on the taut flesh, making her whimper as she twitches forcefully, gripping my erection like she'll never let go.

Her orgasm fills me with excruciating pleasure, and I strain to hold my load a bit longer. As the last of her aftershocks subside, I roll on top of Camille once more.

She clings to me, seeming to have gotten a feel for how our bodies can move together. And as she lies flat on her back, I kneel, lifting her hips to change the angle.

16

Camille

"Oh God!" I whimper as Dimitri thrusts inside me, slamming into my G-spot.

"Say *my* name," he reminds me on a growl.

Because he's my god now. I know it without a doubt.

Keeping my hips aloft, he pounds mercilessly into my pussy.

"Oooo, Dimitri," I moan through clenched teeth, my eyes rolling back into my head as my pleasure becomes almost too intense. My fingers curl reflexively in the sheets as tingling euphoria ripples up my spine.

Shifting to hold me with one arm, Dimitri presses the pad of his thumb against my clit, stimulating me with slow circles as he penetrates me deeply. "Good girl, *malen'kiy kotenok*," he praises, rewarding me for saying his name.

I tremble violently, my body utterly spent from how many times I've come in the last twenty-four hours. I've lost count. All I know is that I'm putty in his godlike hands. He knows each spot and angle that drives me wild.

This new position tightens my well-used pussy, intensifying the friction between us even as the arousal from my first two orgasms allows him to slide inside me with ease. Tension builds at the base of my neck, sending tingling euphoria out to my extremities.

And though I've only just come, I know I'm close to a third release in a matter of minutes.

Dimitri grunts, and I open my eyes to peer up at his chiseled face, I can see the tension in his straining muscles, the taut lines of his neck. He's close too.

Giddy anticipation warms my core at the thought of feeling him come inside me once again. I love his pulsing release that matches the power of my own, urging me to come harder as he fills me up.

Pinching my clit between his finger and thumb, Dimitri rolls the tiny bundle of nerves, demanding my release. And the intensity of my orgasm erupts across the back of my eyelids as I see stars.

My clit twitches exhaustedly as my walls clamp down around his cock, milking him to his own release. His iron length swells and pulses before blasting inside me, pouring hot cum deep inside my pussy.

I whimper as we throb together, my body guiding him further and further into my depths.

And Dimitri slams home, his pelvis crushing my clit as his hips jerk erratically.

"Christ," he groans, letting me sink onto the bed as he eases out of me.

I sigh contentedly, looking up at Dimitri through hooded eyes. I've never enjoyed sex this much in my life. I could get lost in the euphoria of it, falling into the pleasure like the sweetest fresh spring on a hot summer day.

Leaning over me, Dimitri steals a quick kiss then rolls off the bed.

"Where are you going?" I ask drowsily, my sex-addled thoughts clouding my brain.

Releasing a low, rumbling chuckle, he heads toward the bathroom. "The shower. Care to join me?"

I hum appreciatively at the thought of seeing water slicking his muscular body, though it's hard to imagine him looking sexier than he already does. And washing the sticky remnants of his whipped cream snack from my body sounds nice.

Rolling lazily onto my side, I prepare to climb off the bed.

My eyes find the clock resting on the bedside table, and in an instant, all thoughts of sex vanish from my mind.

"Shit!" I gasp, suddenly wide awake as I race toward the shower.

"Everything alright?" he asks, his face registering mild amusement as his eyebrows raise and his lips curve.

"I'm late," I state, shocked that it could already be past eleven. "I'm very, very late."

Did breakfast and sex really take over two hours?

I completely lost track of time.

Dimitri steps aside as I jump into the shower, and I'm grateful for his instant hot water.

"So... no shower sex?" Dimitri teases.

I throw him a thunderous look. "I don't even have time to go back to my apartment." My stomach drops as I realize I have nothing to wear because my dress is lying in shreds on his bedroom floor.

He hands me a towel as I step out of the quickest shower of my life—just a quick wash with his wonderfully spicy body soap followed by a frantic rinse. Then he vanishes from the bathroom.

I follow Dimitri into the bedroom as he heads to his closet. And as he sorts through his clothes, I quickly fasten my bustier around my midsection. He returns to me a moment later with a blue pinstripe dress shirt and a leather belt.

"Put this on," he offers.

And I'm so desperate, I don't refuse. Shrugging into the oversized shirt, I button it quickly at the same time as he rolls the sleeves. Then he cinches the belt around my waist, giving me an impressively adequate tunic dress for what we have on hand.

"I think I might have leggings in my car," I realize as relief floods me. Though it's not my typical style, I'm just grateful to have an outfit to wear. And as humiliating as it might be to walk through Dimitri's lobby in something this short, it will have to do.

"Well then, let's get you to it," he says, a smile stretching across his ridiculously handsome face. Snatching his joggers and T-shirt off the floor, Dimitri dresses as we head out the door.

We make it into the elevator and start to sink toward the lobby before I realize I'm still not wearing panties. I bite my lip, glancing down at the hem of the dress shirt to see if it even covers my ass in its entirety.

Just barely, with maybe an inch or two to spare. Dear God.

Dimitri takes note of my inspection and a dark laugh issues from his throat. "I think those panties might be the best souvenir I ever collect," he observes playfully.

And before I think twice about it, I give his shoulder a light slap.

He chuckles, unbothered by my temper, and pulls me roughly against him as he palms my ass over the long shirt. "No one will notice once you're wearing leggings," he points out.

"*If* I have leggings," I qualify, praying to the karma gods that the pair I tossed onto my back seat is still there. I put exercise clothes in my car at the start of the year in the hopes that it might help my New Year's resolution to get to the gym more. Clearly, that hasn't worked.

Dimitri releases me as the doors ding open onto the lobby, and I self-consciously pull his shirt down lower over my hips as I scuttle toward the door.

We get to Le Fleur in good time, Dimitri testing out the speed and agility of his car before stopping just behind my little green Bug.

"Thank you for the fun night," I gush as he pulls up to the curb. "And the outfit."

"My pleasure," Dimitri says. "I will see you again soon?"

"Uh-huh." I agree, scrambling out of his car as I attempt to not flash anybody.

His motor purrs quietly as he waits for me to unlock my car and slide into the back seat.

Hallelujah! I do have leggings—but no fresh socks or tennis shoes. Hopefully, I've stashed something in my office. I do that sometimes, on the rare occasion that I have a business meeting before a night working in the kitchen.

Not bothering to take off my high heels, I yank my leggings up over my hips, then straighten my outfit as I slip back out of my car. Dimitri's black Lamborghini still idles behind me, and I give him a quick wave as he flashes me a smile.

As I rush through the front doors of Le Fleur, his car pulls smoothly away, merging into traffic. And I don't have time to process all that has taken place in the last twenty-four hours.

"Well, hello," Hannah greets me, her voice teasing as she looks me up and down.

I glance down at the ridiculous combination of high heels, athletic pants, and a dress shirt that's easily five times too large. Not many things in this world make me feel small, but I suddenly realize just how big Dimitri must be.

"Don't you look... nice today," she says tactfully, her smile splitting her face. "Bit of a late start?"

"Shut up," I say flatly, making a beeline for my office. "Sorry, I'm late," I tack on, over my shoulder.

Hannah follows me, unwilling to let me off that easy. You would think that the one perk of having no living parents would be that I might get away with a walk of shame unscathed. But not with Hannah as my best friend. She's more like a sister to me, and when it comes to teasing, she knows how to make me blush.

"Is it just me, or did you do something different with your hair?" she asks, her eyes combing over what I'm sure must be a rat's nest. "And do you smell different? Also, is that a new shirt? It's cute—kind of... elegant casual? Relaxed chic?" she teases, closing the office door behind her as I duck behind my desk to look for shoes.

Popping my head up over the flat surface—and receiving a stark reminder of how Dimitri and I had sex there too—I give my friend a withering glare. "What are you, the question police? If you must know, I spent the night at Dimitri's," I state.

Hannah looks slightly surprised, her teasing expression deflating a little. "You slept with him? Wasn't this your first date?"

Considering my lack of relationship status all through college combined with how long it took me and Roy to reach that level of intimacy, I'm not shocked that she's incredulous. Under normal circumstances, I would agree. Dimitri and I are moving *way* faster than I'm used to.

But these aren't normal circumstances. And my relationship with Dimitri is anything but ordinary. I sigh heavily, flopping back in my roller seat as I resign myself to telling Hannah what's really happening. Screw being late. If the kitchen hasn't managed to pick up my slack by now, a few more minutes isn't going to save the night.

"I mean, not that I'm judging, Cami. Don't get me wrong. The guy is gorgeous, rich, charming, and *very* persistent. You just aren't normally the kind of girl who dives headfirst into those kinds of things" Hannah comes to sit on the edge of my desk, her face genuinely concerned.

"No, you're right," I say hesitantly, meeting her eyes with great reluctance.

She waits patiently for me to continue, her hazel gaze watching me closely.

"Okay, so here's the thing, you know how I'm pretty sure Roy was murdered?" I ask.

"Yeaaah?" Hannah says slowly, her tone telling me she fails to see how that's at all related.

"Well, apparently, he was a complete bastard who took out a loan with a particular, prominent Russian-owned bank. He put Le Fleur up as collateral and forged my signature. Then proceeded to gamble the entire loan away," I state.

"There's no way," Hannah argues. "That's totally illegal."

"Yeah, well Dimitri seems to think the contract's pretty binding. And now that Roy is dead..."

Hannah gasps. "The bank came for your restaurant?"

"Enter Dimitri Federov, co-owner of Federov Capital."

Hannah's jaw drops. "He's a banker?"

"Well, his family owns the bank. He's more of a business acquisitions expert. And he offered to buy me out of Le Fleur rather than letting me pay off the loan."

"Whoa, whoa, whoa," she says, holding up her hands. "You're thinking of actually paying this guy? For a loan you didn't even sign?"

"I don't know what else to do, Hannah. I mean, I genuinely think he might have killed Roy because Roy stopped paying off his debt. And now he's coming after me. My business."

"This is, like, mafia stuff, isn't it? You need to go to the police with this," she insists.

"And tell them what exactly? Hello Officer, remember me? The girl whose boyfriend died in a house fire. Yeah, well, I'm pretty sure I know who murdered him, and oh, by the way, the man responsible happens to be a very prominent businessman. You might have heard of him. He owns about half the restaurants in San Francisco. Also, he's blackmailing me for my restaurant. Yes, he has a very official-looking document that says it's rightfully his. Yes, it has my signature, but I swear I didn't agree to the loan. No, I can't really afford to pay it off, but that doesn't give me any motivation at all for making it sound like he's responsible for my boyfriend's death. Oh, and by the way, you don't need evidence proving this or anything do you? Great." I give Hannah a flat look.

"Well, hell," she mutters, her shoulders slumping. "But wait, why the hell are you sleeping with this jerk again? It sounds to me like you should be sprinting the other way."

"Evidence," I state pointedly. "I want to go to the police, and I'm sure if I can prove that he killed Roy they'll believe the contract was a forgery. But until then, I'm trying to buy myself some time and get close enough to Dimitri to find out what really happened."

"That's your plan?" she asks incredulously.

"It'll work," I insist. "He's already starting to open up to me. And it's not like I'm really into Dimitri or anything. But pretending to like him might be the only way I can get out of this without losing Le Fleur." My gut twists as the words leave my mouth. Because honestly, I'm not so sure they're completely true anymore. At least the part about liking Dimitri.

After yesterday, I feel like I'm walking on a tightrope, dangerously close to falling while I try to keep my sights on the end goal at the far side.

Hannah sighs heavily, rising from my desk and pulling me from my chair. "Just please promise me you'll be careful. This guy sounds dangerous. I mean, if Dimitri's capable of killing Roy and he finds out what you're doing? Don't go getting yourself killed, okay?"

I swallow hard as Hannah really drives the point home, reminding me of just how high the stakes are. "I'll be careful. Promise," I say.

And when she hugs me, I give her a grateful squeeze. I'm glad I told her the truth, but now more than ever, I realize I need to keep my focus. I can't get lost in my feelings for Dimitri. Not with my life and my livelihood hanging in the balance.

17

Dimitri

Staring out the window from the fiftieth floor, I rest my chin in my palm as images of Camille flash through my mind. Her curvy body laid bare before me, the arch of her neck as she found her release, the perfect O of her full lips as she fell apart around me.

Sex with her is out of this world.

But I find that it's not the only thing I find so appealing about her. The girl's a natural beauty, sure. And yet she doesn't seem to have the ego that normally goes along with a face like hers. She's humble—shy even.

Until I bring her desire to life.

Then she becomes a queen of confidence, her appetite overcoming any embarrassment as she unleashes an otherworldly strength and sensuality. I love turning her on and setting her loose to satiate her needs.

And her tenacity. It's not by chance that she's so successful as a young chef and business owner. Where most might buckle under the pressure she carries, Camille seems to shoulder it with a pride all her own.

The more I learn about Camille, the more I want to discover.

She entered my life like a firework and has captured my attention like no girl ever has before. It's driving me insane.

I want to see her again.

"Dimitri," Maksim growls, demanding my attention once again.

"Hmm? Sorry," I sit up in my chair, tearing my eyes away from the window and the middle distance where I found Camille's tantalizing image in my brain.

"I asked how things were going with the acquisition of Le Fleur," my older brother states, his stormy expression clearly demonstrating his irritation with me.

Not that I can blame him. My attention has been entirely nonexistent all day.

But now, I'm suddenly all ears. My stomach knots at the mention of Camille's restaurant and the conversation I know is coming. I promised my brothers a restaurant and a done deal during our last meeting. And so far, I've failed on both counts. Miserably.

But Camille's story about why she opened Le Fleur moved me, and I find it hard to talk about buying it from her now, as if something she cares about so deeply is just another Federov family business strategy. Even bringing up the topic feels like I'm dishonoring her father's memory.

And she clearly loves him more than anything. Because he's why she's fighting me tooth and nail to keep Le Fleur.

"What is it with you today?" Maksim demands. "It's like you're a hundred miles away. I ask you a question, repeat it for you, and still no answer. I might as well be discussing our portfolio with a wall."

"Maybe it's the chef," Alexei suggests, hitting the nail on the head.

And suddenly, I'm defensive, bristling as my younger brother puts his finger on my sore spot. He can detect it with the sharp accuracy of someone who's known me my whole life—or at least the entirety of his. And he's not afraid to push my buttons like most people in San Francisco would be.

"What would you know about it?" I snap, shifting in my chair as I consider any viable options for getting off the excruciating topic.

"Oh-ho!" Alexei teases, leaning away from me as he senses the anger boiling up in my chest. "I think, Maksim, that our brother may have finally met his match. It's never taken you this long to close a deal before, Dimitri. Does that mean your feelings for the chef are getting in the way of your big business brain?"

"Why is it that these meetings always seem to devolve into childish sibling taunting?" I demand.

Scowling at Alexei, I refuse to answer his astute observation. Because Camille's effect on me has everything to do with why I haven't closed the deal. *I* told *her* not to talk about business on our date. I don't think I've ever uttered those words before. To anyone.

But now that I know how much Camille's restaurant means to her, I'm even less inclined to bring up the purchase again.

"Is that what's going on?" Maksim demands, leaning forward in his chair.

I turn to study my older brother, his sharp gray eyes the same as our father's, his stern expression like a mirror image of our old man.

I want to deny it, to tell them both they can just go to hell for doubting my abilities to close a deal. But after my night with Camille, I'm not so sure I can. And it's best to come clean to them now, to be transparent with my brothers, because this is their business too. And my decisions affect them just as much as they do me.

Still, even if I choose not to close the deal with Camille, I won't let Maksim step in to do it for me. On this, he will respect my decision. I'll make sure of it.

"Yes," I state simply.

They don't need to hear the how or the why of it all. Just that my feelings for Camille are hindering my intentions to uphold the contract.

"Really?" Maksim's stern expression shifts to mild surprise. His dark eyebrows arch and the tension in his shoulders relaxes.

Then, to my astonishment, he actually starts to grin.

"Well, I'm happy for you if you've actually found a girl you're serious about," he states, his tone shifting to match his expression. "I was starting to wonder if you would ever settle down."

"Not all of us hook a model and propose after six weeks, Maks," Alexei points out, rolling his eyes at Maksim's impulsive romance with Symphony.

Maksim throws our baby brother a cold look before turning his attention back to me.

"I don't know that I would go so far as to say I'm settling down just yet," I explain. "We've had one date. But I'll admit I'm in uncharted territory with this girl. She's... different."

And by that, I mean interesting. Engaging. Real. Someone willing to fight for what she cares about. And still willing to swing at curveballs. I might have come into the situation on the opposing side of Camille, but somewhere along the way, she not only managed to bring me over to her side. She has me wondering just what makes her tick.

"Well... that's great," Maksim acknowledges, seemingly willing to concede the topic without an argument.

I didn't expect that.

"Great," I state.

"Yeah, great," Alexei pipes in, his tone playfully mocking.

"Don't you have some security tape footage to review or something?" I demand, giving him a side-eye.

Alexei shrugs. "But then who would do the very important job of tormenting you?"

Growling in frustration, I look back at Maksim, whose expression has turned businesslike once more.

"That still doesn't give me an answer about what's going to happen with the restaurant," he states.

And just like that, my temper rises once again.

"For fuck's sake!" I snap, rising from my chair and launching it across the room. "If the loan is such a big damn deal that we can't take a loss this one time, then I'll cover it with money from my personal account."

Maksim and Alexei stare up at me with astonished surprise. Neither says a word.

I don't think they expected me to respond quite so forcefully.

In truth, I didn't expect it either.

But I just admitted to having feelings for this girl, and all my brother can think about is the bottom line. He doesn't seem to give a crap about how taking Camille's restaurant from her might destroy my relationship with her.

Not that I've taken the time to explain that to Maksim.

But my temper's white-hot, and I can't seem to rein it in. "You know what? I'm done for today. You can figure the rest out between the two of you. Just don't fucking touch the restaurant deal. It's mine."

Then I storm toward the door.

"Dimitri," Maksim calls after me.

"Hey, come on! Don't be so sensitive," Alexei adds.

But I slam the door behind me and make my way to the elevators.

I'm not usually prone to theatrics, but when it comes to Camille, I'm starting to realize not everything I do is entirely sane. I want to see where things go between us, and I'm ready to do whatever it takes.

If that means eating a five-hundred-thousand-dollar debt, I'm willing to do that. Because after learning more about who she is and how she came to be the person she is today, I'm less inclined to try and take her restaurant away.

And I'm struggling, now more than ever, with the notion of making her pay for her dead boyfriend's debt when she didn't even know about it in the first place.

18

Camille

It's a long, hard rush, the front of the house packed and keeping the kitchen busy. And standing in front of the grill, I'm dripping sweat for most of the night. By the time the kitchen closes, I'm exhausted. It doesn't help that my muscles have needed some major recovery time after my date with Dimitri.

The first two days, I felt like I'd gone on a powerlifting spree, but now, on the third day, my aches and pains have started to fade. The hot images of our night together, less so.

"Phew!" Louis says, wiping his brow and flashing me a smile as he starts to clean up the stove.

I return the smile and get to work cleaning as well.

"Cami?" Hannah's familiar voice calls to me from the doorway, and when I look up, she jerks her head in an indication that I should come talk to her.

Setting aside my wire scrubber, I do.

"What's up?" I ask, stripping my rubber gloves.

Concern etches her face, and I wonder if we might not have a disgruntled customer wanting to speak to the chef.

"He's back," she says, all her playful teasing replaced by genuine concern after what I told her the other day.

My heart skips a beat, and I tell myself it's because she looks so worried.

"I'll come talk to him. Thanks." I give her a reassuring smile.

"He's at the bar... Cami..."

"I know, I know, Mom. I'll be careful," I tease, taking the words from her mouth.

Hannah frowns but leaves me as she heads back up to the host stand.

Wiping my face with the cuff of my chef's robes, I take a deep breath before pushing through the swinging door and heading toward the bar.

Dimitri leans against it, not using a chair as his hand cradles a glass of chilled vodka. He looks as handsome as ever, his hair styled perfectly, his fine gray suit paying homage to his striking gray eyes. He sees me coming and flashes a winning smile.

"Busy night?" he asks, indicating the splashes of sauce that made it onto my protective clothing.

I laugh. "Every night is a busy night. What brings you here?" I ask lightly, ignoring the butterflies that flutter in my belly.

"I'd like to take you somewhere," he states, leaning dangerously close to me.

I can smell the piney scent of his cologne mingling with the spice of his body wash. I would recognize that scent anywhere after it lingered on my skin the entire day after our date. And as I breathe deeply, the enticing scent makes my mouth water.

"Now?" I ask, forcing myself to focus on Dimitri's handsome face. My eyes flick down to his perfectly shaped lips, and I swallow the urge to kiss him.

A wolfish grin curls those beautiful lips, and when my eyes lift to meet his, I can tell he's caught me looking.

"Well, when you're done closing," he qualifies playfully, then glances around the empty restaurant.

It's nearing eleven o'clock, and most of the staff have gone home by now. Just a few kitchen members still on their side work and the bartender finishing up.

"Um, okay. Give me twenty minutes?" I still need to finish cleaning and change out of my uniform. That should give everyone else plenty of time to finish their tasks and head home.

"Take all the time you need," he says, though his eyes flash with an impatience that makes my stomach quiver.

But as I turn to leave, his fingers catch my palm. Spinning me back toward him, Dimitri pulls me close.

"No kiss?" he teases, his liquid metal gaze shifting from my eyes to my mouth.

A breathy giggle escapes me, and though I know I should keep things professional at my restaurant, when he leans in to claim my lips, I don't pull away.

Fire sizzles through my veins as he kisses me slowly, enticingly, awakening my excitement as our lips move together in a tantalizing dance. He pulls away all too soon, though he still leaves me gasping for breath.

A coy smile stretches across his face. "To inspire you to finish quickly," he teases, releasing me.

Molten excitement bubbles through me as I turn and leave. I move with newfound purpose as I finish scrubbing my station clean and wish my fellow chefs a good night as they head out the door.

I tell myself that my excitement is for the opportunity to do some more digging about Roy's death. Not that Dimitri is here. No, I'm determined to find my answers tonight—either by asking Dimitri or, if all else fails, by digging through his things for evidence after he's gone to sleep.

And any sex we might have will only be to keep him off my trail.

"Do you want me to stay?" Hannah asks, stepping into the kitchen doorway and looking pointedly toward the handsome Russian waiting for me at the bar.

"No, I'll be okay. But thank you," I say warmly.

Hannah nods, seeming reluctant to leave me alone with him now that she knows the truth of it all. Still, she doesn't argue because she can see the determination in my eyes.

"Have a good night, then," she says with a half-hearted wave.

"You too! See you tomorrow."

I get back to work, finishing my cleaning. Then I do a final sweep to ensure the back door is locked and everything's turned off. Kitchen tasks complete, I head quickly to my office to take off my robes and freshen up as best I can. Then I meet Dimitri by the bar once more.

"Ready?" he asks, his eyes raking down my body appreciatively.

Excitement blossoms in my belly.

Dressed in a soft hunter-green oversized sweater and stretchy jeans that mold perfectly to my curves, it's not the dressiest outfit for a night out, but he didn't really give me much warning. And it's certainly comfy. "Ready as I'll ever be," I say.

He places his hand on the small of my back, gesturing for me to lead the way. We head toward the door together, me turning off lights as we go. And the usually spooky task of closing on my own suddenly feels so easy with Dimitri beside me.

Holding the door for me, he lets me exit first, then steps aside as I fish the building's keys from my purse. A creepy sense of déjà vu trickles down my spine as I put the key in the lock and slide the deadbolt home with a soft thunk.

Skin tingling, I get that same haunting sense that someone's watching me. My neck swivels on instinct, turning to look at the corner where someone was watching me the other night. Sure enough, the black car sits there again, still and silent. Like a panther crouching in preparation to pounce.

The hair raises on the back of my neck as I make out the shadowed figure in the driver's seat. And though I can't see their face, I'm sure they're watching me. I can feel the person's eyes following my every move.

I shiver violently.

"What's wrong?" Dimitri asks, his brows furrowing as he turns to follow my gaze.

And just like the other night, as soon as the stranger knows he's been spotted, he flicks on his headlights and starts his engine. He pulls away from the curb a moment later and disappears around the corner, leaving me trembling anxiously.

"Someone's been watching me," I breathe, trying to keep the fear from my voice. But I don't quite succeed.

I get the distinct feeling that my stalker's intentions are malevolent. Like he's waiting for the perfect opportunity. The opportunity for what, however, I haven't a clue.

"The person in the black car?" Dimitri asks, his expression sharp as his eyes flick from me back to the corner where the car disappeared. His face grows troubled, the sharp line of his jaw tensing.

I nod. "That's the second time I've caught him parked there. He did the same thing last time, waiting to watch me lock up. Then just... leaving. I don't know why he's watching me. But it gives me the creeps."

Another violent shudder racks my body as goosebumps race across my flesh. Last time, I managed to talk myself out of my unsettled feeling. But this time, I'm sure it's no coincidence. It's not some drunk who fell asleep. He's here for me.

Dimitri's arm wraps around my shoulders, pulling me protectively against his chest as his eyes scan up and down the street for any movement. Nothing. The street is empty except for us.

"Does anyone else know about this?" he asks, urging me toward his car.

"I called Hannah when it happened the first time. But I wasn't entirely sure what it all meant then. I thought maybe it was just coincidental... or that you might have sent someone to keep an eye on me." I force my voice into a light tone as I add the last part, making it sound like a joke. A laugh bubbles nervously from me afterward, and I cringe at how bad it sounds.

Dimitri stiffens, his steps slowing, and he looks down at me. When I glance up, his expression appears more angry than troubled now.

"You thought I would have someone follow you?" he demands, his eyes flashing as he bristles visibly.

Yes. "N-No," I stutter, my heart skipping a beat. It does seem like a rather ridiculous thought now that it's out in the open. "Sorry. Bad joke," I say, trying to diffuse the situation.

And yet, intense relief floods me at the offense he took at the idea.

Dimitri softens slightly, and we continue on toward the car, his arm still holding me firmly to his side.

"I assure you," he says after a moment, his voice less angry now, "I do a perfectly fine job of following you without paying someone to sit outside your restaurant."

I laugh genuinely this time, the knot easing in my stomach to know he's not mad at me.

"After all, you're with me now, aren't you?" he teases, glancing down at me.

"Fair point well taken," I say, smiling.

I'd had my doubts when I first saw the black car waiting outside the restaurant for me. The timing seemed off to think it might be Dimitri. Still, it's nice to clear the suspicion from my mind. And then another dark question takes its place.

If it isn't someone Dimitri hired, who is following me?

My anxiety spikes once more at the question I have no answer for. In some ways, the complete lack of identifiable suspects is almost more unnerving. Yes, the thought of a Russian gangster sending someone to watch me would be utterly terrifying.

But fear of an unknown predator intensifies my worry, fogging my brain. It's like walking into a dark room where I know something dangerous lurks inside, but I don't know what it is or where it might be.

Dimitri's arm releases me as he opens the passenger door of his car, and I slide gratefully into the seat, trembling uncontrollably. He's around the front of his car in a flash and sinking into the driver's seat a moment later.

Somehow, his presence comforts me, his strength and size easing my distress, at least momentarily. And I'm suddenly intensely grateful that he came to see me tonight.

19

Dimitri

"Are you still up for going somewhere with me?" I ask with concern, glancing at Camille in the passenger seat.

She's visibly shaken, her face pale and her eyes wide as her head moves on a swivel, scanning the deserted street. Though she doesn't look as terrified as she did when she spotted the black car on the corner, she still looks deeply perturbed.

"I think so," she says, turning her blue eyes to me. "Honestly, it'll be nice to have a distraction, take my mind off of things."

I nod and start my car, then pull out onto the street.

"Where are you taking me?" she asks.

And though I love to tease her, this time, I think her nerves could use a break, so I won't keep our destination a secret. "A club," I state simply.

"*Your* club?" she guesses, her astute assessment coming from keen observation.

I chuckle. "One of them, yes," I agree.

Camille smiles, her color coming back to her cheeks as the stress eases from her shoulders slightly. Then she turns her attention to the window once more. Though she said it would be good to take her mind off of things, she's clearly not quite ready to let go of her worry about her stalker.

In the silence that follows, I consider what just took place.

Though I didn't press the matter, it bothers me that Camille could think I would send someone to follow her. I'm not a good person. I've made my peace with that. I'm dangerous, aggressive, and certainly willing to ignore the laws of society to get what I want.

But it's different with Camille, and while I know it's unreasonable to expect, I want her to believe that. To trust me without question.

What bothers me more than her suspicion of me is the fact that Camille's being followed. She seems at a loss for who it might be or what they might be after, and that concerns me. I don't know what her stalker's intentions are, but Camille is clearly freaked out by their inexplicable presence. And I don't like that her safety might be compromised.

I'll ask Alexei to look into it first thing tomorrow. His security team is good at uncovering information about nefarious people like that. And until I can get to the bottom of who owns the black car, I won't let Camille close the restaurant alone. It's too risky.

Pulling up in front of the nightclub Carmelo, I stop before the valet stand and climb out of the car. Camille does the same, looking up at the club's pink name scrawled in neon across the green stem of a martini glass.

"Have you ever been here before?" I ask, offering Camille my arm.

She shakes her head and places her hand in the crook of my elbow as she glances toward the long line of people curving around the block—countless clubgoers waiting to get in.

"Well then, you're in for a treat," I state, guiding her right past the line of waiting people, and up to the front door.

"Mr. Federov," the bouncers greet me with an inclination of the head. They give us a double-door entrance as they swing the glass panes wide.

Thrumming club music spills out onto the street and envelops us as we enter the dim space lit only by colorful neon sconces. Camille's eyes grow wide as we follow the short hall that opens up onto a massive dance floor with a bar lining one wall. A DJ occupies the stage along the back wall, his tables glowing with brilliant lights as he turns dials and slides knobs with confidence.

"This place is amazing!" she shouts over the loud music, her gaze rising to take in the multiple tiers of balconies—our VIP sections—that look out over the crowded dance floor.

"Come," I command, taking her hand in mine and leading her toward the stairs.

My hand swallows her delicate fingers, and Camille clings firmly to me to avoid getting lost in the sea of people. Finding the section reserved specifically for my family when we want to visit, Camille and I settle onto the plush leather couches. I order a bottle of Cristal as Camille looks down at the dance floor with apparent interest.

Her body rocks gently to the beat as she gets into the music. I can tell already that she's a good dancer. She moves with natural fluidity, seeming to feel the rhythm without even thinking about it.

"You come here often?" she asks, leaning close to my ear so I can hear her without her shouting.

"Now and again. It's been a minute," I admit. "A certain chef has kept me somewhat preoccupied lately." I smile at her wickedly and am rewarded with a shy grin.

Our champagne arrives a moment later, and I clink glasses with Camille before taking a sip. Relaxing back into our couch, we sit and talk for a while, enjoying our bubbly as we watch the dancers below. But as the alcohol kicks in, Camille seems more and more drawn to the throbbing beat that moves the club.

"Want to dance?" I offer, and she nods eagerly.

Taking her by the hand once more, I rise from our couch and lead her down the stairs to the dance floor. Bodies rock and sway around us, the dancers oblivious to who I am as they bump and jostle without a care in the world.

I find I don't mind too much once I take Camille in my arms. Because every time they do, it brings her firmly in contact with my body. Camille's hips sway seductively, and she moves with easy confidence. I can see why she likes to dance. It comes naturally to her as she moves like no one's watching. She looks sexy as hell as her arms snake around my neck.

And when she turns to grind her round ass against me, her back leaning against my chest, I'm instantly aroused.

"I could watch you dance all night," I murmur against her ear, my lips brushing the edge of it as I lean close.

She hums suggestively and grinds back more forcefully with her hips, taunting me. And though she doesn't say a word, I know it's a challenge, daring me to keep dancing with her even as she intentionally drives me wild.

Fingers digging into her hips, I push my growing excitement forward, pressing it between her ass cheeks. I'm rewarded with an appreciative moan. As if we're playing a game of chicken, Camille rolls her hips dramatically in response, upping the ante and making me throb with need.

Then she reaches back behind her head, finding my hair with her fingers. Tilting her face to look up at me over her shoulder, she levels me with a smoldering gaze. Then her fingers curl, tangling in my locks as she pulls me toward her juicy lips.

I lean in, eager to taste her, and just before our mouths collide, Camille stumbles roughly back against my chest, a sharp gasp bursting from her lungs. I catch and balance her easily, my arms already around her waist, and fury bubbles up inside me as I shift my gaze to the disrupting force.

A young guy, probably in his early twenties, stands before us, his eyes wide with horror as he openly stares down at Camille's chest. He holds a half-empty drink forgotten in his hand. "I am so sorry!" he shouts over the music.

Camille seems too stunned to respond, and though my blood boils at the way his eyes stay riveted to her breasts, I glance down to see what happened. A large stain darkens the chest of her sweater as the wet fabric clings to her voluptuous curves. Her chest heaves in shock, as if she were just doused in ice water. In truth, the comparison can't be too far off.

"The fuck is your problem?" I growl, furious. Grabbing a fistful of the guy's polo shirt, I haul him forward. Irate at his reckless actions that led to drenching Camille with his drink, I'm ready to pummel the idiot bloody.

"It's fine, Dimitri," Camille says firmly, stepping in quickly as she collects herself.

I snarl, baring my teeth at the careless dolt, unwilling to let it go that easily. The guy cowers beneath my violent gaze, cringing at me with blatant fear.

Gentle fingers wrap around my wrist, silently asking me to release the guy's shirt. "I'm fine, really. It was an accident," she insists, moving between us until I have to look at her. "I'm sure he didn't mean to, right?" she asks, looking back over her shoulder at him.

He nods vigorously, looking contrite. "I'm so sorry, man. I swear, it won't happen again."

"You've got that right," I growl, giving him a shake.

"Please, Dimitri?" Camille says when I still don't release the guy's collar. "It's not a big deal. My shirt will dry. I just want you to dance with me."

Her wide-eyed look of innocence eases my temper, and though I'd love nothing more than to punish the idiot for spilling his drink on Camille, I reluctantly release him.

"Get lost," I command darkly, and the guy vanishes a moment later, fleeing into the crowd like his life depends on it.

Lips stretching into a smile, Camille looks coyly up at me. "Where were we?" she teases.

Seeing that she's perfectly fine after getting over the shock of wearing a cold drink unexpectedly, I can relax once more. Pulling her into my arms, I hold her close, ignoring the way the liquid seeps from her sweater into the layers of my suit.

Looping her arms around the back of my neck, Camille arches into me, and her hips start to sway. I move with her, relishing the feel of her body conforming to mine, her full breasts brushing against me.

When she pulls me down to her, I claim her lips greedily, kissing her passionately as we move to the pulsing beat. Her tongue strokes into my mouth, deepening the kiss, and we start to make out.

Forgetting to dance, I hold Camille tightly against me, my hands exploring her curves as she moans lustily against my lips.

"Take me home?" she suggests, pulling away just enough to look me in the eye.

Her blue gaze bewitches me, and though I had hoped the night might eventually end at my place, I'm suddenly eager to leave the club early.

Stealing one more fiery kiss, I lace my fingers with Camille's and pull her toward the door. She giggles conspiratorially, tripping after me as I guide her through the crowded mass of bodies.

My Lamborghini is waiting for us as we step outside the club, leaving the ear-throbbing music behind. I open the car door for Camille and then climb behind the wheel.

It's a good thing the streets are fairly quiet at this late hour. Because I plan on breaking records to get back to my penthouse tonight.

20

Camille

My heart leaps into my throat as Dimitri peels away from the curb, his tires squealing with the effort to find traction. I gasp, one hand gripping the door, the other finding his hand on the stick shift.

The purr that rumbles from his chest makes my stomach do a somersault, and I remove my hand from his, realizing he might need it to drive. His gaze flicks to mine, and the ravenous hunger there sets my skin on fire.

Then his hand shifts from the stick shift to the button of my jeans. My breaths come fast and hard as he opens the button and lowers the zipper of my pants, revealing a small triangle of my lacy green panties.

With one hand on the steering wheel and his eyes on the road, Dimitri careens around the corner. And at the same time, his fingers work their way beneath the fabric covering my pussy.

Shocked by the explosion of excitement that rockets through me, I slide forward in my seat as his fingers find my clit.

I'm already soaking wet.

And Dimitri groans appreciatively as his fingers stroke my slick seam.

Normally, I might be terrified by such reckless driving, but as Dimitri slowly starts to finger me, two thick digits pressing inside my entrance, I find it hard to focus on anything else. Whimpering, I roll my hips to crush my clit against his warm palm.

"Greedy," Dimitri teases, his voice dripping with excitement.

"Says the man who just put his hand down my pants while driving," I answer breathlessly.

Dimitri chuckles low and dark, his hand increasing its pace as his fingers use my wet arousal to increase the friction against my clit. I moan lasciviously, letting my eyes sink closed, and I block out the terrifying sight of buildings flying by, reveling in the way Dimitri touches me.

"You like that?" he rasps, his sexy Russian accent making the question that much more provocative.

"Yes," I moan, squirming in my seat.

"You like it enough to come before we make it to my apartment building?" he teases, his fingers hooking to stroke against my G-spot.

"Fuck! Yes!" I scream, my back arching of its own volition.

I don't even know how far away we are from his place because, right now, I'm so consumed by my intense arousal that I'm sure I'll come any second. Something about the extreme speed and the way Dimitri touches me with such possessive confidence fills me with a powerful cocktail of adrenaline.

"You better, *kotenok*. Come before we get where we're going. If not, I might just have to punish you," he promises me darkly.

And though I'm deliciously intrigued by the playful threat, I'm so turned on already that I know I won't be able to hold off to find out exactly what he has in mind.

My pussy tightens around Dimitri's fingers as I barrel toward release, and as he crushes the heel of his palm against my clit, I topple over the edge. Crying out, I fall apart around him, my clit throbbing, my pussy pulsing as I come hard and fast.

Dimitri hums with approval, pushing his fingers inside me as far as my jeans will allow. He pauses there, feeling my walls squeezing him mercilessly. And I shudder with the warm, tingling relief.

As I tremble with the last of my ecstatic waves, he slowly withdraws from my pussy, his fingers running over my clit as he removes his hand from my pants. Capturing his palm, I guide his fingers toward my mouth. And when Dimitri glances over at me, I take them slowly between my lips.

Sucking his middle finger playfully, I lick up my tangy juices as I show him just what I want to do with his cock. Because he's fingered me, fucked me, eaten me out, and made me come so many times, I'm eager to return the favor.

Carnal fire blazes in his silver gaze as Dimitri watches me suck his fingers clean. And a low growl rips from his chest. His tires squeal a moment later as we come to an abrupt stop.

Startled, I glance out through the windshield to realize we're in a basement parking garage.

Unbuckling my seat belt with trembling fingers, I clamber out of the car, anticipation driving me forward. Meeting me at the back of his car, Dimitri pulls me roughly against him, his hands groping and grabbing my ass firmly as he grinds against me with his cock.

Our lips meet in a violent kiss, and I wrap my arms around his neck, letting him lead me blindly toward the elevator. We pause our lustful exploration only long enough for Dimitri to find the call button. Then he claims my mouth once more as he shoves me forcefully against the cement wall.

I moan, my fingers scrabbling over the buttons of his shirt, determined to strip him of his clothes so I can see his broad, muscular chest. When I reach the bottom, I fling his shirt wide to reveal his rippling abs. Keeping me pinned to the wall with his hips, Dimitri continues to kiss me as he leans far enough away to slide his hands up beneath my loose sweater.

Strong hands palm my breasts and knead them passionately.

I gasp as the elevator dings and the doors slide open. Dimitri steps back from me, his hand finding mine as he hauls me into the empty enclosure.

As soon as the doors close behind us, I drop to my knees, my hands finding his belt as I undo his pants. Dimitri's fingers comb into my hair, pushing the loose strands away from my face as he watches me with molten desire.

Drawing his cock out of his pants, I swallow hard at the glorious sight of his erection. Licking my lips, I only hesitate a moment before wrapping my mouth around the large tip. He's too big to take all the way, so I grip the base of his cock with one hand. And as I swallow him down my throat, I stroke the exposed length in the same motion.

Air hisses between his teeth as his fingers tighten around the roots of my hair, sending tingles racing down my spine.

I've completely lost control. I'm so attracted to Dimitri that I'm doing things I never pictured myself doing. And I love it.

Giving head in an elevator?

I never realized how exhilarating it might be. But it feels intensely liberating to act upon my deepest desires, and Dimitri doesn't seem inclined at all to stop me.

Low, hissing Russian escapes his lips as I guide his cock in and out of my mouth. And though I have no clue what he's saying, it sounds like an endless string of cusses. The sexy sound of the foreign language turns my insides to Jell-O. And warm moisture slicks my folds.

His hands gently cradle the back of my head, urging me to take more of his thick cock—as much as I can. And I do, finding a rhythm as I slowly let his cockhead press harder and harder against the back of my throat.

"You are so *fucking* sexy," he growls, rocking with my motion.

From the way his hips jerk, I can tell it's taking all his effort not to claim my mouth more forcefully, and I hum around him appreciatively. My jaw is already screaming with the effort of opening so wide.

But I love the way his cock twitches responsively from my attention.

And then the doors ding open, revealing the entryway of his grandiose apartment.

Dimitri guides me to my feet, his strong arms an iron support as I rise from the floor.

He moves me bodily out of the elevator, and as soon as we're inside the apartment, his lips greedily find mine once more.

His fingers curl around the hem of my sweater, and in one fluid movement, he pulls it up over my arms and head. Tossing it aside, he rakes his eyes down my body to my lace-clad breasts and the open button of my jeans.

We come together like magnets snapping into place. And I shove his shirt and jacket over his shoulders, unceremoniously removing his clothing without regard to their fine quality.

His fingers deftly reach behind me to unclasp my bra.

I fling it away from me as his thumbs hook inside the waist of my jeans and panties, and he shoves them down my legs. Stepping out of them, I'm suddenly stark naked in his entryway. But I don't have time to get self-conscious.

In another instant, Dimitri's pants are on the floor, and his hands are on me. Massaging me as they explore the curves of my body, his warm palms sear my flesh and drive me wild.

I do the same, my fingers spreading as I run my hands up his washboard abs and over his impressive pecs, soaking up the glorious rock-hard strength of his body.

Gripping his shoulders for support, I lean up onto my toes and nip playfully at his lower lip, sucking it between my teeth as I pull him down to my level.

Dimitri groans, following me with his head, and his arms wrap firmly around my waist. Then, one hand guiding my leg up onto his hip, he hoists me from the ground. In the same fluid motion, he turns to press me firmly against the wall as I wrap my legs around him.

I gasp as his hard cock grinds against my clit, pinned between our bodies as he holds me suspended in the air.

"I need you. *Now*," he growls against my lips.

Clinging to him with my arms and thighs, I nod. My pussy aches to feel him inside me. And I don't think I can wait until we make it to his bedroom.

Tongue penetrating my lips, Dimitri kisses me passionately, his lips demanding, his tongue greedy.

One arm holds me tight as he reaches around my thigh with the other to align his cockhead with my entrance. Smoldering excitement rises in my belly. I don't think I've ever wanted someone to pound my pussy so badly.

The silky skin of his tip glides between my folds, collecting my slick arousal and making me shiver with anticipation.

Then Dimitri shoves forcefully inside me, burying his cock up to the hilt.

And his low, agonized groan sends a jolt of euphoria exploding through my body.

21

Dimitri

I groan as I slam inside Camille's tight pussy, my intense need for her overcoming any self-restraint I might possess.

"Yes!" Camille gasps, her head rocking back against the wall as if with intense relief.

Consumed by my lust, I pound into her hard and fast, my need to claim her overwhelming me. And her walls tighten deliciously around me as I thrust. Mewling gasps escape her, growing louder as I fuck her without mercy.

The sight of her provocative hips swaying in the club, the way she ground so playfully against my cock—she was practically begging me to take her right there on the dance floor. And I knew if we stayed much longer, that's exactly what would have happened.

Her flirtatious foreplay turned me on so intensely, I had to know if it got her going as well, and fuck she was wet when I put my hand down her pants in the car. Whatever this attraction is that Camille and I share, it's something more powerful than I've ever felt before.

It took all my strength not to come in her mouth on the ride up. She looked so fucking sexy on her knees in the elevator; her sweet, juicy lips wrapped around my cockhead like it was the best popsicle she's ever tasted.

And all that buildup has left me captive to the raging excitement pounding through my veins. Lips consuming hers, I claim her body possessively, taking her pussy greedily, my cock throbbing from the cries of pleasure that pour from her mouth.

"You like getting me riled up in public?" I rasp, my tone playfully accusatory as I punish her pussy with driving force.

"Mmm," Camille moans, too enraptured to respond.

"Did you want me to finger you right there on the dance floor?" I press, and the thought drives me wild. Touching Camille, claiming her body right there for everyone to see—to know she's mine. That her delicious tits belong to me, not some asshole who spills his drink on them.

But I wouldn't do that because I want these seductive moans all to myself. I want to be the only one who knows what her cries of ecstasy sound like.

Her breaths come hard and fast, warm air washing across my face as she clings to my shoulders, taking my punishment with greedy enthusiasm.

"Tell me what you want, *kotenok*," I growl.

"Let me come, oh, please, I need to come," she whines, her full breasts heaving against my chest as they bounce with each forceful penetration.

She looks like a goddess, her perfect body oozing sexuality, her face consumed with her lustful need. And the sheer beauty of her is intoxicating. My balls tighten as I find myself on the threshold of release.

Reaching between us, I press the pad of my thumb against her clit, stimulating her as I continue to rock inside her pussy.

"Come for me, *krasivyy*."

Shuddering violently, Camille obeys. Sobbing with the intensity of her release, she clings to my shoulders as her walls clamp down around my throbbing erection. The strength of her orgasm triggers my own release, and I grunt as I shove deep inside her, filling her with my seed.

Pulse hammering through my veins, I keep her pressed against the wall, buried up to the hilt inside of her. We breathe heavily together as her pussy flutters and my cock throbs. And slowly, our pleasure subsides.

"Holy hell," Camille breathes as I finally ease her feet back onto the floor.

I chuckle as she puts words to the intensity of our climax. I'd lost my mind, my need to have her was so strong. And now a deep contentment floods me as I hold her close. Everything about Camille is alluring—her wit, her fire, her body, her voice, the way she carries herself with silent confidence. Her eyes alone could seduce me.

And though I've only just come, as I peer into their endless blue depths, I'm ready for more.

Camille squeals as I scoop her up into my arms, carrying her toward the stairs and my waiting bed.

"What are you doing?" she squeaks, clinging to me as I climb the steps with ease.

I love her apparent fear of heights, because every time I carry her up my glass stairs, she grips me tighter, pressing her warm body against mine as if she's afraid we might fall. Smiling wickedly, I don't respond because in my mind the question is more rhetorical. *What else would I be doing besides taking her to my room to have my way with her a second time?*

But even this small display of anxiety brings out the protector in me, and I tighten my arms around her, securing her against my chest. Her pulse flutters in the vein of her neck, and I lean in to kiss it, eliciting a gentle gasp from her lips.

Overwhelmed by my need to both claim and protect Camille, I find my emotions ruling my actions for the first time in my life. It bothers me to think something scares her. That someone's watching her disturbs me deeply, and I nearly lost my mind when someone spilled a drink on her. I don't typically jump in to rescue people, but with Camille, I don't even have to think about it. It's instinct.

Having her here, safe in my arms, is the best kind of salve. Her soft body pressed against my chest fills me with a kind of peace I've never found in my life. And I would do just about anything to keep this feeling.

Carrying Camille across the threshold of my room, I let the hallway light flood across the dark space, illuminating my bed. And there, I lay her down. Gently easing her onto the mattress, I crawl on top of her.

Her knees spread automatically, accommodating my hips as I settle between her full thighs.

Hovering over her, I study her beautiful face; the soft button of her nose, so delicate over her full, luscious lips. Brushing stray wisps of hair from her cheek, I lean in slowly. Camille trembles beneath me as I press a tender kiss to her perfect mouth.

Her fingers trace up my spine, grazing the muscles of my back as she tickles my skin with a gentle touch. And as our tongues stroke out to meet each other this time, it's with a soft, inviting caress.

Each touch is slow and enticing, feeling each other with a curiosity not driven by desperate need but by something more intimate and tender. My cock twitches back to life, and Camille's breathing grows shallow, her nipples hardening as they press adamantly against my chest.

I palm one full breast, pinching her taut nipple between my fingers as I massage the supple flesh. And her nails graze lightly down my back, raising goosebumps in their wake until her hands grip my ass.

She pulls my hips more firmly against her, and I groan as my cock hardens against the peak of her wet slit. Hips rocking, she slides my cockhead between her folds, her pussy lips enfolding my shaft as she grinds against me.

"You are something else. You know that?" I breathe against her skin as I kiss my way down to the hollow of her throat.

"Hmm," she hums appreciatively, her motion growing more pronounced as my lips excite her.

The sound sends electric anticipation up my spine, and my cock twitches, swelling further.

Intensifying the friction between us, I rock my hips in time with hers. The lengthened strokes feel insanely good, driving my arousal.

"Oh God, Dimitri, I want you," she moans, her fingers pressing into my skin.

"You get me all night," I promise.

And she responds with a greedy moan.

Sliding down her body, I claim her nipple with my lips. Her fingers find my hair, giving a gentle tug of appreciation. Alternating between rolling the tight pebble of her breast and sucking it into my mouth, I relish the silky softness of her flesh and the eager way she responds to me.

Gasps of pleasure burst from her, and her body squirms deliciously.

As I switch my attention to her other breast, my hand slides down her waist, feeling every inch of creamy skin until I find the line of her hip. Tracing the sensitive line inward, my fingers find her warm, wet folds.

Running my fingers along her warm, wet seam, I throb at the sheer amount of arousal coating them. Camille shivers, her hips rolling in response. And when I press the pad of my thumb against the small bundle of nerves at its peak, she cries out.

Her pussy lips twitch as her clit flutters beneath my thumb. And when I ease two fingers inside her warm depths, her walls tighten with anticipation. Going slow, I press deep inside her, reveling in the way her body responds to me; her core tightening, her juices flowing over my fingers.

I take my time, going slow and gentle because I want to feel every twitch and shiver that my touch elicits. And though I don't want to confess my feelings for her, I'm coming to the realization that I would do things for Camille that I've never been willing to do for anyone.

I don't just want to make her scream my name. I want to give her as much intense pleasure as her body can sustain. I want to keep her safe. I want to make her happy. I would do anything to give her the life of her dreams.

"That feels *sooo* good," she murmurs.

And when I look up at her striking face, her eyes are closed in an expression of euphoria, her eyebrows twitching ecstatically. I hum around her nipple, and her pussy tightens deliciously. Her lips part, releasing a sharp groan as her back arches.

She's close. I can feel it in the way her muscles vibrate with tension. Trembling beneath me, Camille strains against the bed like a Delphian prophet, her fingers spasming, gripping handfuls of the sheets as she edges closer to release.

Intensifying my pressure just slightly, I coax her closer to fall into bliss.

"Yes! Oh God, Dimitri!" she cries, and then her pussy throbs around my fingers, her clit twitching under my thumb.

Her breaths come hard, her breast pressing firmly against my lips as she gasps with the orgasm that consumes her. My cock throbs with the need to feel her falling apart around it. But I force myself to be patient. Because I want to take my time with her tonight. I want to feel every riveting sensation.

Camille's pussy tightens around my fingers again and again, urging me deeper inside her as her body begs me to fill her with cum. And God, I want to. But I refuse to remove my fingers from her until the last of her aftershocks subside.

Slumping against the bed, Camille releases a heavy breath. Her eyes flutter open to look at me with glassy contentment. And when a soft smile stretches across her lips, I can't help but return it.

She's so beautiful, so breathtaking. I lean in to kiss her lips, and her hand cups my cheek in the sweetest gesture of tenderness, her thumb tracing a line across my flesh that sets it ablaze. Intense emotion consumes me, and as I line my body up with hers, I can feel the connection humming between us.

22

Camille

Dimitri's endurance is astounding. Though he finished when he took me roughly right there in his entryway, he's already hard as a rock and ready for more. But while the fierce, passionate sex we've been having is super hot, this new intimacy is something else entirely.

And as his cock presses inside of me for a second round, easing slowly into my depths like he's determined to make me feel every glorious inch, I know I'm a goner. Because this soft, new tenderness strikes straight at my heart.

It no longer feels like fucking. We feel like we're making love, and my heart swells with the intensity of my feelings for Dimitri. I can't deny them any longer. While I thought I was playing him, tricking him to distract him from wanting my restaurant, I've been falling for him. Hard.

And it hits me with stunning force as Dimitri rocks slowly against me, setting my nerves on fire and pleasure crackling up my spine. Slow and intentional, he's taking his time. And somehow, this torturously slow pace is exponentially more erotic.

On the coattails of my second orgasm, I'm already intensely sensitive, my body overstimulated from the amount of pleasure he draws from me like an artist. No one's ever made me feel this good before. And yet, Dimitri does every time I'm with him.

Not just erotically either. He makes me feel beautiful. He makes me feel desired. He makes me feel safe and protected. *And* he makes me feel sinfully euphoric.

Breathing in shuddering gasps, I tingle with excited pleasure. Each gentle thrust awakens my body, and I'm enraptured by his soft lips. His taut muscles graze against me, his strong arms trapping me in a tantalizing embrace.

And I can feel the protective possessiveness radiating from him. I'm his. And if I wanted it, he could be mine. I sense it deep within my soul.

"You are so sinfully delicious," he rasps against my lips, his voice coarse with lust.

I whimper, my pussy tightening in response to his sexy words. And as his thick, hard erection slides in and out of my depths, I build swiftly toward another orgasm.

Dimitri groans, his cock throbbing inside me in response, and the roll of his hips grinds against my clit with each deep, intense penetration.

"I'm gonna come!" I gasp, shocked as my core tightens with my impending release. With the slow, erotic pace, my climax crept up on me. And now, suddenly, I can't hold back. Tingling euphoria trickles down my spine, and I rock into him, unable to control my body.

Dimitri grunts, the sound low and primitive, and it drives me over the edge.

Crying out, I explode around his cock, my pussy throbbing, gripping him like a vise.

"*Fuck,*" he hisses beside my ear.

And then he jerks forward, pressing deep inside me as he releases a burst of hot cum. It feels so good, so intensely euphoric to fall apart around him as he finds his release buried in my depths.

Moaning with the overwhelming pleasure, I tremble in his arms, consumed by my ecstasy. Dimitri breathes heavily, his chest pressing me into the mattress as his cock pulses with each burst of seed filling me.

And then slowly, we come to a stop. Breaths heaving simultaneously, we still; my arms wrapped around his strong body as he crushes me gently with his muscular weight.

He presses a soft, chaste kiss to my lips and eases out of me, his gray eyes soft as he looks at me. Rolling onto the bed beside me, he wraps an arm around my waist and pulls me firmly against his chest, spooning me from behind.

Blissful drowsiness weighs my eyelids down as he brushes my hair away from my shoulder to kiss the tender skin behind my ear. This, right here, is utopia; wrapped in Dimitri's strong arms, his warmth radiating into my back as he holds me close.

Before I even know what I'm doing, I'm half asleep, drowsing with my bone-deep contentment. As I start to drift away, a last fleeting thought flashes across my mind.

Tonight's the night I'm supposed to get my answer about Roy.

My body stiffens as I think of my old boyfriend and how the man whose bed I'm currently warming could most likely be responsible for his death. My defenses fly back up as I realize I've gone too far. I let my guard down and allowed myself to feel something I shouldn't have. I'm falling for Dimitri.

But could I live with myself if I fell in love with someone who's not only old enough to be my father but who's wrapped up in a life of crime—specifically a man capable of murder over an unpaid debt?

The age difference is almost a nonentity in my mind. While society might consider it too wide a gap, I find Dimitri closer to my intellectual interests and full of virility and life that few younger men possess.

And I think I could learn to be okay with his ruthless businessman side because he's not selling drugs or trafficking women—nothing that blatantly immoral. He's just the kind of man who knows what he wants and goes for it.

But if he's capable of killing someone over money, then I really need to reassess what I'm doing here. I need a moment to think.

"Is everything alright?" Dimitri asks, sensing my sudden tension.

My heart flutters and I sit up quickly before he can feel it pounding in my chest.

"Yeah. Absolutely. Totally fine." That wasn't *at all* convincing. Clearing my throat nervously, I grasp desperately for an excuse. "It's just... getting late, and I better go. I have an early day at work."

In truth, I'm suddenly terrified of learning the truth about Roy's death. Because if Dimitri really did kill him, I'm not sure how I could live with the feelings I'm developing. I started spending time with Dimitri in the hopes of uncovering what really happened so I could lock Dimitri away. But now I just don't know what to do. *How am I supposed to move forward from here?*

I need time. I need space to clear my head. To think.

Because these newfound emotions are entirely too dangerous.

Gathering the sheets around my breasts, I scan the room frantically for my clothes before remembering they're all downstairs, in the foyer.

"Stay," Dimitri insists, watching me as I haul the top blanket off his bed to wrap it around my body.

I can't walk through his house completely naked. All the intimacy from before feels too exposed now. Too vulnerable. And I create a makeshift toga out of the warm blanket, clinging to it like a shield as Dimitri rises from the bed.

"Are you seriously leaving now?" he asks, a deep crease furrowing his brow.

"Yeah. I really need to go," I insist, stepping through the bedroom door.

Dimitri follows me, not bothering to put on a stitch of clothing. And his glorious masculinity makes my mouth water even as I run for my life.

"Can't I just take you back first thing in the morning?" he offers, his tone baffled.

"No! No, you've been distracting me far too much lately. I have a lot to catch up on tomorrow. And I know if I stay, we won't be sleeping, which will leave me completely useless."

Stepping lightly down the stairs, I ignore the way my stomach flips at the sight of the ground far below me. In seconds, I'm back in the entryway and snatching my jeans off the floor.

"Well, at least give me a moment to get dressed, and I'll drive you back to your car," he says, scooping up his pants.

"No really, it's fine. Totally unnecessary. I'll just take an Uber. You're already home and"—glancing down at his beautifully tattooed, naked body, I swallow hard—"halfway ready for bed," I finish lamely.

Dimitri chuckles, watching me dress as he finally concedes. "I don't like that you're leaving."

The confession sends tingles racing up and down my spine, and my breath catches in my lungs. I don't really want to leave. I would much rather stay and forget all about the dark shadows lurking between us.

But I can't just forget about what's happened. Dimitri killed Roy. He's trying to take my restaurant from me. He's not a good person. And somewhere along the way, I lost sight of that. I fell for his gentlemanly charm and dangerous good looks.

I can't keep turning a blind eye.

I know that.

But if I'm too scared to learn the truth about who killed Roy, then does that mean I'm willing to relinquish Le Fleur?

Not a chance.

"I'll see you soon?" Dimitri asks, stepping close as I straighten my sweater and pull my hair out from its neck.

I gasp at his sudden proximity, the warmth of his naked flesh pressing against my breasts. One strong arm wraps around my waist as the other hand pinches my chin, raising my eyes to look at Dimitri's chiseled face.

A question lingers in his eyes, And I know he finds my behavior suspicious. I can see it. I need to be more convincing.

Releasing a breathy laugh, I force myself to calm down. "Yes, I'll see you soon," I promise, smiling despite the nerves that make my stomach quiver.

And then he leans in to kiss me. Fireworks explode through my body at the tenderness of his lips. With a sharp gasp, I freeze, unable to move, unable to breathe with the intensity of my attraction.

The passion with which he touches me is intoxicating, and my mind goes blank as my body melts into him. Arms snaking around his neck, I kiss him back. A moan of appreciation vibrates between our lips.

And he lingers there, tasting me with a dizzying gentleness.

When he finally steps back, I stagger, completely unbalanced by the best good night kiss of my life.

"You're sure you won't stay?" he presses, his voice low and enticing.

Wide-eyed, I shake my head mutely, not trusting my voice.

"Then, sweet dreams, *kotenok*."

"You too," I breathe, then turn to press the call button.

The doors open instantaneously, and I step into the elevator before turning for one last look at his gorgeous body. The striking intensity in his eyes stops my heart.

23

Dimitri

Sitting in my office, shuffling papers mindlessly for the fifth time in a row, I release a frustrated sigh. Tossing them onto the desk, I run my fingers through my hair, the product making it stand up wildly.

I didn't sleep much last night. I can't shake the feeling that something was up with Camille when she left in such a hurry. After some of the best sex I've ever had. I might have thought her anxiety had to do with her stalker, except everything was fine up until that point. She'd seemed more than eager to come with me back to my place.

Hell, she'd even sucked my cock in the elevator without any prompting on my part.

But when she left, she seemed troubled. By the way she brushed off my concern, I got the sense that she didn't want to talk about it. Digging the heel of my palms into my eyes, I try to alleviate the headache that's been growing steadily as I try to puzzle through her strange departure. I'm not going to be able to get Camille off my mind until I know.

Glancing at the clock, I'm sure she'll be at work by now. She said she had an early day. But I'm waiting for Alexei to get here. I want to tell him about the black car that was following Camille before I go see her.

"Hey, Di."

Someone slaps the frame of my office door, and I lift my head to glance over. Alexei stands in my office doorway, peeking in on me, an amused look on his face.

Speak of the devil.

"Whoa, you have another late night with your French chef?" he asks, cracking a smile.

Hackles raising, I growl in irritation, and my kid brother laughs.

"Touchy, touchy," he teases. "I guess I'll leave you to your thoughts, then."

"No, wait," I insist as he turns to go. "I actually need to talk to you about something."

Cocking an eyebrow, Alexei enters my office and shuts the door behind him.

"Someone's watching Camille," I state darkly.

Alexei frowns, the expression making him look far more like Maksim than usual. "Who?"

"That's what I want you to find out," I state. "A black car's been sitting outside her restaurant the last few nights she's closed. Apparently, it drives off as soon as she sees it."

"And she has no idea who it might be?"

"None," I confirm, frowning as it reminds me of her suggestion that she thought it was me.

"I'll look into it," Alexei states, dropping his usual banter as he takes on his security role.

As much as my brother enjoys his jokes, when it comes to protection and safety, I trust no one more.

"Thanks." Rising from my chair, I sling on my suit coat.

"You're leaving?" Alexei asks, surprised.

"I need to go talk to Camille," I say.

Alexei chuckles, his scowl shifting into amusement. "Man, you've got it bad."

"What?"

"*Feelings,*" Alexei teases. "You really like this girl."

"Shut up," I say, giving my brother a light shove as we both head toward the door. But I can't help the smile that follows.

If I'm being honest with myself, I do like Camille. More than I've ever liked a girl before. And after last night, I can't deny it. The connection we have is out of this world. And I want to spend every waking minute with her.

But that's not why I have to talk to her now. I need to know what's going on. I can't get rid of this unsettling feeling that something's wrong. Something she doesn't want to tell me.

The drive to her restaurant is a short one, and I park just down the street. On instinct, I scan the street as soon as I climb out of my Lamborghini. My eyes stop on the corner where the black car was waiting last night, but there's no sign of it.

Le Fleur is bustling with energy as soon as I enter. Though the restaurant's not open for a few more hours, I can feel the full day's work leading up to the night's rush.

Only one person stands up front as she pours over a serving schedule. But the loud clink of dishes and chopping knives issues from the kitchen, filling the front room that usually boasts a room of diners and their conversations.

"Mr. Federov," the hazel-eyed blonde hostess greets me as I walk through the door.

She's the same girl who walked in on me and Camille in her office —just after the first time we had sex. Hannah, I think her name is, though Camille only said it that once. Hannah scrutinizes me with an intelligent, if suspicious, gaze. Very different from the look of open interest she gave me the first night I came to Le Fleur.

I can hardly blame her. I've been monopolizing her boss's time and attention for weeks now. And from what I understand, Hannah's as good a friend as they come.

"Is Camille here?" I ask, though I already know the answer. I saw her little green Bug parked just outside.

"Yes, but she's busy. You should probably come back later," Hannah says, and the edge to her voice raises my suspicion.

Whatever was bothering Camille last night, it seems her friend might connect it to me. And I wonder if Hannah knows something I don't. But if Camille has a problem, I want to speak with her about it directly.

"I'm sure she won't mind the interruption," I state. "I'll be quick." Stepping around the host stand, I intend to hunt Camille down myself if Hannah won't help me.

She doesn't try to stop me, though she levels me with a seething glare. Jaw tense, she turns back to the host stand, facing away from me. Puzzled by the intensity of her reaction, I pause, glancing back at her in question.

"Camille, you dummy..." she mutters under her breath just loud enough that I can catch her words. "... taking this whole act *way* too far."

"Excuse me?" I demand, red flags going up as an alarm blares in my head.

This girl definitely knows whatever it is Camille's not telling me. But more than that, my brain catches on the word *act*. That has to mean something, and I can't think of a single good thing it could mean.

Hannah whirls, her eyes widening in horror. "N-nothing," she stutters, clearly shocked that I'm still near enough to have heard.

"No, no, you definitely said *something*," I insist, stepping closer to her once more. "What's this about an act?" I demand.

"I didn't—you must have—that's not—" Hannah scrambles for words, her eyes darting around the room as if searching for something that will save her.

Slowly, she backs away from me, her body diminishing, curling in on herself as I step forward.

"Don't lie to me," I state evenly, my temper rising.

Hannah's back collides with the wall beside the host stand, the obstacle cornering her as my body cuts off any avenues of escape.

Nearly hyperventilating, she grips the edge of the stand for support. Her eyes terrified, she watches me close the distance between us.

"Tell me what you said," I command, using my size to intimidate the truth from her. Because she's clearly not going to give up her friend's secrets without a fight.

"P-please," she gasps, tears springing into her eyes. "I didn't mean anything by it."

Then why wouldn't she want to tell me what she said? Slamming my fists against the wall on either side of her head, I lean close, narrowing my eyes into a fierce glare. Hannah releases a terrified sob and flinches from my wrath.

"You think I can't see you're lying?" I hiss.

"I'm s-s-sorry," she sobs, trembling as her resolve buckles.

"What did you *say*?" I repeat. "Don't make me force the truth from you," I threaten darkly.

"That she's taking her act too far," Hannah gushes, her words tripping over themselves in their haste to leave her lips. Then her eyes widen in shock, mortified by her lack of strength to hold out.

"What act?" I press, easing back now that she's no longer resisting me.

But my blood boils at the implication behind her words.

"Camille might have mentioned something about s-sleeping with you to make you forget about buying her r-restaurant..." Hannah breathes, her face twisted with the pain of betraying her friend. She can't seem to meet my eye, her gaze focused intently on the floor.

Snarling, I step back from Hannah as if her words were a physical strike.

The pain that lances through me is intense and unbearable. Here I am, falling for Camille, thinking we have a deep connection that might turn into something real. *And she's been playing me this whole time? Sleeping with me as a distraction technique?*

Breathing fast and hard, Hannah dares to look up at me, and she pales at the fury she finds in my eyes.

Clenching my fists, I tremble with rage, and my gaze shifts toward the kitchen. In an instant, it all comes together. Camille's initial resistance to my advances, her outright refusal. Then the sudden, inexplicable shift when *she* kissed *me* for the first time. While I thought she was playing hard to get, Camille was assessing a window of opportunity. A way to manipulate me.

My brother Alexei's teasing prods come back to me now. How I've finally met my match. *It's never taken you this long to close a deal before, Dimitri. Does that mean your feelings for the chef are getting in the way of your big business brain?*

Everyone could see it but me. Of course Camille doesn't want me. I walked into her life demanding her business just weeks after her boyfriend's death.

How could I have missed something so blatantly obvious?

I know the answer before I've even finished thinking the question. Camille is my weakness. I have a soft spot for her that I've never had for anyone before. She tricked me, weaseling her way into my mind. My heart.

And all the while, she's only been interested in protecting her precious restaurant.

I know there's more to it than that. This restaurant means everything to her. It's her dream—and it's closely tied to the memory of her father. But right now, I can't think beyond her betrayal. Camille's only been with me in an attempt to manipulate me.

And that truth cuts deep.

Anger mingling with hurt, I stomp toward the kitchen, seething.

24

Camille

As I stand at the stainless steel counter of Le Fleur, slicing steaks of filet mignon for tonight, I still haven't decided what to do about my feelings for Dimitri. They're so intense and real, and yet, I can't wrap my mind around the concept that he probably killed Roy.

Logically speaking, I know it's true. It all adds up—the timing, the motive. But for the first time, I want that house fire to have been an accident. I don't want to learn that Dimitri killed Roy because my heart is telling me we have something good and deep and meaningful.

And if I knew that Dimitri didn't kill my boyfriend over an unpaid debt, maybe, just maybe, this could become something magical.

I can feel the connection between us. It's unlike anything I've ever known before. And my attraction to Dimitri is undeniable. So, after learning that my emotions are in line with my physical desire, I'm suddenly reluctant to prove anything that might destroy what we have.

But if I don't find evidence against Dimitri, I don't know how I'll save my restaurant.

I can't keep pretending everything is good between us. Even though he hasn't brought it up since our first date, I know the day will come when Dimitri calls my payment due.

Won't he?

The chatter of the kitchen staff draws me from my reverie as Rorey teases Betsa loudly about her most recent date. I smile as Louis pipes in, joking that Rorey's only giving her a hard time because he's jealous.

I chuckle as the boisterous chatter takes my mind off Dimitri if only for a minute. It's nice to hear my love life isn't the only drama around here.

Something thumps loudly from the front room, and I frown, turning my attention to the swinging door in confusion. *Did Hannah drop something heavy?* I debate going to check on her and glance down at my workstation and the partially cut meat.

Then, without warning, Dimitri bursts into the kitchen with such force that the swinging door slams against the wall.

"*You've been using me?*" he rages, his eyes blazing as he rounds on me in an instant.

My heart stops, my knife clattering to the floor as I nearly leave my skin in fright.

And as he closes the distance between us, his expression is thunderous. For the first time, I'm terrified of Dimitri. His anger seems to fill the entire room, burning the oxygen from the space around us as his impressive body suddenly makes me feel small.

Leaning back against the counter in a feeble attempt to put distance between us, I glance around the room at my silent kitchen staff. They stand frozen in place, their eyes wide with fright, no one moving a muscle.

"Could you... give us a moment?" I ask meekly, my voice quivering.

And though I can see the worry on their faces, not a single person hesitates as they dash toward the dining room.

Dimitri hovers over me, his eyes watching as the last of my employees vanish through the swinging door, leaving us alone. Then his steel gaze slowly shifts back to me. Heart pounding in my throat, I look up at the gorgeous and insanely furious Russian towering before me.

"Tell me you didn't *fuck* me to distract me from calling in your debt," he growls, the words scathing as they leave his mouth.

His gray eyes flash with an intensity that makes me wonder if he might not kill me here and now. And if his accusation is that specific, it means he knows, so lying won't save me.

"I-I can't," I breathe, my eyes shifting to the floor. The knife I was using to prepare meat lies where I dropped it.

Stepping within inches of me, Dimitri pinches my chin between his finger and thumb. Then he lifts my face, forcing me to look at him. "I want to hear you say it," he says, his voice low and flat and deadly.

"S-say what?" I gasp, my heart hammering.

"Tell me what your plan was. How did you see this playing out between us?"

Swallowing my fear, I try to steady my mind. And though I'm terrified to confess, I hope I can find some sense of peace on the other side. Because I've been so conflicted. *But what if he won't forgive me?*

"I knew you wanted me..." I state quietly, barely daring to breathe. "And you mentioned at our first brunch that my turning you down was only making you want me more. So, I thought, if I had sex with you, you might forget about my restaurant and maybe I could figure out what really happened to Roy..."

My stomach drops as every detail spills from me, and I don't know if I'm relieved over it all coming out or if I'm just horrified about where things will go from here.

Dimitri's nostrils flair, and he scoffs as he releases my face, stepping back from me in disgust. Seeing the defensive walls slamming up around him, I scramble to finish my explanation. To tell him how everything changed when we started spending time together. How I really *do* want to be with him, that I love spending time with him, and that my feelings for him *are* real. Despite my original intent.

But I barely get past the first two words before he's boiling over, his rage spewing from his mouth in a violent string of Russian curses as he cuts me off.

"You *suka*," he snarls, pacing across the kitchen in his fury. "You're just as shallow and manipulative as the rest of the women I've ever met. I thought you might be different. That you might have a fucking soul. But I should have known better."

Shocked by the vitriol in his voice, I gasp. And my defenses fly up. "Hey, that's not fair—" I cut in, pushing off the counter to engage in the argument. I can admit my actions weren't entirely honest and are generally beneath me. But they weren't without reason. He threatened to take my business from me, and his anger now doesn't seem to be taking that into account at all.

But Dimitri's not having it. Stopping in his tracks, he gets right in my face again, his immense presence terrifying in his anger. And once again, I step back as my argument dies in my mouth.

"You think you can use me?" he demands. "I can have whomever I want. Whenever I want. I have the wealth, the power, the name. You don't think I could find the price that would make you spread your legs for me? Who are you to think you can manipulate *me*?"

The blow hits low as he directly targets my self-esteem, and tears sting my eyes. But I refuse to let them fall. He can't take away my worth, and it cuts deep that he would even try. Jutting my chin defensively, I cross my arms over my chest.

"I wouldn't accept all the money in the world to sleep with you," I counter coldly. But the truth is so obvious that my bluster is pathetically flimsy. Because I *did* sleep with him. Many times. Without receiving a single dime. And fuck, I liked it.

"You don't think you have a price, Camille?" he asks, his silver eyes molten. "Your price is your restaurant. Or don't you know? You sold me your body on a prayer that I would let you keep it. So while you want to pretend you're too good to be a whore, you bartered your body in exchange for a bit of time."

My blood turns to ice in my veins, and I take another step back as the fight leaves me. His words are so hurtful I have no defense against them, no ability to stop them from burrowing deep inside me.

And suddenly I'm spiraling, my pain and regret so tumultuous that I can't see my way out of this deep, dark hole. I can't believe I fell for Dimitri. That I couldn't see the violent hatred within him. It makes me question my sanity for developing feelings for him. When I suspected from the start what he's capable of.

One thing's for sure. My instincts last night were correct. I needed to get out, to get some space, and get my head on straight. Because nothing good can come from falling in love with this man.

"You do not use me, Camille. You're here only because I have allowed it. And don't think for a moment that you have manipulated me."

His tirade finished, Dimitri storms from the kitchen, slamming the swinging door open once more. I get one last glimpse of his broad shoulders before he vanishes from my life.

And the silence that follows is deafening.

Stunned, I stare wide-eyed at the door for a long moment, my heart pounding so forcefully I can hear it in my ears. I can hardly believe how quickly things unraveled between us. I never imagined that's how things would go if Dimitri learned my plan.

Despite the massive hole in my chest that leaves me aching hollowly, I can at least be relieved he didn't get violent. But now that I've seen the level of anger he's capable of, there's no doubt in my mind that he could kill someone who stood between him and his money—like Roy.

I shiver as I think about just how reckless my plan was.

But worse than the intense fear his wrath drew from me, I find the loss of our momentary bliss somehow more devastating. Because, despite the fact that our relationship was based on lies, I truly felt like I might have found the perfect man for me.

That just goes to show how terrible my taste is in men. I went from a man who racked up a debt that put my restaurant in jeopardy to a man capable of killing someone. A man willing to utterly destroy me. It seems as though I find toxic relationships even when I'm not looking for one.

My heart skips a beat as the swinging door opens slowly, and I steel myself for another vicious tongue-lashing. Then sweet Louis peers tentatively around the edge of the door.

Intense relief consumes my sous chef's angular features as he steps into the kitchen, the rest of the crew following one by one.

"You okay, Chef?" Louis asks tentatively.

I nod numbly, not quite sure how to move my lips.

Breathing a sigh, he releases the tension in his shoulders. "We thought you might be dead," he admits, following it with a nervous chuckle.

And just like that, my emotions come crashing down around me like a bucket of ice-cold water. Tears flood my eyes as a sharp sob bursts from me. And my poor staff stands stunned as I bawl openly in front of them.

Hugging my stomach, I crumple in on myself, crying uncontrollably.

Unsure of how to help the situation, they gather around, hands patting my shoulders, concern written across their faces. Louis wraps an awkward arm around my shoulders, trying to comfort me.

25

Camille

"Good night, Chef," Louis says, his eyes still filled with concern.

"Good night, Louis," I say, forcing a smile.

Against all odds, we made it through an insane night at Le Fleur. The orders were nonstop, creating a rush that left me utterly spent. I'm so exhausted that my arms are heavy as I clean the grill, my tasks dragging out longer than usual.

"Cami?" Hannah asks tentatively from the door.

"Hey, Banana." I use my nickname for her—one I use sparingly because I know it has deep emotional meaning to her. But I want to put her at ease because she's checked on me countless times tonight.

"Is everyone else gone?" she asks, stepping into the kitchen.

I nod.

"I just wanted to say I'm so, so sorry. I feel absolutely awful for having said anything." Hannah twists her fingers together in a guilty knot.

"You don't have to keep apologizing. Really. It's my own damn fault. I'm the idiot who decided to attempt such a stupid plan in the first place." Giving her arm a squeeze, I try to reassure her for the hundredth time.

Hannah sniffles. "But I'm the one who told him about it. And you could have gotten hurt."

"Girl, please. The fact is he didn't hurt me even though he was madder than a wet hen. And I know how absolutely terrifying Dimitri can be." In truth, though he's never laid a hand on me that I didn't desperately want him to, his very presence is intimidating, and his anger tonight was larger than life.

"Yeah," Hannah agrees, her face still looking guilty.

"Please don't blame yourself," I insist, grabbing her hands. "I don't blame you in the least, and I know you wouldn't have told him without a reason."

Hannah nods, her eyes brimming with fresh tears. And I pull her into a hug.

Wrapping her arms around my waist, she gives me a tight squeeze. "I was just so scared. And then I thought he might hurt you, and I just didn't know what to do…"

"Hey, we're okay. It's okay. People fight," I say.

"Yeah, but most people don't have arguments with the man who killed their boyfriend," Hannah points out, pulling back to look me in the face.

"Fair point well said," I concede with a smile.

She releases a tearful laugh. "Are you sure you're okay?"

"If you ask me that one more time, I just might lose my mind."

"Okay, okay." Hannah gives me one last squeeze and steps back.

"You all done for the night?" I ask.

She nods and glances over her shoulder. "Everyone else went home." Then she turns to look at me. "You want me to stay and lock up with you?"

"No," I scoff. "I'm fine. I'll be out of here in no time."

"Alright. I'll see you tomorrow."

"Night!"

Hannah leaves through the swinging door, and with a heavy sigh, I turn back to my task at hand. I'm sorely tempted to just leave it for tomorrow. But if I don't clean it up tonight, it's going to be ten times more challenging in the morning.

Putting some elbow grease into it, I get down to work.

And in the peace and quiet, I can finally process what happened between me and Dimitri. It was stupid of me to think I could manipulate him. And in truth, I feel bad. Since we started dating, he's shown me nothing but kindness and respect. He's shown me what it feels like to have a true connection with someone.

Roy never gave me that.

But tonight was a side of Dimitri I've never seen before. I saw his potential for aggression when he took on that kid at the club—the one who spilled a drink on me. But when it comes to us, he's always seemed unshakeable, his charm flowing effortlessly no matter what I threw his way.

So his spiteful words hurt me deeply, their unexpected delivery as painful as the words themselves. But now that I've had time to think on it, I wonder if he might not have said those things out of his own hurt.

My chest aches at what a mess I've made of everything. What seemed like such a great idea at the start now feels like an intense betrayal on my part. I'm so conflicted and lost about where to go from here.

Because now that I've lost Dimitri, I find I'm almost ready to concede everything to be with him. I don't know what's wrong with me. *Is it so messed up that the one person in the world I want to turn to for comfort right now is the man who's causing all this pain?*

But for weeks now, Dimitri's been the one to make me feel safe and cared for and heard. And without him, I don't know what to do with myself. *Can I go back to the life I knew before him?*

I'm not so sure.

Heart heavy, I look around the kitchen and consider my work done. Groaning as my muscles protest from a hard night, I slowly make my way to the office and change out of my chef's robes.

Then I make my final sweep through the restaurant, checking doors and stoves and lights to ensure everything is locked securely and turned off. My body is on autopilot, but my mind remains on Dimitri as I scan the front room to make sure it's all in order. Then I flick off the lights and step out the front door.

It's a brisk night, the wind whipping my jacket around me, and I shiver as I pull it closed before digging into my purse. Finding my keys a moment later, I lock up and head to my car. Emotionally wrung out, I'm too tired to know where to go from here.

Home obviously. But with Dimitri, things aren't so clear.

Do I apologize?

Even if I tried, I'm not so sure he would forgive me.

Do I accept that I've ruined things beyond repair?

That might just end with me losing Dimitri *and* Le Fleur. Because now that our relationship seems to be over, it wouldn't surprise me if he holds me accountable for Roy's debt.

With bleary eyes, I slide behind the steering wheel of my little green Bug and close my door. Turning on my car, I start the heater, blasting it to thaw my icy flesh. I take a moment, trying to clear my head. And I massage my tired eyes.

Then, with a resigned sigh, I buckle my seat belt and put my car in drive.

It's late enough that the streets are empty, and I can pull away from the curb without having to merge. Driving to the end of the block, I stop for a red light. And wait. Chuckling to myself, I glance up and down the deserted streets, wondering just what the point is of me sitting here on my own, not another car in sight.

But as tempted as I am to just roll on through the intersection, I can't bring myself to take my foot off the break. To ease my impatience, I reach down and fiddle with the radio. Finding a station I like, I turn it on full blast and start to belt out the familiar song trickling from my speakers.

While I'm not much in the mood to sing, it will help take my mind off Dimitri—and keep me awake for my short drive home. When I look up, I'm shocked to find the light's already green.

When I switch my foot to the gas pedal, my little car jumps

forward, as ready as I am to get the heck out of dodge so I can curl up in my own bed.

As I enter the intersection, movement to my right catches my eye. My heart skips a beat as my stomach lurches uncomfortably. And I have just enough time to turn my head and spot a black car barreling toward me.

No headlights.

Its tires squealing as it quickly picks up speed.

"Oh, shhi—"

The force with which I'm struck sends me slamming sideways into my door. A strange popping sound follows like one giant bubble bursting. And with it, the oxygen seems to be sucked from my car.

The world spins around me as I scream in sheer terror. Clinging to the steering wheel, I pray for it to stop. Then something enormous slams into my face and chest.

The air leaves my lungs in an instant as I feel like I've been punched in the gut. And suddenly, I'm pinned, blind to the world around me. Mercifully, my car stops, giving a final jerk before it lands securely on its wheels.

Vision dimming around the edges, I blink, trying to make sense of what I see. But everything is white. Slowly, painfully, I turn my head to the left as something squeals loudly—like a large beast in agonizing pain.

My heart stops as the black car enters my vision once more. Only this time, it's tearing away. Its red taillights glare at me, ominous in the dark night. Panic floods me as I realize what happened.

The bastard hit me. Intentionally.

Through the thick fog that clouds my brain, I try to think of what I should do next. But my head's spinning so intensely, I can't think straight. I'm probably still dizzy from getting turned around so many times.

All I know is that I'm in danger. This wasn't an accident, and if the driver of the black car realizes I'm not dead, they might come back.

Terror grips me, and through the intensity of my fear, one

thought bursts brilliantly through my mind, shining a light that chases all the monsters away.

Dimitri.

Digging in my pocket for my phone, I ignore the way my head screams in agony. And relief floods me as I pull it out to find it survived.

I dial Dimitri and press the phone to my ear, praying he'll pick up.

It rings and rings and rings until I'm certain I'll be sent to voicemail, and my stomach sinks as a fresh wave of rejection comes crashing down on me. Tears sting my eyes, and the knot in my throat makes it impossible to swallow.

"Camille?"

The sweet sound of Dimitri's voice—guarded as it might be—brings me crashing back to reality. And as I open my mouth to respond, a shattered sob bursts from me.

26

Dimitri

Alone in my penthouse apartment, I sit on my couch with my head in my hands.

I feel awful for what I said to Camille. I've never once thought less of her because she doesn't have the money I do or the same level of prestige that comes with my family name. And I know she's not a whore. I've never met a woman with more self-respect. And she has far too much pride to sleep with a man for money.

I only said it to hurt her as much as she hurt me. And now, I regret it immensely.

At the same time, I can't just go back and apologize. Because she's the one who used me. She played me, and I hate knowing that I fell for her so hard and so easily when she's felt nothing for me this whole time.

In truth, her plan worked far too well. Not only had I stopped pressing her to sell Le Fleur, but she also had me thinking it was my idea. I'm such a fool.

Frustration blasts through me as I think about how ridiculous I've been. Thinking that wooing Camille would be a fun challenge—that

I could make her fall for me. And all the while, she had other plans. I played right into her hands, even though I'm supposed to be the master of this game.

I never should have fallen for my own lie—that I might have actually found the woman of my dreams.

No, I need to forget about Camille.

I want to wipe her completely from my memory.

Scrubbing my face with my hands, I release a deep breath and stand.

I don't know how I'll get it done, but I'm determined to never think of the girl again.

Heart heavy, I march toward the stairs, surprised to find how dark it is outside my wall of windows. I've been so lost in my thoughts, I don't even know what time it is. Well past midnight, based on what my watch says.

Which is why I find it shocking when my phone starts buzzing in my pocket.

Brow furrowing, I pull it out to see who's calling, and my heart stumbles uncomfortably in my chest.

Freezing halfway up my stairs, I stare down at Camille's name lighting up my screen.

I should ignore it. Send her straight to voicemail. I don't want to hear anything she has to say. *Does she think some half-assed apology is going to make things right between us?*

Or maybe she's calling to rub it in a little more. That while I've been sitting here, twisted into knots over what I learned today, she's had a great night at the restaurant and is just happy to be out from under me. Literally.

But try as I might, I can't ignore her.

Closing my eyes, I take a fortifying breath. Then I answer.

"Camille?" I ask, pressing the phone to my ear.

And my heart stops at the broken sob that echoes across the line.

"What's wrong?" I demand, my anger vanishing under the immensity of my concern.

But though she tries desperately to get the words out, Camille can't seem to get past the first letter of her explanation because she's crying too hard.

"Breathe, Camille, breathe. I need you to calm down and tell me what's wrong." My stomach knots painfully as I stand, useless, on the stairs, unable to help her when I can't even discern what happened.

Static crackles across the line as she follows my instructions, taking several deep breaths before trying again.

"I—*hic*—was in—*hic*—an accident," she sobs, her words cut short by hiccups, making her nearly impossible to understand.

"A car accident?" I press, my blood turning cold as my hand white-knuckles my phone.

"Y-yes," she stutters, breaking down once again. "I'm s-so s-sorry. I d-didn't know who to call."

"The police," I state instantly.

"R-right," she hiccups. "How stupid of me. I'm s-sorry. I'll l-let you go."

"No, wait," I insist, adrenaline bursting through me at the thought of her sitting in her damaged car on the side of the road. "Are you hurt?" I ask, my heart aching.

"I d-don't think so," she says, her voice sounding confused. But my questions seem to be calming her down. She's not crying hysterically any longer at least, and her breathing is evening out.

"And the other driver?" I ask.

"H-he took off. I think he ran a red light, but it all happened so fast... I can't remember."

"Where are you?" I demand, turning on the stairs and making a beeline for my elevator.

She gives me an intersection not half a mile from Le Fleur.

"I'm coming to get you," I state as the vague sound of a siren issues through the phone.

"Dimitri?" she whispers, her voice sounding choked.

"Hmm?" I pound the call button, willing the elevator to come faster.

"Th-thank you," she breathes.

Then the call ends.

Pulse thrumming, I jump into the elevator as soon as the doors open and ride it impatiently down to the garage. Camille's broken voice keeps running on a loop in my mind. She sounded so scared, so lost.

And in this moment, I don't care that she's hurt me deeply. I desperately need to know she's safe and unharmed. It worries me that she can't remember what happened. Maybe that's just because it happened so fast, but she sounded too shaken up for a quick fender bender. Quite possibly, she might have gotten a concussion or blacked out.

I'm in my car in a flash and racing toward the intersection where it happened.

Red and blue lights pour through my window as I arrive on the scene. And my stomach drops at the unnerving sight. Camille's standing beside a police car, an officer by her side. Her tear-stained face looks haggard, her eyes puffy. And her auburn hair is a mess of curls around her face. I might be wrong, but it looks as though she has a trickle of blood running down from the side of her forehead. And she's hugging herself like she might fall apart if she doesn't hold her pieces together.

The officer seems oblivious to her emotional state as he scribbles on the pad of paper in his hand. Three other police cars block off the intersection, and uniformed officers seem to be taping off the scene.

The amount of broken glass strewn across the intersection tells me this was far more than just a love tap. Someone slammed into her at a speed far higher than San Francisco allows.

Then my eyes spot the tow truck as it starts to crank her little green Bug up off the street. My gut clenches as I see for the first time the massive dent that's buckled the entire right side of her car.

If anyone had been in her passenger seat, they surely would have been crushed. And though the driver's side looks surprisingly intact, all the windows have been shattered as if popped by the sheer force of impact.

Fighting the vomit that threatens to rise up my throat, I park my car along the street and climb out. Slowly picking my way around the crime scene, I head toward Camille and the police officer she's speaking to.

As I approach, he flips his notebook closed and gives Camille a nod. Then his eyes shift to me. A moment later, Camille turns her head as if sensing my presence.

The sweetest look of relief bursts across her face, and seemingly without thinking, she starts to walk toward me. After several steps, she hesitates, biting her lip before she turns back to the officer.

And though I can't hear what she says, I'm close enough now to hear him respond, "We have everything we need."

Then Camille turns back to me, her feet carrying her swiftly in my direction as I duck beneath the caution tape.

She's on me a moment later, and her eyes glisten with tears as she flings her arms out to wrap them around my neck. I pull her to me without hesitation, holding her close as I breathe in the sweet floral scent of her shampoo mixed with salty sweat.

As she breaks down in my arms, tremoring against my chest, I stroke her soft curls and murmur assurances, trying to soothe her.

"Thank you for coming to get me," she whispers when she finally has her tears under control again.

When she tips her face up to look at me, my heart twists at the sad state she's in. She looks exhausted, her eyes red and swollen from crying, and a good-sized knot colors the line of her hair over her left eye. Though the blood's dried by now, a small trickle had run down her temple.

With tender hands, I inspect the wound, shifting her hair to see how far back the cut goes. Camille flinches slightly, her left eye closing as air hisses between her teeth.

"We need to get you to the hospital," I observe.

"No, I'm fine. Really. It's just a little bump on the head," she insists.

"Camille," I scold authoritatively.

"Dimitri," she shoots right back, giving me the same intent glare I try to level at her. "It will only cost me money, and I feel fine. Just a little rattled."

Still, I hesitate. She looks more than a little rattled, and I don't like the thought of leaving her alone when she might be concussed. From the state her car is in and her confusion on the phone—not to mention the good-sized lump on her head—I'd say the odds are pretty likely.

Sighing heavily, I propose a compromise. "Fine, if you won't let me take you to the hospital, then at least let me take you back to my place for the night."

Camille's eyes widen, and her lips part in shock as color pools in her cheeks. I'm immensely grateful to see it return when she was looking so pale.

Before she can argue, I explain, "I want to keep an eye on you overnight. Just to be safe. You might have a concussion." I don't want to voice my other reason—that I desperately need to keep her close because my instinct to protect her is in overdrive right now. Just the thought of dropping her off at her house has my shoulders knotting with tension.

"Oh, right," Camille says, her gaze dropping to the ground. "Well, if it wouldn't be too much trouble..." she starts. Then she looks up at me once again, a flicker of hope lighting the blue depths of her eyes.

And it stirs something deep inside me.

Something that sends warmth flooding through my body.

"I insist," I state, wrapping an arm securely around her shoulders and guiding her toward my car.

She feels horribly unsteady, like her knees might buckle at a moment's notice. But I can tell from the way she carries her head that no amount of persuasion on my part is going to get her to a hospital.

And while I'll never admit it, I'm grateful I won't have to let her out of my sight.

27

Camille

Dimitri keeps glancing in my direction on our drive to his penthouse. Like he thinks I might fall into convulsions or something if he doesn't keep a constant eye on me.

And when we get to his building, his arm is around my waist, supporting me as soon as I stand from his car. He's so gentle, his concern so blatant that it melts my heart. I almost think his actions might be his way of trying to apologize for the way we left things in Le Fleur's kitchen today.

He doesn't say much, and in the quiet, I feel like I can re-center myself for the first time. The crash itself is still a blur of terrifying sounds and a sense of utter helplessness as I was tossed around like a ragdoll.

But a nagging thought tickles the back of my mind like I've forgotten some critical detail.

I'm almost a hundred percent certain by now that the driver in the other car ran a red light. But I don't think that's what my brain is trying to recall.

As soon as we're in Dimitri's apartment, a sense of calm envelops me. I'm safe here, and as I breathe a sigh of relief, my muscles finally relax. My knees buckle unexpectedly, and I gasp as I head toward the floor in an instant.

Then strong arms are scooping me up as Dimitri holds me against his firm chest. I blush as our faces come close together, and his masculine scent of leather and pine fills my nose.

"Sorry," I say, though I'm not entirely sure what I'm apologizing for.

But Dimitri doesn't set me back on my feet. Instead, he carries me like a bride up his glass stairs to the bedroom. My heart hammers in my chest, not from the climb this time but from our proximity.

And when he takes me into his impressive master bath and sets me down on the edge of his clawfoot tub, I almost breathe a sigh of relief. Because having him that close does strange things to my body.

He starts the water running in the tub, pouring Epsom salts and bubbles into the mix as I watch.

"What are you doing?" I ask. When my brows furrow, the torn skin at my temple tugs, and I flinch from the pain.

Dimitri's gray eyes miss nothing, and they flick toward the lump on my head with concern. "Drawing you a bath. You're probably going to feel like hell tomorrow. I figured an Epsom salt soak might help a little."

Then he turns to his bathroom cabinets to shuffle through them.

I'm grateful for the moment of privacy as tears sting my eyes at his empathy. This is the man I fell for—someone who's there the moment I need him, giving me things I never even knew I needed.

Turning on the sink, he runs a washcloth under the water. Then, tools in hand, he turns back to me. My breath catches as he kneels in front of me. With a tender touch, he wipes my face clean with the warm, damp cloth.

My eyes flutter closed at the glorious sensation. Like the gentlest of massages. I can feel the slight tug as he goes to work on the blood sticking to my skin. But his attention is so slow and careful, it doesn't hurt at all.

Then he returns to the counter to collect a cotton ball, which he applies soap and water to.

"This might sting a bit," he warns, turning back to me.

I twist my face in preparation for the pain and suck in a sharp breath when he dabs lightly at the lump on my head. It's definitely bruised and sore, but as I acclimate, I find the pain to be perfectly within reason.

Dimitri finishes my medical treatment by applying antibiotic ointment to the cut and covering it with a bandage. Then he turns to the tub and shuts the water off.

"I'll give you some privacy," he states, and it makes my stomach twist painfully to see the different squares we're in now. Yesterday, he would have stripped me down himself without a moment's hesitation.

Fighting a fresh wave of tears, I nod.

"Just... keep talking to me so I know you haven't passed out and started drowning."

I laugh in spite of myself. "Okay."

As soon as he leaves the bathroom, I strip down and climb carefully into the tub. A deep groan of appreciation escapes me as the warmth enfolds my knotted muscles, helping them unravel one by one.

"Everything okay in there?" he calls from the other room.

"So good," I moan, sinking back against the tub.

I stay there for a solid half hour, Dimitri checking in and reminding me to speak whenever I've been silent for too long. But the bath feels heavenly. And when I finally step out of the water, it's growing close to lukewarm.

I dry off quickly and wrap my towel around my body before checking my reflection in the mirror for the first time. I look thoroughly exhausted, and the lump on my head is turning purple already, but the bath has brought good color to my skin. And overall, I'm rather impressed by the shape I'm in.

"Knock knock," Dimitri says by the door, and I turn to find him holding an oversized T-shirt and pajama pants. "I thought you might prefer to sleep in something a bit more clean and comfy," he states, handing them over to me.

"Thanks." I smile as my heartstrings tug once again.

His sweetness is almost more painful than the car crash. And it's a stark reminder of what I've lost. Changing into Dimitri's borrowed clothes, I contemplate just where I stand in all this.

Can I live with a man who would be capable of killing someone like Roy?

The question has been nagging me since Dimitri and I made love last night. But now, a second question surfaces that makes my chest ache with loss.

Can I live without Dimitri if he did kill Roy?

I'm suddenly not so certain.

With that thought fresh in my mind, I step out of the bathroom, cleaned up and ready for bed.

"Feel better?" Dimitri asks, his eyes skimming quickly down my body before flashing up to my face again.

"Like a brand-new person. Thank you."

He gives a soft smile. "Then let's get you in bed."

My heart skips a beat at the suggestion, though I know he probably doesn't mean it in the way I hope he does. He gestures to his king-sized bed, helping me under the covers and ensuring I have enough pillows to ease my aches and pains.

Then, with a nod, he straightens. "I'll be in to check on you throughout the night," he promises.

And my stomach knots at the meaning behind his words. He's not planning on staying in his room. Heart aching, I can't stop myself from reaching out to grasp his hand. Dimitri pauses, his eyes flashing down to our connected fingers then up to meet my eyes.

"Stay with me?" I breathe, my vulnerability making it impossible to speak above a whisper.

Intense agony flashes across his face, and then it's gone. He nods, and I scoot over, making room for him. When Dimitri settles onto the bed beside me, I snuggle close to him; breathing in his wonderful scent, soaking up the warmth of his body.

His arm wraps around me, pulling me close as I use his chest as a pillow. And it feels so good, so right. My body heats, my heart quickening when his fingers stroke lightly along my arm. And I dare to think he and I might just be okay.

Tipping my head, I press a light kiss to his neck, and Dimitri doesn't refuse me. So I do it again. His hand stills on my arm, and I shift, propping myself on my elbow to look into his face.

His expression is unreadable, his eyes a silver pool of emotion, and I lean in tentatively to kiss his lips. Electric attraction crackles through me at the connecting point, and my heart flutters as his hands gently grip my arms.

Daring to take it further, I trace my tongue along the seam of his lips. Dimitri inhales sharply, and then his lips part as he kisses me back. Giddy excitement washes through my core, and I shift to lean my weight on his chest, not quite straddling him, but slowly working my way there.

Tongues dancing out to meet each other, our kiss deepens in an instant, and I whimper as relief consumes me. Maybe we're not beyond fixing after all. His hands cup my face gently, and he forces our lips apart so his eyes can peer deeply into mine.

They search my face, then flick up to my bandage, as if seeking some sign that my injury might be putting me at risk.

"I'm fine," I insist. "I just want you." My tone is pleading as I fear an impending rejection.

But after a moment's hesitation, Dimitri seems to give in, his resolve crumbling. Pulling my lips to his once again, he kisses me passionately. Strong hands explore my body with shocking tenderness as they follow my curves down to my hips, and he guides me the rest of the way on top of him.

I do so eagerly, my legs spreading to straddle him as I lie on his chest, never breaking our kiss. His touch is greedy, roaming from my full hips and round ass, up my tapered waist, and to my back.

His hands slide beneath the soft fabric of the oversized T-shirt. And when he guides the shirt up over my head, I raise my arms willingly. It's his shirt next as my fingers curl beneath the hem, working it up over his abs. He sits up, his muscles flexing deliciously, to allow me to remove his top.

His strong arms wrap around me, pulling me against his chest, my breasts pressing up in voluptuous mounds as he crushes them between us. And then his hands are working at the tie holding up my pajama pants.

Air gasps from my lungs as I do the same to his, my fingers shaking with anticipation. Just hours ago, I was sure we would never do this again. Now, my heart races as my body deeply craves Dimitri and the intensity of our connection.

Our lips remain locked as we blindly strip our remaining clothes, the act clumsy, and yet somehow that much more exciting. He wants me. He still wants to be with me, and that knowledge makes all the rest of my troubles fade into nothing.

Tongue delving between his lips with newfound confidence, I kiss him hungrily, and Dimitri groans, his chest vibrating against me as our bodies tangle into a perfect knot. I can feel the iron bar of his cock swelling and throbbing between us, begging to be inside me.

Shifting my hips, I reach down and grab his impressive erection to guide it to my entrance.

Sexy Russian words slip between his lips as I sink slowly down onto his swollen girth, and my body tingles with euphoria at the intense penetration. His hands grip my hips tightly as he guides me onto his cock.

"Oh God," I groan, the feel of him sliding into my already wet depths is so intensely arousing that I'm ready to come.

Sitting up, I deepen his penetration, my hands resting lightly against his muscular pecs as I start to roll my hips. Dimitri groans, and the sound sends a shiver racing up my spine. Grinding against him more forcefully, I find my rhythm.

My muscles are bruised and exhausted, and yet I'm so turned on, I can't find it in me to care. I need Dimitri so badly, I would do anything to be with him right now. Reaching up with one hand, he cups and fondles my breast, awakening my sensitive nipple as he pinches and rolls the tip until it's a hard pebble.

He does the same with his other hand, cradling both my breasts as he gropes me deliciously. And as I rock on top of him, I lean into his palms, my hands covering his to show him just how much I like his touch.

Arching my back, I let my face tip toward the ceiling, my moans growing louder as I build swiftly toward release. Dimitri drives me wild, leaving me so intensely craving him that I can't seem to get enough.

His hands shift, sliding out from under mine as he guides my fingers to take their place. I obey the silent command, squeezing my breasts so the supple flesh oozes between my fingers. And Dimitri's hands follow the curve of my waist down to my hips once more.

Then one hand moves to the peak of my thighs, and his thumb gently presses against my clit. I cry out as jolts of electric pleasure crackle up my spine, and my hips rock adamantly on his cock, intensifying the friction as I increase my pace.

"Come for me, *kotenok*," he rasps, his voice low and commanding.

And I have to obey. Moaning with the intensity of my release, I come hard and fast, my walls clamping down on his cock as if desperate to keep him inside of me.

28

Dimitri

My balls tighten at the sinful sensation of Camille orgasming on top of me. Her sensual beauty is intoxicating, and I'm so entirely consumed by her that I can't stop myself.

Every time she kisses me, I lose my head completely. Though I'm sincerely worried she has a concussion, she doesn't seem to care in the least, and I can't think straight when she starts touching me.

As soon as our lips met, I was a goner.

I couldn't resist. I had to have her.

I know I'm going to regret this, but her scintillating lips light my body on fire. And her tight pussy sends my body into overdrive, making me determined to claim her one more time.

Only this time, I'll guard my heart. Because I know better than to think this is anything but lust between us. Her body might be from heaven, but she has the ability to send my soul straight to hell, and I won't fall for her again.

The pleasure of her release is agonizing, and my cock throbs as she milks me forcefully, begging me to come with her. But I won't. Not until she's good and thoroughly fucked.

If we're going to do this, then I want to leave our last night together branded in her mind.

Camille slows, her hips coming to a stop as she unravels on top of me. In her ecstasy, she seems incapable of maintaining her glorious pace.

But I'm not done with her yet.

Wrapping an arm around her waist, I shift our weight, rolling on top of her. She gasps at the sudden shift of gravity, and her lips part sensually as I press her into the mattress, my weight pinning her down.

Leaning in, I capture her lips in a violent kiss, and Camille moans, her fingers combing into my hair as she kisses me back with fervor.

Relishing the sensation of her aftershocks fluttering around my hard cock, I drive inside her at a steady pace.

While I want to fuck her brains out, I also don't want to take it too far in case she's actually injured. So, as ravenously as I need her, I try to restrain myself.

Lost in the throes of passion, Camille seems like she could care less about her head. Her cries issue from her lips with tantalizing pleasure, and her breasts heave against my chest.

"Yes, oh God!" she gasps, her legs wrapping around my hips as I thrust deep inside her.

And I can feel her tightening around my cock as she builds swiftly to a second climax. She feels so good, her wet folds slicking my shaft, allowing me to slide in and out of her tight hole with ease. And my dick throbs as the blood pounds through my veins.

Gasping, Camille explodes around me, her pussy throbbing and her clit twitching against my pelvis as I maintain my rhythm. Intense satisfaction consumes me as I leave her putty in my hands. She might have thought she could use me, but I'm the one who controls her body. Her pleasure. And I want to show her just what she gave up the day she decided to manipulate me.

Camille rolls her hips beneath me, her excitement driving her motion, and her slick arousal drips from her slit. Moaning lasciviously, she trails kisses up my throat, raising the hair on the back of my neck.

"*Blyat,*" I cuss as my own excitement builds to the point of combustion. I won't be able to hold out much longer. Her pussy feels too sinfully good.

"Please, Dimitri, please, please," she begs, her tone almost tearful with need.

And though she's already come two times, she's begging me for more. Snarling, I hammer inside her, losing myself completely. Camille cries out with every thrust, the sounds of her pleasure building pressure as my balls throb and tighten.

"Oh God, I'm coming!" she gasps as if shocked that she could come so many times in quick succession.

And though I want to keep pounding inside her for as long as I can, I know I won't be able to ride out another of her earth-shattering climaxes. With a low grunt, I shove inside her to the hilt as I find my own release.

Cum spurts from me in powerful bursts as we throb together. And hot wetness fills her until it trickles out around my cock. As I pour every ounce of myself deep inside her depths, a new hollowness takes its place inside my chest.

And suddenly, my intent to prove just how badly she messed up backfires. Because now I only feel more manipulated. Clearly, she's willing to use me for her own pleasure, even after she made it clear she doesn't have feelings for me.

After everything, I've somehow managed to fall into her snare once more.

My cock throbs with a final traitorous burst of pleasure. And I pull out of her unceremoniously. Still breathing hard, I roll away from her, snatching up my joggers and hauling them on.

I'm out of bed a moment later, grabbing my shirt off the floor and pulling it roughly over my head.

"What are you doing?" Camille asks, her voice stunned as she sits up to watch me dress.

"Leaving," I state bluntly, my tone flat.

"Why?" she breathes, shifting to tearful in an instant.

But I'm too mad to respond.

"Do you not want to be with me anymore?"

She sounds so broken and sad, and it brings my temper raging back to life.

"That's rich coming from you. You're the one who's been pretending to feel something for me to get what you want," I sneer, stalking toward the door.

Scrambling from the bed, Camille snatches up my T-shirt that looks almost like a dress when she wears it, and she pulls it on as she chases me from the room. "Dimitri, wait. Please, let me explain," she begs as she follows me down the stairs.

Whirling at the base of them, I turn to face her, my anger pounding through my veins as I lash out. "Explain? What could you possibly have to explain? I think it's all pretty fucking clear, Camille. And I'm not really in the mood to be your toy—or your fucking dildo."

Then I turn to storm away once more.

"Dimitri," she sobs, her delicate fingers wrapping around my wrist.

My heart twists at the sound of her anguish, and though I'm beyond furious, I can't leave her like this. Body rigid, I turn to face her again. She cries silently, tears tracking down her cheeks as her eyes implore me to listen.

"It's true that my initial plan was to use sex to get close to you so I might save my restaurant, but somewhere along the way, I fell for you. I'm in love with you, Dimitri. I have been for a while now. And I can't stand the thought of losing you because I was so stupid at the start."

My heart throbs at her confession. Those words mean more to me than I ever thought they could. Somehow, it changes everything. I don't know what to say because knowing her feelings are real makes all the difference in the world. I could find a way to get over her betrayal if she truly loves me. Because I'm crazy about her.

"You love me?" I ask, my voice laced with disbelief.

"More than I ever imagined possible," she confesses, stepping forward to place her hand over my heart. Her blue eyes peer up at me, her emotions fathomless as she silently implores me to believe her. "The only hurdle I don't know how to get past is the fact that you're willing to kill people," she murmurs, her tears flowing more freely now.

"Wait, what?" I frown at the comment that comes out of left field.

"Well... Roy," she starts as if trying to tiptoe into a subject she knows will make me mad.

And I freeze, slowly connecting the dots as I put together what she's trying to say. She's made offhand comments here and there, hints about wondering who might have killed her boyfriend, but I hadn't thought anything of it because I had nothing to do with his death.

Like a massive bomb, Camille has dropped explosive information on me, and I stand stunned, trying to form a coherent thought as I try to put my words together. I want to defend myself, to clear the air and clarify that Roy died from his own stupidity—not at my hand.

But more than that, I want to talk about *us*. About just how much it means to me that she would say she loves me. Because, without a doubt, I'm in love with her too. In truth, I've been crazy about Camille since the moment I met her. I want her more than I've wanted anything in my life.

My lips part, the words sticking in my throat as I struggle to express myself through my utter astonishment. But before I can speak in my defense, the elevator into my apartment dings open.

Camille jumps as we turn to face the unexpected guest, and Alexei steps into my house. I frown, confused by the unusual intrusion. It has to be close to three o'clock in the morning. And from the look on his face, something's terribly wrong.

"Why aren't you answering your phone?" he demands in Russian, his tone sharp—not an ounce of his typical banter present.

"I…" I hadn't heard it ringing, and I glance around me, wondering where I even put it.

"Whatever, it doesn't matter. Forget the phone. We need to go," Alexei snaps.

"What? Why?" I rasp, automatically switching to our native tongue, my heart jumping into my throat.

"Mom's in the hospital," he says curtly, his impatience visible.

"*Blyat,*" I cuss, my feet carrying me forward before my head has time to process what's happened.

"Dimitri?" Camille asks behind me, and her voice sounds so lost and vulnerable that it makes my heart ache.

Turning to meet her eyes, I can see the fear written across her face. And she looks so fragile and small, it tears me up inside.

"Stay here," I plead in English. "I'll be back." I glance toward my brother, doubt flashing through me, but the intensity of his concern solidifies my resolve. "I have to go," I state, turning back to Camille. "But just… stay put."

Then I join my brother as he steps into the elevator. I catch one last glimpse of Camille before the doors close, and her expression looks utterly broken. It rips my heart to shreds.

29

Camille

The shock of having someone enter Dimitri's apartment in the middle of the hardest conversation I've ever had leaves me stunned.

I don't know who the guy is, but based on how similar his features are to Dimitri's and the fact that the two are right around the same age, I would assume they're brothers. He looks maybe a few years younger than Dimitri and several inches shorter. But he's just as handsome and, if possible, even more muscular.

Their brief exchange takes place in hurried Russian, of which I know not a single word. And I stare wide-eyed when Dimitri walks away from me like it's the easiest thing he's ever done.

As Dimitri and his brother vanish into the elevator together, I suddenly feel immensely hollow.

I have no idea what just happened. Maybe it was Dimitri's plan to leave with him all along. And seeing as they carried out their entire conversation in Russian, I can only assume it must have been about something they didn't want me to understand.

Feet frozen to the floor, I stand staring at the elevator doors for a long moment after he's gone. Dimitri left me alone in his massive apartment, not a word of explanation. Not an ounce of remorse.

Stay put. That's all he had to say to me.

I poured my heart and soul out to him, exposing my vulnerability and deepest emotions in an attempt to mend the rift that's grown between us.

And he gave me nothing in return.

It was all in vain. Dimitri's lack of reciprocation and gruff tone as he told me to stay speaks volumes. I'm like a pet he doesn't have time to discipline just now. It doesn't matter if I'm in love with him. He feels nothing for me anymore.

Perhaps some lingering concern, and maybe a sense of responsibility for my safety—God only knows why—because he did come to pick me up when I needed him, even after his massive blowout.

Still, the way in which he drew away from me as soon as we finished having sex says it all. Physically, he might be attracted to me, and if I push the envelope, he's even still willing to fuck me. But that's all it is now. He's completely removed himself emotionally. He *doesn't* want me anymore.

Maybe, once, we could have been happy together. But too many things stand between us now. My betrayal, the fate of my restaurant. Dimitri's hurtful words before he left Le Fleur. Roy's murder.

I take a deep, shuddering breath as I consider everything that just took place between us. Because I finally mustered the courage to say it, to reveal my fear that Dimitri killed my boyfriend. And the fact that he didn't deny it is all the confirmation I need.

An innocent man would have shown some surprise or shock. A defense would have come easily—an objection that I got it all wrong. But Dimitri didn't say a word. Instead, he stiffened, watching me with inscrutable eyes as he refused to confess his guilt.

Though I'm sure now that I'll never know exactly what happened to Roy—how Dimitri killed him—I don't need to keep digging. I've gotten as much information as Dimitri is going to give me. And I know with confidence that Dimitri murdered him.

Heart heavy and tears streaming down my cheeks, I force myself to turn and make my way back up the stairs to Dimitri's room. Stopping in the doorway, I sob as I look at the bed where I've spent so many hours learning about what it means to have someone satisfy me so completely.

Funny, but in my attempt to discover what happened to Roy, I learned so much about myself. What it should feel like when someone truly wants to please me. If nothing else, I can thank Dimitri for that. Because I'll never settle for someone like Roy again. Someone selfish, who could care less *if* I finish, let alone how many times.

I ache to have the happiness back that I found with Dimitri. I crave it with every fiber of my being. But if I'm being honest with myself, it wasn't real. Because the connection we had was based on lies and deception. When it comes down to it, my attraction was driven by our physical connection and how good he could make me feel. Admittedly, he's masterful at that.

But the rest is just a fantasy I made up in my head to make myself feel better for falling in love with a killer.

But now it's done.

I need to face the facts.

And pick up the broken pieces of my life so I can carry on.

Slowly stripping his oversized T-shirt, I hold it to my nose, breathing in his scent one last time before I fold it neatly and set it on the bed. I fold his pajama pants, too, making the act methodical and deliberate because I'm dangerously tempted to take them with me. To cling to one small piece of our happiness for as long as I can.

But it's better to rip the bandage off in one go.

Heading to the bathroom, I don my own clothes. They're gritty from a hard night in the kitchen followed by a traumatizing car wreck. But they'll have to do until I get home.

My eyes catch on my face in the mirror, and I'm shocked by the hollow, haunted look in my eyes. The emptiness that comes with knowing this is the end of my soul-consuming romance.

And though it kills me to leave, I know I have to go.

Because saying goodbye to Dimitri is only going to make things harder. And I'm not sure I have the strength to wait until he comes back.

Summoning an Uber, I press the call button for the elevator. Then I ride it down to the first floor. I pull myself together on the trip down, taking deep breaths and wiping the tears from my face.

Distraught, I know my life will never be the same. I can't go back to the way things were before Dimitri entered my life. I'm a different person now.

All I can do is move forward from here. And though it tears me up to know I have to live without him, I'm determined to survive this too. Slipping into the back seat of my Uber, I peer out the window as dark thoughts consume my mind.

I have new challenges to contend with now that my plan to prove Dimitri's guilt has completely unraveled. I'm back to square one on losing Le Fleur. Because I'm confident Dimitri won't let it go without a fight. And he has the documentation to prove that my restaurant is his by right.

The best I can do now is to go back to paying off the lien in installments. I pray that will be enough to satisfy him. And maybe, just maybe, he'll let me keep Le Fleur.

My Uber pulls up outside my tiny house, and I slip from the back seat with a mumbled thank you. Fishing my keys from my purse as I walk slowly up the sidewalk to my door, I'm struck by the sense that this place no longer feels quite like home to me.

Not in the same way Dimitri's apartment does.

Sure, this house is familiar, and it contains the majority of my possessions. But it feels so... vacant without the protective presence that fills Dimitri's grand home.

Locking the door firmly behind me, I drop my purse right there on the floor. Stripping down as I head to my bedroom. I don't bother finding fresh clothes before slipping under my covers.

Curling into a tight ball, I hug my knees, and I let my emotions flow freely as I allow myself one night to fully feel the loss that consumes me.

Tomorrow, it will be back to work, and I can put all of this behind me. But right now, I just need to process the intense emotions swallowing me in a deep black hole.

30

Dimitri

Relief floods me as I step into the hospital room and find my mother sitting up in her bed, her feeble body looking ghastly thin in a flimsy hospital gown. Maksim is already there with her, and he shifts the pillows behind her to help make her more comfortable.

"What happened?" I demand as Alexei and I stride into the room, letting the door click closed behind us.

"I guess she had a bad bout of food poisoning that left her weak and light-headed," Maksim explains. "She collapsed, and one of her servants found her on the floor. They've hooked her up to an IV, and she's doing much better now."

"I'm fine, boys. Really," she insists, her voice warbling weakly.

Alexei steps close to her bedside, kneeling as he grips her tiny hand in his big ones. As he presses her knuckles to his lips, she combs his hair back from his face. Of the three of us, he's always been a momma's boy, the good son who goes to visit her every Sunday.

But it still kills me to see my mother so fragile. She's getting older now and hasn't been the same mentally since Father died. She's been sick a lot lately, so when Alexei said she was in the hospital, I didn't even think. I just went.

"What are you doing walking around when you're light-headed?" I ask, my voice gruff with concern.

A knowing smile spreads across my mother's face as she meets my eye. She knows me better than anyone and isn't fooled by my harsh tone. She sees it for what it is—the expression of my deep love for her and the gnawing concern that comes with my fear for her safety.

"Well, I can't sit around all day, dear. And I wasn't light-headed until I got up." Reaching a hand out to me, she beckons me silently toward her bed.

I step forward to take her hand, and feeling her warm fingers against my palm reassures me that she's okay. I give her palm a gentle squeeze before releasing it and stepping back again.

"We're just glad you're feeling better," Maksim states, standing with me as Alexei continues to stay close by our mother's side, his hand on her shoulder.

A light knock sounds on the door, and we all turn to watch as a doctor steps inside the room, wearing a white lab coat with a stethoscope hanging around his neck. "Good morning," he greets, though the sun hasn't yet risen. His eyes flick to me and Alexei, noting the new people who have entered the room. "My name is Dr. Fields. I ordered the initial tests for Mrs. Federov here when she was admitted. How are we feeling, ma'am?" he asks kindly, riffling through the papers pinned to his clipboard.

"Right as rain, Doc," she assures him with a smile.

He gives a nod, and his brows press together as he reads her chart.

Crossing my arms over my chest in a mirror image of Maksim's posture, I ask, "What's the diagnosis?"

"Food poisoning for sure. Mrs. Federov, do you go berry hunting?" he asks, his eyes shifting to meet hers through his spectacles.

"Beg your pardon?" she asks, confused.

"Berries, do you ever pick them and eat them? Maybe while you're exploring wooded areas on a walk or something," the doctor rephrases.

"Never," she confesses, her expression baffled.

"The reason I ask is that your bloodwork would indicate you've been exposed to a poisonous fruit, specifically one related to the chokeberry plant—also known as American nightshade," he explains.

I glance sideways at Maksim, my instincts setting off a warning bell in my mind. It could be a coincidence, but when would my mother ever be exposed to poisonous berries by chance?

"Oh, well, I have several berry bushes growing on my estate, and my chef made me a blueberry tart for dessert just yesterday," she says as if that clears up any confusion.

But the explanation only intensifies my suspicion.

"If that's the case, I would recommend you avoid eating any fruit from those bushes until you've had a professional confirm they're edible. Chokeberries can easily be mistaken for blueberries by someone who doesn't know the difference. But you're fortunate you didn't eat more than you did. The level of toxins in your bloodstream is considerable. Any more, and the dosage easily could have been lethal."

My heart stutters at the thought of how close I came to losing my mom. Looking at her kind face, fury bursts to life inside my chest. I don't care if it was a mistake or not. I'm going to rip that chef limb from limb.

"Will she recover?" Alexei asks, his voice laced with anxiety.

Dr. Fields nods. "Fortunately, fluids and electrolytes go a long way to helping the body flush the poison, and if she's feeling better, we may not need to take any further action. However, I want to keep her here for the next twenty-four hours at least to ensure her recovery is stable and she continues to improve."

Maksim nods. "Of course."

"I'll be back to check on you again in a few hours," the doctor says, meeting my mother's eye. "If you need anything, just press the call button."

"Thank you, Doc," my mother says, her hand patting Alexei's knuckles comfortingly.

As soon as the doctor steps out of the room, the door shutting behind him, Alexei turns to us. "That chef needs to go," he states firmly.

"Alexei!" our mom scolds, looking up at her youngest son. "I'm sure it was an accident. Anton is a good man. If we speak to him, we'll find out it was an honest mistake, like Dr. Fields said."

"No, Alexei's right," I state, my instincts telling me this was no accident. "We can't take that risk. Even if he didn't do it intentionally, he clearly doesn't know enough about the risks he's taking, and you're in no condition to be his guinea pig."

Maksim nods. "I want him gone. Today."

"Agreed," Alexei and I say simultaneously.

"You boys are overreacting," Mom insists.

"Mom, you know this isn't something we can take lightly," Alexei states, his tone kind but firm. "We have too many enemies. And we're not about to gamble your life on the off chance that some idiot chef made a mistake."

"Besides, we grew up eating the berries on that property, and we never once had something happen like this. You can't tell me he happened upon the one chokeberry plant that we've been missing all these years," I add.

"It could have cropped up without us knowing. That's a big property, boys, and as well as the gardeners maintain it, they could easily overlook a new plant that starts growing on the perimeter," my mother insists.

Maksim and I share a sharp look, and I nod.

"The gardeners can go as well."

"Dimitri!" our mom scolds.

"This isn't a discussion," Maksim backs me.

And seeing she's clearly outnumbered, my mother crumples, her shoulders sagging in defeat.

"You'll take care of it?" Maksim asks, turning to me.

I nod. "I'll head straight there." I know Maksim has a major deal to close in hours. I was supposed to be part of the meeting, but he'll have to do it on his own. And Alexei won't be leaving our mother's side until we're certain our mother isn't in immediate danger.

Pointing toward the hospital's roof, Maksim says, "Take the chopper."

Raising an eyebrow at him, I ask, "Really?" We all love our mother, but that mode of transportation to get here seems a bit excessive, even for my older brother.

He shrugs. "Symphony and I were spending the weekend in Carmel," he explains.

My eyebrow rises an inch higher. "So, where in the hell is she now?"

"She decided to stay since the hotel and spa were already booked," he says, his tone warning me not to go there.

But I'm wound so tight, I can't help myself. "Your mother's rushed to the hospital after collapsing, and your fiancée thought it made more sense to stay and have a spa weekend alone than come offer emotional support?" I ask pointedly.

Maksim bristles visibly. "Do I look like I'm in need of emotional support?" he growls.

"You look like you need a reality check, to me, brother."

"Boys, no fighting!" Mom pleads, and immediately, I'm contrite.

I definitely shouldn't be provoking him in her presence. "You're right. Sorry, Mom," I say gently, turning to her. I press a kiss to my mother's forehead and leave a moment later.

Heading up to the hospital's rooftop helipad, I tell the pilot my destination as soon as I climb aboard. Moments later, we're in the air, heading north to the family estate.

Loath as I am to be the one in charge of firing the staff responsible, I'm the best one for the job. Because this could prove to be a targeted attack, and I'm the one who knows how to get answers.

I'll be questioning the staff extensively until I get to the bottom of this, and if I find out that someone intentionally poisoned my mother, I guarantee they'll be eating the rest of that blueberry tart to see what happens when you fuck with the Federov family.

It isn't until after I land in Sonoma and search for my phone to call Camille that I remember leaving it in my apartment. Frustrated and hoping she'll understand when I get back in town with an explanation, I get to work interviewing my mother's staff as soon as they arrive for work.

It takes days of grueling interrogation to get to the bottom of it. Another to dispose of the guilty chef's body after he finally confesses to bringing the berries with him for her tart. But try as I might, I couldn't get an explanation for his act of betrayal. He would take that to his grave.

To prove his guilt beyond a doubt, I make him finish every last bite of the poisoned dessert. Watching him choke on his own vomit within the hour is the most satisfying moment of the painstaking ordeal.

In the end, I don't care what his reason is for trying to kill my mother. Anyone who could harm a hair on that saint-of-a-woman's head deserves to die the slow and painful death Anton did.

But my job's not done yet. After the guilty party is taken care of, the next step is vetting new employees and hiring only those I can fully entrust with my mother's care.

It takes me three full days working around the clock to settle the whole debacle. Though I know my brothers would do an equally thorough job in protecting our mother and seeing that she's surrounded by staff we can trust, I'm glad to have been the one to handle it myself.

It gives me a sense of assurance I wouldn't have if it had been left in anyone else's hands.

But by the time I reach my penthouse apartment late in the evening after my final day, I'm damn near ready to collapse from exhaustion.

My house is empty when I arrive. And I can't blame Camille for having left. Three days are far too many for her to stay away from her restaurant—even if she has a concussion. I just hope she took care of herself in my absence. Though knowing how stubborn she is, I wouldn't be surprised if she was back to work the morning after her accident.

I find the clothes she borrowed folded neatly on the corner of my bed, and for some reason, it disappoints me to know she didn't wear them home or keep them.

But one emotional dilemma at a time.

Once I get some sleep, I'll find Camille first thing in the morning, and we can have the conversation I've been dying to finish ever since she told me she loves me.

31

Camille

Flames lick up around the steak as I flip it on the grill then turn to the chicken dish I'm preparing beside it. The Thursday night rush brings me a sense of relief as it takes my mind off Dimitri and the nervous knots that have bound my stomach all day.

"Plating!" Betsa calls, moving through the kitchen to collect the sol I'm pan-searing before turning to Louis for the sauce.

I've been coasting on an adrenaline high ever since I sent the courier to Dimitri's house with a check containing my payment toward the lien. I haven't heard from him since the night of my accident. It's been days since he told me to stay put, and I wonder if he even meant it a little or if he was just waiting outside his apartment building, watching for me to leave before he went back inside.

It took me time to build up enough nerve to send him my payment. But today, with Hannah's support, I was finally ready to solidify my intention to break it off with Dimitri. Which means I have to face the debt Roy strapped me with.

Transferring a pistachio-crusted pork chop to a bed of potatoes, I turn to collect gravy from Louis's sauce station, then I bring the dish to the heat lamp.

"Order up!" I call, ringing the bell.

Quick footsteps tell me a server is on the way, but I don't pause to chat. I have plenty more orders to fill.

Turning back to the stove, I check my steak before moving on to the next ticket on the line.

But a muffled disturbance from the front room catches my ear. Heated voices steadily grow louder, and I glance toward the swinging door with a frown.

"No, you can't go in there!" I hear Hannah shout, and then the swinging door bursts inward, revealing Dimitri's impressive figure.

Dressed in a fine, tailored suit, his hair done to perfection, and that well-trimmed stubble coloring his strong jaw; he looks as devastatingly handsome as ever. His broad shoulders fill the doorway for a moment, obscuring Hannah. Then his silver gaze locks on me and he strides in my direction.

A sliver of panic slices through me, and at the same time, my irritation spikes at the fact that he's decided he needs to see me now—after nearly four days of utter silence—in the middle of my dinner rush.

"I'm sorry, Cami," Hannah gushes, her face flushed with aggravation. "He wouldn't listen. Do you want me to call the police?"

Heart pounding, I force my face into a mask of calm as I feel the tension of my kitchen staff escalating. We don't have time for another one of Dimitri's blowouts, and from his face, he's pissed. At least this time, he doesn't look like he's on a rampage.

"It's fine, Hannah," I state, then I flick my eyes to Dimitri as he steps into my personal space.

I can sense Louis gawking beside me, and I cast him a warning look.

"You better not let that sauce break," I say, indicating he should go about his tasks like nothing out of the ordinary is happening.

And though I'm trembling from Dimitri's growing fury next to me, I try to do the same. "What do you want?" I ask the tall, menacing intruder, doing my best to keep my tone steady as I turn my attention back to the grill.

"Why are you sending me money?" he demands, shoving the check in front of my face. His voice is flat and filled with rage.

"Isn't it obvious?" I ask, trying to keep my cool, though my hands shake as I remove the steak from the grill to the cutting board so I can slice it into medallions.

"Don't fucking play with me. You haven't answered any of my calls."

"Are you joking?" I demand, slamming my knife down and turning to face him fully. "Since when have you picked up the phone? The last I heard from you, you were hightailing it out of your apartment *three days ago* with no explanation. Just *stay*. I'm not your dog, Dimitri. I have a life, a business, responsibilities. And you want to be pissed at me for not picking up the phone?" Scoffing, I turn back to the stove.

"You're not even going to let me explain?" he growls, his hands fisting as he crumples the check.

"Why should I? You know, you say a lot more with your silence than you seem to realize. I don't need you to lay it out for me like I'm a child. I got the message. We're done. So just take the money and leave me alone."

But he doesn't. He stands motionless, his anger flowing from him in waves as he stares me down.

Tears sting my eyes, blurring the order tickets hanging in front of me that I need to fill, and I know I'm not going to be getting anything done while he's hell-bent on arguing with me.

Growling with frustration, I turn to face Dimitri head-on. "Can't you see I'm busy?" I demand. "I think we're finally on the same page, so why can't you just take the check and let me be?"

"Just take the check? Are you fucking kidding me?" Dimitri grabs my wrist and shoves the crumpled paper into my hand. "If we're back to talking business, then fine, sell Le Fleur to me. That's the deal I'm offering."

"No," I state adamantly, the pain and rejection escalating my temper until I'm right in Dimitri's face, glowering at him, even though I know how reckless it might be. "You will never get Le Fleur. This restaurant is *mine*. I'll pay off the stupid debt. I just need a little more time."

"Even if I let you, this payment is inferior," he snarls, indicating the crumpled check in my hand like it offends him. "You owe several months of payments plus interest for being late."

Like a switch, he's flipped to being a cold, ruthless businessman. And I feel the intensity of the pressure he'll be putting on now that I'm not spreading my legs for him. This Dimitri is something I don't quite know how to manage. But I hate more than anything to see the steel in his gaze, the icy detachment that tells me there's no hope for us from here.

And in an instant, I feel the crushing weight of knowing without a doubt that we're done. Tears stream down my cheeks unchecked as my anger and loss mingle into one overwhelmingly intense emotion.

"Fine!" I scream. "I'll give you the money if it means I never have to see you again!"

Dimitri's nostrils flare as he looks down at me with unbridled fury. His chiseled face looks striking even in his rage, and it tears me up to face him, to look into the eyes of the man I was falling for and know that he hates me. That my confession of love meant nothing to him.

"That works for me," he states coldly, stepping back from me and straightening his fine black suit. "I expect to receive what you owe by the time the banks close tomorrow." His eyes flick up to the kitchen staff, who stand terribly still behind me.

Then he turns without another word and stalks through the kitchen door.

Shaking from head to foot, I clench the crumpled check tightly in my fist and will my tears to stop. But they only fall harder. Biting back a sob, I brush angrily at my cheeks and turn to the stove.

The chicken's burnt, its skin charred beyond saving, and as I rush to scoop it off the heat and into the trash, I lose it completely. Dropping the skillet back onto the stove, I brace against the counter with my palms and cry.

I hate it. Falling apart in front of my staff. Losing my confidence to keep my business running. Watching Dimitri walk out of my life. It's all too much.

How have I sunk this far in such a short time?

The bruise on my temple throbs as my pulse roars through my ears, reminding me of Dimitri's tender touch as he washed my face after the accident. That's the man I want in my life. The one who would drop everything to take care of me when I need him.

But I can't reconcile this other person. The cold, calculating businessman who can cut me loose without a second thought because I made one mistake. That's who killed Roy. That's who's going to take everything from me.

Unless I can find the money to pay Dimitri by tomorrow, I'll lose Le Fleur.

"Chef?" Louis asks tentatively.

God, what my staff must think of me. Not only is this the second fight they've witnessed in a week—followed both times by my meltdowns—but now they also know I'm strapped with a debt that could cost me my restaurant and I was having an affair with the guy I owe money to. How much longer can I expect them to stay if they think Le Fleur will end up in Dimitri's hands?

"I'm fine, Louis," I assure him, waving off his concern as I quickly collect myself, trying to salvage what's left of my dignity.

I attempt a smile, but from his look of concern, I can tell it's not at all convincing.

"I'm so sorry you guys had to see that," I say, turning to look at everyone in the kitchen. "It won't happen again."

"You have nothing to apologize for," Betsa says adamantly, stepping closer to grip my hand.

Rorey, my pâtissier, nods emphatically, and Louis agrees.

"Thanks," I breathe, giving them a sincere, if watery, smile this time. "Phew!" releasing a deep breath, I fan my face. "Let's pull ourselves together and have a good rest of the night, right?" I say, rallying with an upbeat voice.

My team smiles back at me, returning to their stations a moment later with a renewed sense of purpose. But as I turn back to my line of tickets and get to work recreating the ruined chicken dish, I can't help but feel the heaviness in my heart.

Because as strong as I want to appear, it took everything in me to stand up to Dimitri. To face him again when I left it all on the line for him and he had nothing to say to me. Maybe I could understand if he needed a minute to collect himself, but…

He just left.

For three days.

What could possibly be so important that he couldn't respond to "I love you" before vanishing from the face of the earth like that? I think that says it all.

I need to accept the facts. Dimitri and I are over.

32

Dimitri

Pacing in front of my wall of windows that look out across the dark bay, I snarl in my anger. I've been fuming for hours since my confrontation with Camille, and I can't seem to find a moment's peace.

That Camille could possibly think I'm the bad guy here, that she has any right to treat me with malice or contempt when she's the one who lied to me—it fills me with a rage that turns my vision red.

I'm done.

Done trying to make sense of her. Done caring about her sob story and the restaurant she cares so much about. She can make me out to be the villain all she wants, but she's the one who used me. She lied to me, manipulated my emotions, and now she wants to pretend like I'm the one without a soul.

I might not be heartless enough to take Camille's restaurant from her, but I'm sorely tempted out of spite. If she wants to make me the bad guy, why should I try to stop her? It pisses me off to know she got so far under my skin. I'm nearly ready to retaliate. But one thing's for sure, I'm not letting her off the hook now. Not when she wants to pretend I'm the jerk.

Desperate to blow off steam, I need to talk to somebody. Because pacing alone in my apartment isn't doing anything to resolve my anger.

Pulling my phone from my pocket, I dial Maksim, though I know it's late.

"*Da,*" he answers, his tone distracted, like he didn't take the time to look who was calling.

"I'm done being Camille Anderson's puppet," I growl, cutting right to the chase. "I'm going to let her pay off the loan."

"The chef?" he asks in confusion.

"Yeah. It turns out she's been playing me this whole time. She thought sleeping with me would deter me from taking her restaurant."

"Well... she wasn't wrong, was she?" he observes with mild amusement.

"It's not funny," I snarl. "And you're not helping." I pace more adamantly across my marble floor, my fist clenching by my side as I grip the phone more forcefully by my ear.

"Sorry. Continue," he says, though I can hear the smile in his tone.

The full story floods from me in an instant, the dam of emotion releasing as I tell my brother everything. "Well, now that I've found out she was just using me, she wants to make it seem like I'm the asshole. First, she gives me some sob story about her restaurant being a dream of her dead father's, and yet she let her deadbeat boyfriend take out a loan, posting her restaurant as collateral. I mean, the contract has her signature. She signed off on it. And that makes her responsible to pay it off since her boyfriend got himself killed."

"Right," Maksim agrees patiently.

"But I'm the idiot who let her blind me to the truth. She played me for *weeks*, making me think we might have something. I was willing to pursue that and forgive the loan. And then, it turns out the whole fucking thing was a lie. And when I confronted her about it, she gave me some teary explanation that she had a change of heart—not that she was going to tell me about any of this, mind you. I had to find out about it from her friend."

"That's rough," Maksim observes.

"No fucking joke. And that's not the worst of it. The night Mom got taken to the hospital, Camille told me she loves me. And then the next thing I know, she sends me a check without a word of explanation! So, I go to her restaurant to get the logic behind it, and she tells me we're done. She wants nothing more to do with me and I should leave her alone. She's just as illogical and manipulative as all the rest of them. This is why girls are too much fucking trouble."

The line's quiet for several seconds as I feel my temper de-escalating slightly, and I slow to a stop, turning to lean against the glass as I look out at the dark sky lit by the Golden Gate Bridge.

"This was tonight?" he asks finally.

"Yeah. I'm going crazy over here trying to decide if I should just take the restaurant to teach her not to fuck with sharks."

"She's got you that mad, huh?" Maksim asks, impressed.

Growling in frustration, I shove away from the glass and slump onto the couch. "I won't. But I'm not letting her off the hook either. If she wants to make payments, then that's what I'll take. But I'm done after that. No more letting women get under my skin."

"I've never heard you get so worked up about a girl before. That has to say something," Maksim observes calmly, then he lets the simple statement sink in.

"Yeah, well it'll be the first and the last time," I growl.

"Alright," my brother says, but his tone would indicate he doubts it.

"What?" I demand, my irritation spiking.

"It's nothing really. I just think you're not being honest with yourself if you're saying you're done but still willing to take payments on a loan that's months overdue."

"You think I should just take the restaurant then?" I snap.

"I didn't say that. I'm leaving this deal in your hands, brother. I just want you to make your decision with your eyes wide open. It sounds to me like you still have some unfinished business with the chef."

My brother's words give me pause, and I knead my temples as I take a moment to absorb what he's saying.

"Look, take the night. Think it over. Maybe you'll have a different perspective in the morning. Maybe not. But clearly, she's got you mad enough that you shouldn't make a final decision tonight."

"Alright," I grumble. "Thanks for letting me unload."

"Hey, we're in this as a family. We don't get where we are unless we have each other's backs."

"Thanks, Maks. Really."

"Anytime."

Ending the call, I stare at my phone for a long moment, considering my brother's words. I feel better after having vocalized my pain and frustration. And maybe he's right. I need to make a logical decision, not an emotional one.

As I lock my phone, the time flashes across the screen: 11:18 p.m. Camille must be about done closing I would imagine. She'll be locking up soon.

Irritation flashes through me that Camille would be the first thing that crosses my mind. Admittedly, I just finished talking about her. But why would I move directly to what she would be doing right now?

Shouldn't I be thinking about the meeting I have in the morning and how I've wasted valuable sleeping hours fuming over someone who doesn't want to be with me?

Rising from the couch, I shove my phone in my pocket and head toward my stairs. But something doesn't feel right. The hairs stand up on the back of my neck as my mind tracks back to the fact that Camille should be closing now.

And in a flash, the black car sitting on the corner comes to my mind.

The person who's been watching her.

I've been so caught up in my mother's poisoning crisis, I haven't even checked in with Alexei to see if he's followed up on the suspicious car.

And that's all it takes for my mind to leap to Camille's accident. The one where a driver ran a red light in the middle of the night, T-boned her, and then drove away.

It's too much to believe it's a coincidence.

And if this stalker stepped up his game from watching Camille to hitting her with his car, how long will it be before he makes his next move?

I've left her vulnerable and exposed for days now, not stopping to consider that her life might actually be in danger.

And suddenly, my hurt and anger seem inconsequential in the face of something bad happening to Camille. I don't care what she's done. I can't stand the thought of someone attacking her.

I have no clue who the person is or why they might be so interested in Camille, but now's not the time to be riddling out the answer. If I'm right, the rest of Le Fleur's staff should have left by now, which means Camille's there all by herself.

Heart pounding, I head toward my penthouse elevator, calling Camille as I go.

The phone rings and rings, but she doesn't answer.

Anxiety knotting my gut, I step into the elevator and pound the button to take me to the garage, then press the arrows to shut the doors.

"Hey, this is Camille. I couldn't answer the phone right now. If you're calling during restaurant hours, you know why! But leave a message, and I'll get back to you as soon as I can."

The phone beeps, sending me to voicemail, and I release a long string of Russian cusses as I end the call and try again.

"Pick up, pick up!" I growl as it rings for a second time.

But it's pointless. She's not going to answer me. Whether that's because she hates me or because she's already dead, I don't know. But the possibility of the latter is too horrible to bear.

Giving up on the phone when it sends me to voicemail a second time, I shove it into my pocket and watch the floor numbers slowly tick down.

As soon as the door opens onto the parking garage, I sprint to my Lamborghini. The motor purrs to life a second later, and I'm peeling out in record time.

Because I can't get rid of this horrible, gut-wrenching feeling that I'm going to be too late.

33

Camille

Sitting in my office, I pour over the receipts for the week, checking my math before filing them away. I know I should be doing this when my head's in a better space, but right now, I can't imagine going to sleep, so I might as well get this done before my deadline tomorrow.

It will help exhaust my brain anyway, so I won't stay up all night debating whether I made the right decision about Dimitri. Cutting him from my life was one of the hardest choices I've ever had to make. But it's the right one.

I think.

He's a criminal, a murderer. And he doesn't love me. I need to get my head on straight. But that doesn't ease the painful ache, the hollow, gaping hole in my chest that throbs every time I think his name.

The restaurant's quiet, Hannah having left nearly an hour ago, which leaves me alone with my thoughts and the business account that's not going to balance itself. I need to find the money to pay

Dimitri with tomorrow, and I would rather not wait until the morning to get it done.

Rip the bandage off so I can stop thinking about the emptiness to come. I never imagined that I could fall so hard for someone. Even Roy, my longest-term boyfriend, doesn't hold a candle to the feelings I've developed for Dimitri in so short a time.

I don't know how I fell so hard for my own deception. Then again, I hadn't anticipated someone could move me the way Dimitri did. He showed me what it really means to connect with someone—even if we weren't meant to be.

I need to stop torturing myself with fantasies.

He's not the prince charming I keep making him out to be.

He's a cold-blooded killer, who not only murdered my boyfriend but is also coming after my restaurant to fulfill a debt that's not mine to pay.

Heaving a sigh, I set down the next bundle of receipts and scrub my face with my hands. Then I pause.

Do they smell like gasoline?

Cupping my hands over my nose, I inhale deeply, wondering why I might smell like gas if I don't even have a car right now. Mine's totaled, and until I can afford to get another one, I'll be Uber-ing around town. So it makes no sense that I should smell like gas, and all I inhale is the lavender lotion I keep in the women's bathroom.

Frowning, I glance toward the office door.

Then my stomach knots.

I was so lost in my head when I closed up the kitchen. I'm not one hundred percent sure I turned off the stove. Not that the gas should have made it this far by now, but I can't afford to be making mistakes like that. The industrial appliance has the capability to light this place up if I happen to leave a burner on overnight.

Rising from my chair, I rush toward the door and open it.

The smell is definitely coming from the kitchen. And the fumes only grow more potent as I make my way there.

"Shit," I gasp, racing down the hall toward the swinging door as the fire alarm blares to life, shrieking in my ears. I can't believe it's bad enough to set the smoke detectors off so quickly.

Bursting into the kitchen, I'm appalled at the sight before me.

It's not just one burner I forgot to turn off. Each is on full blast, the gas roaring from the stove as foot-high flames lick the air hungrily. Smoke clouds the ceiling and creates a brownish haze inside the room.

As a chef, I'm used to heat, but this is something else entirely. In seconds, I'm drenched in sweat, the hot air dry and scorching. It sucks the moisture from my skin, baking me with its rapidly growing intensity.

Coughing as the fumes burn down my throat to hit my lungs, I cover my nose and mouth with one arm. Then I step into the room. I have to turn off the stove before the fire spreads, or worse, the building explodes. My entire life is in this restaurant, and if the building goes down, I can't imagine where that will land me.

Heart fluttering in my chest, I creep cautiously forward, torn between my instinct to run and my need to save my restaurant. And every second, the flames climb higher, dancing toward the vent that's supposed to release the smoke outside. Someone must have closed it because the smoke billows out around it, avoiding escape.

At the stove, I hold my breath and uncover my face to reach for the knobs. I need to cut the flow of gas. But just as my fingers close around the dials, a burst of heat explodes before me, the noxious air lighting around my palms as the heat singes my cheeks.

Screaming at the sudden painful blisters rising on my fingers, I fall back onto the floor. My hands throb from the seared flesh, but worse, my vocal reaction forced so much smoke into my airway, I can hardly breathe.

Coughing violently, I know I have to do something, but I don't dare try to touch the stove again.

Gripped with terror, I look desperately around the room for something, anything, that will help my predicament. And my eyes land on a fire extinguisher.

Lungs burning, I crawl on hands and knees toward it, desperate to save Le Fleur.

Another burst of flames ripples outward, making me flinch, and suddenly, the fire takes on a life of its own. Crackling across the ceiling, the cutting boards lining the wall, the countertops; it consumes anything it can find to burn as kindling.

"No, no, no," I sob, crawling faster.

But the air is so thick with smoke that I'm overcome by another coughing fit, this one so powerful and relentless that it leaves me gasping and light-headed. And when I finally get my lungs under control once more, the room swims before me, making it nearly impossible to identify which of the fire extinguishers is the real one.

Shit.

I know I'm in a bad spot. The gas has been on for far too long, filling the room with fumes that both turn my stomach and muddle my brain. The fire is spreading more quickly than I thought possible.

And I'm so dizzy from the pain and smoke inhalation that I'm not quite sure where the door is. But all I can think is *I can't lose my restaurant.* Panic overwhelms me as I realize I might die here. And still, it feels like my heart is being wrenched out of my chest to see my kitchen go up in flames.

I sway dangerously, grateful I'm already on the ground as my vision starts to dim. I'm going to pass out. Suffocating heat envelops me, followed by the terrifying sound of plates shattering as they're exposed to temperatures beyond their durability.

But I keep crawling forward, and after several attempts, my fingers close around the metal of the extinguisher. It's excruciating trying to work the nozzle with my burnt fingers, but I prevail, turning the head toward a wall of flame and pulling the trigger.

Nothing happens.

Now what do I do?

My last hope of salvaging my kitchen apparently decided to go on a permanent vacation, leaving me helpless to stop the destruction of my home away from home.

The flames nearly surround me now, their path seeming to encircle me with malicious intent.

I have to get out of here.

But when I turn to find the door, the floor rises up to meet me.

Lungs screaming for relief, my vision darkening, and I find my brain is too foggy to do anything about it. I'm not getting enough oxygen. *Oh God, I can't die here. Not like this.*

And then a dark shadow looms over me.

Fear grips me, and my instincts tell me to run, that I'm in very real danger. But I can't seem to get my body to cooperate. My knees shake and buckle when I try to stand, and I cry out as I push against the floor with my blistered palms.

Strong arms scoop me up a moment later, but I'm too weak to fight them off.

Is this who set the fire?

But then why wouldn't they just leave me to die?

Nothing makes sense to me right now.

My head lolls dangerously as I lose track of what's up and what's down.

My thoughts are disjointed, firing off like threads of a spider web that lead to oblivion.

"Don't you dare die on me," growls a deep masculine voice.

It sends a shiver down my spine. I try to focus on the voice, turning my head in its direction, though the motion makes my stomach turn violently. On the verge of vomiting, I blink several times as I try to make sense of the vision above me.

Dimitri's face swims into view.

Like an avenging angel, he looks beyond furious, the sharp line of his brow telling me he's on the warpath. Just like when he stormed into my kitchen earlier this evening.

But it doesn't make sense.

Am I hallucinating? Calling to mind the last clear image I have of him in my head? The light shining around his visage like a halo would suggest as much. I must be dreaming him into being.

Why else would he be here? Now?

He can't be. This is my mind's desperate attempt to call him to me before I die. Because I can feel it. The sudden cold, the intense darkness. It surrounds me, cutting through my body like a knife.

I'm surprised that death by fire could feel so horribly cold, and I shudder violently as it consumes me.

For a split second, it feels as though the icy grip of death has awakened all my senses, intensifying my nerves until I can actually feel the solid muscle of my hallucinatory savior. I smell the piney scent of his cologne. Taste the salt of his sweat on my lips.

"Stay with me," he murmurs, his voice a distant echo.

And then inky darkness envelops me, dragging me deep into oblivion.

34

Camille

The incessant beeping of my alarm clock slowly pulls me from a horrifying dream in which a haunting shadow loomed over me. Knife in hand, the unknown figure had laughed as he cut deep lines in my palms, setting my skin on fire. But it was the joy with which he hurt me that terrified me the most. Like my pain brought him a sense of satisfaction that I couldn't possibly make sense of.

Groaning, I force my eyes open, desperate to wrench myself from the nightmare.

Brilliant fluorescents greet me, glaring down at me with apathetic, harsh light.

Sharp pain lances through my skull at the sudden, violent assault, and I squint. But I refuse to completely close my eyes and allow that creepy shadow to enter my vision once again.

Slowly, the world around me swims into sharper definition. That sound I mistook for my alarm is, in fact, a heart monitor, which quickens its pace as my brain finds focus, alerting me to the crisp white sheets and the stiff railing that surround me. A plastic mask hisses against my face, forcing fresh air into my nose at regular intervals.

My hands pulse with a singular heartbeat, and when I lift them slowly, painfully, I find they're not only bandaged with clean white gauze but there are also several tubes running from my arms, liquid dripping from a bag suspended beside me as it trickles into my veins.

I'm in the hospital.

Breathing deeply, I try to recall what the hell happened to land me here.

A car accident?

No, that was days ago. *Wasn't it?*

I can vividly recall the evening that followed my crash. The sex Dimitri and I had followed by a fight that still leaves me aching with loss and rejection.

Feeling confined by the mask covering my face, I grasp for it, clutching it between my two throbbing palms and wrenching it from my head. And though my lungs burn from the sterile air of the room, I feel less claustrophobic now.

Slowly, images filter back into my mind. The empty dining room of Le Fleur, flames licking up the wall of the kitchen, smoke billowing across the ceiling like a dark, ominous cloud; and then that haunting, shadowy figure that strikes fear into my heart.

I frown as the image of Dimitri's face hovering above me stands out among all the rest. Like a god of fire, his face is surrounded by a golden light that flickers across his skin in stunning detail.

I remember now. I was at the restaurant, and there was a fire. The kitchen had gone up in flames in an instant. And when I'd tried to put it out, I'd fallen victim to the smoke. The fire had spread so fast, I hadn't had time to consider my own safety. I'd been so consumed with trying to preserve my precious dream.

Did Dimitri carry me from the restaurant?

No, that doesn't make sense. He was there earlier in the night. But he stormed out after our fight. The last thing I'd said to him was that I never wanted to see him again. And he'd said that was just fine with him.

Pain lances through my chest as I choke down the knot in my throat.

Not daring to let myself hope, I force my body into a sitting position, though my hands scream as I use them to push myself up. And still, I look around—just in case my vision might be true.

One thing's for sure. I'm definitely in the hospital.

But there's no sign of Dimitri.

I must have imagined him.

Intense disappointment seeps through me, and I fight to contain the tears that sting the backs of my eyes. I don't know who brought me here, but I'm shocked by the level of hope I had that my vision had been real.

Then another realization hits me. If my restaurant was on fire and I ended up in the hospital, it means I failed to put the fire out. And I didn't stay conscious long enough to call the fire department. God only knows how long it took for someone to notice the smoke and pull me from the building.

And while I passed out trying to salvage the situation, my entire life may have burned to the ground. I've lost everything I've worked so hard for. My restaurant and my dad's vision, gone in an instant.

A sob racks my body, and the sharp intake of breath rips through my raw lungs like a saw. Coughing violently, I double over, my muscles cramping as my body tries to reject the horrible fact that I can't breathe.

Consumed with misery, I fight to calm myself down, to take small breaths until my agonizing coughs die away. Then I slump back against my pillows, intensely exhausted.

I don't know what I'm supposed to do now. My restaurant, my livelihood, my life is gone. And not only do I need to find a way to rebuild, but I also need to come up with money I no longer have to pay off the loan Roy took out in my name.

Sudden and intense resentment fills me for the position my boyfriend put me in, and then, immediately, it washes away in a sea of guilt as I realize how agonizing it must have been for him if he did, in fact, die in that house fire. What a horrible way to go. *And how close did I come to suffering the same fate?*

Shuddering violently, I close my eyes, willing myself to forget the terrifying feeling of suffocation that overcame me as I started to lose consciousness. Of all the ways to die, I think burning might be the worst. I never again want to feel the helpless, strangling sensation I felt tonight.

I jerk as a soft click alerts me to someone entering my room.

Eyes snapping open, I turn toward the door to find a white-robed doctor stepping inside, a clipboard in hand. He looks older, perhaps in his late sixties, his gray hair thinning above his wrinkled forehead. But his eyes are sharp with intellect.

"Ah, you're awake, Miss… Anderson," he says, delaying a moment as he pinpoints my name on the sheet of paper. "I'm Dr. Downy. How are you feeling today?"

"Fine," I rasp, then clear my throat as I realize I sound like a terminal lung cancer victim. "What happened?"

"Well, you were brought in by a gentleman who pulled you from a kitchen fire. You've been treated for minor burns to your hands and face. Nothing that should cause permanent scarring. Our bigger concern is the degree of smoke inhalation you suffered. It seems you've done a bit of damage to your lungs."

"But what happened to the restaurant?" I ask, my voice gravelly and my throat swollen to the point of pain.

"I'm not sure actually. But considering the state you were in, I would say the fire was pretty extreme. Do you not recall anything?" He looks at me intently over the clipboard, as if my answer might be critical to my mental well-being.

Struggling to draw upon the hazy images in my mind, I see with perfect clarity the stove on full blast, the flames licking the air as though searching for an adequate food source.

"It was a gas fire," I start and clear my throat.

"I know it's uncomfortable but try not to do that as much as possible. We don't want to damage your vocal cords while you're recovering. Here." Dr. Downy crosses the room to raise a glass of water with a straw to my lips.

Suddenly intensely thirsty, I gulp it down.

"I'll get a nurse to bring you more," he assures me, setting the cup aside. "Do you remember anything else?"

I shake my head, then recall my efforts to reach the fire extinguisher. "I couldn't get the extinguisher to work. That's about the time I blacked out."

Dr. Downy nods, looking back at my chart and scribbling something across the sheet of paper. "Well, Miss Anderson, it sounds like you were very lucky. Aside from minor burns and a few mild signs of respiratory distress, it appears you and the baby will be just fine. I expect a full recovery."

My heart stops, my blood turning to ice in my veins as the doctor's words register in my mind.

"I'm sorry, what?" I ask, sure I must have heard him wrong.

"I don't think you'll suffer any permanent damage so long as you take it easy and—"

"No, no. The part about the baby," I press, my anxiety spiking as I break out in a cold sweat.

"Oh." The doctor's face shows mild surprise, and he glances back down at my chart once again, as if to confirm his statement. "It would appear from your blood work that you're pregnant, Miss Anderson," he states.

Then his eyes flick back to mine as if shocked I wouldn't know this already.

But I can't be. I'm on the pill. I have been for years…

But when Roy died, didn't I run out for a few days?

I hadn't thought it mattered at the time. It wasn't like I was planning on hooking up with anyone when Roy was scarcely in his grave.

No, that can't be it. I was back on birth control by the time Dimitri and I had sex. Right?

How long could it possibly take for the pill to build back up in my system?

Oh God.

Stomach dropping, I feel like I might be sick.

Pulse roaring in my ears, I gape at the calm doctor, wondering how he can possibly state something so monumental as easily as he might tell me it's raining outside.

"I'm... pregnant?" I gasp, my heart in my throat.

35

Dimitri

In the pristine white sitting area of the burn recovery wing's waiting room, I pace, phone to my ear as I carry out my conversation in Russian, ignoring the sidelong glances from other family and friends waiting for their loved ones.

Though I brought Camille into the hospital hours ago, she's still unconscious. Something the doctor assured me is a good thing, as her lungs are scorched enough that she'll be uncomfortable when she wakes up. So the longer she sleeps, the less likely she is to aggravate the smoke inhalation.

Aside from that, they're not giving me anything because I'm not related to Camille. And right about now, I'm kicking myself for not just telling them I'm her husband. Because the agitation of not knowing is driving me up the wall. Like a trapped beast, I can't sit still. But I can't leave either. If Camille wakes up, I want to be here, to hear she's okay from her own lips. I need that reassurance with a desperation I never thought possible.

At least they're letting me sit in the room with her. I guess I get points for being the one who brought her to the hospital in the first place. I just stepped out so I wouldn't disturb her with my phone call from Maksim and Alexei.

"The fire was definitely intentional," Alexei states. "We found empty cans of accelerant in the dumpster out back, and the lock on the kitchen door was tampered with. Looks like the fire department managed to save most of the restaurant area, but the kitchen's destroyed and the smoke damage is going to be a nightmare to fix, I bet."

I bristle, furious with the bastard responsible. "It has to be the same person who's been watching her. I'm sure of it. Have you gotten any further on who it is?"

"I'm sorry. I haven't," Alexei says, his tone agitated. "What with Mom in the hospital... it slipped my mind."

Growling with frustration, I pace across the sterile hospital floor. "I get it. But who is this bastard, and why would he target Camille?"

"It's an act of war," Maksim states.

He's been quiet for most of the call, but his statement now makes me pause. He's confident. I can hear it in his tone.

"How do you know?"

"We received a threat, sent to the office this morning. It indicates this is just the first of many attacks to come."

"Who sent it?" Alexei cuts in.

"Doesn't say, but it's a rival Bratva for sure. And they're moving in on our territory. They say we've held the throne for too long and they're coming for our business," Maksim states.

"How does that have anything to do with Camille?" I rasp, running my fingers through my hair as I sit heavily in a chair. "Does this mean she's got a stalker *and* our new, unknown enemy is coming after her?"

"Cowards," Alexei grumbles under his breath.

I'm with my brother. If you want to start a war, look me in the eyes and tell me you're going to take what's mine. Don't go after a vulnerable woman to send me a message just because you see a window of opportunity. It's the coward's way.

"I don't know. It seems too big of a coincidence to not be related.

But, Dimitri, if they're going after her restaurant, it probably means they've been watching you. They targeted her because they think it will get to you," Maksim states, his tone factual, though his observation douses me in guilt.

I'm the reason bad things have been happening to Camille.

Anxiety knots my stomach at the very real possibility.

And it also pisses me off. *What kind of cad would go after an unsuspecting, innocent woman to make his point?* Fury rips through me, making my hands clench and shake.

"We'll find who it is," Alexei assures me.

"You can start by searching for small black sedans with destroyed front fenders," I state.

"That's oddly specific," Alexei observes dryly.

"This asshole totaled Camille's car T-boning her the night Mom wound up in the hospital."

A low whistle issues across the phone.

"Who'd you piss off, Di?" Alexei asks.

I've been asking myself that same question. But I can't think of anyone specific I've tortured recently. Aside from Camille. She's been my main focus for weeks now. But the attack does feel targeted, and if Camille isn't the one they're trying to send a message to, then it definitely must be me.

Shaking my head, I let it hang as I stare down at the floor. "I don't know."

"Well, my team will get to the bottom of this," Alexei assures me.

"Keep me updated," I state.

Signing off, I slip my phone into my pocket as I stand. When I look toward the doors designating the burn recovery wing of the hospital, I'm filled with the intense need to check in on Camille again, to see her sleeping soundly and make sure she's safe.

I hate that my association with her might have put her in the hospital, that she's injured because of the life I lead. I'm used to the anxiety that comes with my mother's vulnerability from being who we are.

We've grown up knowing the danger of running a Bratva. But I've never had a relationship long enough to think about the woman I love finding herself in that same position. And as soon as I think the word, I know it's true. I still love Camille, even if I'm deeply hurt by her decision to push me away.

But after the fire at her restaurant, I can hardly blame her for not wanting to be near me. And I'll respect her decision—just as soon as I'm sure she's safe without my protection.

Heading from the waiting room, I make my way down the hall to Camille's room, my anger at the man responsible for putting her here simmering slowly in my chest. I want to watch the life leave his eyes, to know for sure that he can't ever come after her again. He nearly took everything from me, and it leaves me agonizingly hollow to think of a world without Camille in it.

The doctor is just leaving as I approach, and his steady gaze finds me. "She's awake," he informs me with a soft smile. "She seems strong enough to have a visitor. And I'm sure she's eager to speak with the man who saved her life. Just... keep the conversation light. She's had quite a shock, and I doubt she'll have much strength to talk for long."

I hardly feel like her savior. Apparently, I'm the reason she was targeted. But I don't need to say as much. "Thanks, Dr. Downy."

With a nod, he departs down the hallway, and I take the last few strides to open the door into Camille's room, eager to see her.

If it were possible, she looks paler than she did when I brought her here in the first place, and guilt gnaws at my gut as I take in her state. Now that she's awake, the shock of her reality seems to be setting in, leaving her eyes wide, her hands trembling in her lap.

Then her eyes turn to find me. Emotion explodes through my chest. Relief, gratitude, love; quickly followed by a fierce, consuming need to protect her from the bastard who hurt her.

"Dimitri," she rasps, her voice ragged as her eyes fill with tears.

I cross the room in three long strides to stand beside her hospital bed, and my anger intensifies as I look at her bandaged hands. I want to take one, to hold her and comfort her, but I don't want to aggravate her pain. So instead, I stand helplessly beside her, my jaw tight with the effort to restrain my fury.

"I thought I dreamed you came for me," she murmurs, looking up at me with emotion-filled eyes. "But you're here. That means you did carry me from the fire. You saved me... didn't you?"

A knot constricts my throat, and I grind my teeth looking out the window that casts soft light around the room. Silence falls between us as I struggle to answer because it all comes back to me in a flash.

Camille lying on Le Fleur's kitchen floor, too weak to drag herself from the room, her hands so painfully blistered that she cried out when she tried to use them—it had terrified me. She looked so helpless surrounded by the wall of flames enveloping the kitchen.

I was nearly too late.

And when I lifted her off the ground, for a moment, I thought I might have been. She flopped so lifelessly in my arms, her head lolling like a ragdoll's. I was desperate to get her out of danger, but the few minutes it took me to get her outside, before I confirmed she was still alive, were some of the longest of my life.

Only her faint, thready pulse when I got her to my car gave me a sliver of relief. But the drive to the hospital was no less nerve-racking. Camille slumped unconscious against the seat, deathly pale and trembling violently from her injuries.

My hands shake with rage at the fact that anyone could do something so terrible to Camille just to send my family a message. I want to murder the man responsible. In the most brutal way possible.

"Dimitri?" she asks tentatively. "What's wrong?"

Aside from the fact that she nearly died?

She deserves to know about what's going on. That someone's not just watching her. They tried to kill her. Twice. All to send me a message. Le Fleur's kitchen is ruined because of me.

But she already said she wants to be done with me. I can't bring myself to tell her that I'm the reason bad things keep happening. And I can't just tell her someone wants her dead. It would only scare her —and make her want me to stay away more.

I don't think I can anymore. Even if I want to give her the life she wants, I'm stricken by the intense realization that leaving Camille alone is going to be impossible. It brings me pain just thinking about leaving her side. I plan on finding who set the fire and killing them before they can do anything else to hurt Camille. So maybe she never needs to know.

"Dimitri, talk to me," she pleads.

I shake my head, turning to pace as I fight my inner conflict. It's not something I want to tell her. But it isn't fair to keep it from her either. She deserves to know. To understand the danger she's in because of me.

"Are you angry?" Her voice trembles slightly, her fear rising though she doesn't know the half of it.

Growling in frustration, I comb my fingers into my hair. "Yes," I answer honestly. But I can't bring myself to say why.

36

Camille

My stomach drops painfully. *He knows. Dimitri already knows I'm pregnant.* The doctor must have told him. And he's not happy.

The intensity of my emotion at finding out I'm pregnant was a heady combination of joy and fear. The shock of it at first left me speechless, and in the time since, I've struggled to think back to those weeks between Roy's death and Dimitri's entrance into my life to know how this possibly could have happened.

One thing's for sure. It's Dimitri's. Roy and I hadn't been intimate in... I can't even remember how long. Months for sure. And Dimitri's the only one I've been with since.

But being a parent was not something I had anticipated at this time in my life. And now seems like the worst possible moment to learn I'm pregnant because everything I've worked so hard for just went up in flames. Literally.

Being a parent, though, is something I thought a lot about after my dad died. I've always thought I wanted to have a family of my own someday. My dad was one of my best friends, a person I hold dearest in my heart, and it would be amazing to have that relationship with my own children.

So, though the timing is terrible, I'm ready for the adventure of being a parent.

But it seems Dimitri is on an entirely different page.

"Say something," I plead, my heart shattering at his anger.

Dimitri shakes his head again, his fury apparent on his face as he paces inside my hospital room. Actually, he looks livid, like he's having to work hard to stop himself from breaking something.

He doesn't want to talk to me about our unexpected situation, and pressing him only seems to aggravate his anger.

Intense rejection punches through my chest as I realize how alone I am. Because he clearly doesn't want me or the baby. He might have saved my life, but he still doesn't want me. That's the simple truth.

After all the contention between us, I can see how he would feel that way, but it still hurts deeply to know he doesn't feel the way I do.

For an instant when he came into the room, I thought he might have changed his mind. That the fire had made him realize he didn't want to lose me. His eyes sought mine out with a ferocity that made my heart quicken. And they were filled with intense emotion, which I read as relief to see that I'm okay.

But he can't even speak to me now, he's so upset about the baby.

Well, if he's so mad about it that we can't even carry out a civil conversation, then fine. I can do this on my own. Because I'm *not* giving up my baby. I don't care that it's completely unexpected or that I've just lost my only source of income to a fire. I already love the tiny being growing inside my belly, and suddenly, it's the only thing that matters.

Protective fury rips through me at the thought that he might want me to get rid of it.

He's probably worried I'll insist on him taking care of it. But if he doesn't want anything to do with me or our child, then I don't want him in our lives. We can do just fine without him.

"What? Are you mad that the restaurant burned down?" I rasp

through my rough throat, lashing out at him because he doesn't even have the decency to talk to me about what's going on. "That's the only thing you wanted in the first place, isn't it? And now that it's been destroyed, you don't want me. I don't know why you bothered saving me anyway."

Dimitri scowls, his eyes flashing with fire as he turns to me. And I can't help the tears that spring to my eyes at his inscrutable gaze.

"Well, I'll find a way to give you back your money, so you can stop worrying," I hiss, my voice cracking painfully as salty tears sting the back of my throat.

"Are you serious right now? We're back to that already?" he demands, his first words to me scathing.

Covering my belly protectively with my arms, I glare up at the man who's ripped my heart out and stomped on it more times than I can count. "Isn't that the only thing we've ever really had between us? A loan you came to collect? Well, you can't have my restaurant because it's gone, so I guess you'll just have to accept the payments I can afford to give you. Or are you going to kill me too?" I demand, my voice shaking with rage rather than fear now.

He can damn well try, but I won't let him hurt me or the baby.

"What?" he growls, his fists balling, and my eyes snap down to the aggressive gesture.

"You need to leave," I rasp with as much authority as I can muster.

"Camille, you're—"

"Get out!" I scream, my emotions overcoming me as tears pour down my cheeks.

Dimitri stiffens, taking a step back as if I struck him.

"Get out! Get out of my room!" I shout again, my voice increasing with the intensity of my pain and anger.

Several nurses burst through the door a moment later, pausing as they take in the scene before them.

"Sir, I'm sorry but you have to go," one states, stepping forward to put herself between me and Dimitri.

"I'm not leaving," he snarls, his eyes never leaving mine as I tip my chin defiantly.

"I want you to go away!" I sob, and a horrible, choking cough racks my body, doubling me over as I suddenly struggle to breathe. My body throbs as my emotions pound through my exhausted muscles and aggravate my burning lungs.

"She's in no condition to be getting so upset," the same nurse says as several more come to stand between us.

They attempt to steer Dimitri toward the door, corralling him rather than attempting to force the muscle-bound man anywhere. Jaw set, he looks ready to argue as his gray eyes flash, watching me closely.

Then the fight seems to leave him. "Fine." Without another word, he storms from the room.

And though I put on a brave face, it still feels like he takes my heart with him as he leaves.

Curling my arms around my knees, I bury my face and cry openly, the pain of my racking sobs tearing through my lungs.

A gentle hand strokes my back as one of the nurses tries to calm me.

"Maybe we need to consider sedation," someone murmurs when my tears won't seem to stop.

I jerk my head up to glare around the room, searching for the guilty party. "No, it could hurt the baby," I state.

But I do need to calm down. My lungs feel raw and burnt, and it hurts just to breathe.

"Just lie back and try to take slow, steady breaths," the nurse rubbing my back instructs. "We won't sedate you, but you do need to calm down if you want to avoid causing permanent damage."

Nodding, I do as she says, trying to breathe in through my nose and out through my mouth. A moment later, the nurse hands me a glass of water with a straw. I drink it slowly, relief coating my dry throat as the cool liquid trickles down it.

"Thank you," I murmur, trying to find a comfortable position against the pillows.

But I feel so hollow, and a deep sadness tightens my chest to know

Dimitri's gone. *Why is it that whenever I see him now, we end up fighting?*

It kills me to see how much things have changed between us. He was so mad at me for sleeping with him to save my restaurant. I don't think he's going to get past it. My hope that we might find our way back to each other, that he could forgive me, is gone.

Not even a child could bring us together.

I can't believe he would reject our baby without even a conversation. That he would know with such certainty that he doesn't want a child we made together. We might not be in the best place right now, but I would think a baby might take precedence over hurt feelings.

The anger I saw in him has me terrified that he might go so far as to expect me to get rid of it. Lashing out at him, screaming like I did —it was all instinct, an attempt to distract him long enough that he might not mention the unthinkable.

But now, as the nurses slowly filter back out of the room, leaving me in peace, I feel so utterly alone. And a deep, gnawing sadness seeps through me, weighing my body down.

It's just you and me, little one, I think, looking down at my belly and covering it with a protective hand.

37

Camille

As Hannah pulls up in front of my house, I peer out at the tiny structure and breathe a sigh of relief. Two days in the hospital before they finally felt confident that I could maintain my oxygen levels on my own.

"You're sure you don't want me to come in? I'm happy to help wash your hair. Whatever you need," she says.

"No, I'm fine. Thank you. The doctor said I can unwrap my hands for a shower. I'm sure I can manage." I pull my friend into a tight hug before slipping out of her little blue Honda and heading into my home.

It's been exhausting these past few days, trying to see my way through the tumult of emotions to figure out where to go from here. Dimitri didn't come back to try and talk about what's happened, which solidifies my resolve to do this on my own.

If he can walk away from us that easily, then I made the right call to tell him to go.

At least I've had Hannah, at my bedside and a wonderful support as I tried to work through my emotions. "We'll figure it out, Cami.

This isn't the end of Le Fleur, and a baby is just one more blessing to bring us hope when life feels daunting," she assured me.

I run those words through my head on repeat. Thank God I have such a sweet, loyal friend.

Ready to wash the smoky scent from my hair, I head straight to the shower to clean up, taking my time unbandaging my hands, revealing the raw flesh beneath. My palms have healed considerably, the blisters calmed to look more like red rings than the swollen, angry welts they were before.

I keep my shower quick, cleaning up as best I can without aggravating my hands. I wrap them in fresh gauze when I'm done, as Dr. Downy instructed. Then I change into a loose dress and a warm, open cardigan.

It's nearly late enough to be dinner time, so I head to the kitchen to feed myself, though I find the thought of food less than appealing right now. In truth, nothing's been sitting right since my last confrontation with Dimitri. And though I wonder if it's an early sign of my impending morning sickness, I think it has to do with the horrible sense of loss I can't quite shake.

Tears in my eyes, I press a palm to my belly and wish I could feel the life growing inside me, some sign to show me I'm not alone. Maybe if I went to Le Fleur, it might help me know where I really stand.

Hannah said it's not just a pile of rubble like I'd been envisioning. And it could make me feel better to be back in a place that feels more like home than the kitchen I stand in now. Besides, I'm tired of wondering and worrying. I'm ready to move forward, to see where I can go from here.

Ordering an Uber since I still haven't figured out a car, I collect my purse and step outside to find the evening wonderfully mild. It's not quite dark yet, though the sun casts a golden hue across the city's hills, creating deep-purple shadows where the light no longer touches. After a short wait, my driver and I exchange a brief greeting as I slide into the back seat.

He drives me into town, dropping me off at the corner where Le

Fleur sits, the red brick building looking ghastly vacant and lifeless, though now is about when the rush would usually begin.

Thanking my driver, I slip from the car and stand in front of my restaurant for several silent minutes, looking up at the facade. From here, it would appear nothing is wrong—aside from the bright-yellow caution tape that cordons off the entrance.

But this is my building, and no one's around to tell me I can't go in.

Shifting the tape aside, I slide my key into the lock and open the door. Then I duck to avoid the caution tape as I step inside.

The strong smell of smoke fills my nose, though none of it visibly thickens the air of the dining room. Covering my face with a corner of my cardigan, I flip on the light switch and am relieved when the room flickers to life.

Like a graveyard, the dining room holds vacant tables and chairs, the remains of my business now that it's not safe for customers to be here. Thankfully, the bar seems to be left untouched—where the alcohol and the tanks of CO_2 for the fountain drinks would have made things exponentially worse if the fire had gotten that far.

The swinging door to the kitchen is the first visual indication of a disturbance. It hangs slightly crooked, its weight supported by one bent hinge.

Tentatively, I make my way closer, my heart in my throat as I brace myself for the damage I'm about to see. Because I know the kitchen is ruined. I stayed long enough to see how destructive the fire became.

Carefully, I pull the door open, the hinge groaning dramatically with every inch.

Tears sting my eyes at the sight of my usually pristine cooking space. Black char coats most of the walls, and a hole's been burned clean through the ceiling tiles, exposing the beams that support the roof like the ribs of some giant animal.

Twisted metal showcases just how hot the fire got, and a good number of kitchen supplies have been melted beyond recognition. The freezer and fridge doors look charred from the fire but still intact, and I wonder if they might have managed to survive the destruction.

The pantry is not so lucky. It seems the boxes and jars of dried food and nonperishables were some of the easier fuel for the flames. I don't dare go further to see if anything is salvageable in the mix. The floor is littered with broken glass and fallen shelving.

Sighing, I pick my way across the kitchen to the back exit and open the door to see what the back of the building looks like. Black stains the outside brick there, but I'm grateful to find the structure itself looks decently sound.

With a lot of work, I might be able to save the building, though the damage is extensive. I don't yet know if my insurance is going to cover what happened, but now that I'm here, I'm determined to save my business, the restaurant my dad and I had talked about opening for so many years.

Heading out of the kitchen, I make my way into my office. Miraculously, the fire didn't make it this far, so I still have my laptop and bookwork.

Sighing, I settle behind my desk and open my computer. First things first, I need to know what my bottom line is, what I have saved that can go toward rebuilding. Within minutes, my optimism is considerably diminished.

Without money flowing in from customers dining here every evening, I'm going to quickly fall behind on my mortgage. And it's not like the bank is just going to forgive my loan because my business is on hold indefinitely.

Crunching the numbers again, I fight to contain the crushing weight of my reality. I don't see how I can keep this business running, to keep my employees for the months it might take to fix the ruined kitchen. I'll need an extensive loan unless my insurance covers everything.

And worst of all, with my name and business tied to the loan Roy took out against Le Fleur, I'm sure my credit has been ruined. Beyond tears, I cover my face with my hands and let that awful truth sink in.

I feel the weight of the world settling on my shoulders as the big picture appears before me. I'm sure I want to keep my baby. But I honestly don't know how I'm supposed to do this on my own.

And to top it off, I find myself missing Dimitri desperately. The loss of his protective concern and unshakeable confidence leaves me in a state of constant fear and uncertainty. And missing him only intensifies my turmoil because I know he doesn't want me. Not to mention the very real and glaring fact that he's a murderer.

He killed Roy, and though I selfishly yearn to be back in my blissfully ignorant state before I knew that, when I could pretend like we had a workable relationship, I know I can't have him near my child.

Still, that doesn't lessen my heartache.

Something creaks outside my door, and my heart flutters as my brain irrationally jumps straight to Dimitri. Before I can logic it away, the thought that maybe he's changed his mind and came looking for me flashes through my brain.

Holding my breath, I rise from my chair, my hope overwhelming my caution as I keep my eyes trained on the door.

And then, in an instant, my instincts kick in.

Of course it's not Dimitri. If he wanted to reconcile, he knew where to find me. But I haven't heard a word from him since he left me in the hospital.

Which means, unless the restaurant's fire has created structural damage that I didn't see, someone else is here with me. In the building that is clearly marked to dissuade anyone from entering.

A violent shiver runs through me as my office suddenly feels like a cage. If the intruder finds me here, I will have nowhere to run.

Heart pounding in my ears, I creep toward the door, trying not to make a sound.

Slowly, carefully, I turn the handle and ease the door open a crack—just enough to peer into the hallway.

No one's there.

Did I imagine the sound? Am I hearing things?

My nerves have probably endured too much stress over the past week, and now every little sound is triggering me. But I can't shake the feeling that someone's here with me.

Slipping out into the hall, I tiptoe toward the dining room, hoping I can reassure myself that I'm alone. At the very least, I should lock the front door. But now that I'm freaking out, I'm starting to regret coming in the first place.

I should go.

Reaching the end of the hall, I peer cautiously out into the dining room, scanning the tables and chairs for anything out of the ordinary. The air leaves my lungs in a whoosh as I find myself alone. Relieved, I make a beeline for the front door, ready to make my escape. I can come back tomorrow. In broad daylight, maybe with Hannah here to stop my overactive imagination.

"Shoot." I stop halfway to the door, realizing I left my purse in the office—with my phone and wallet and my ability to call an Uber.

Turning back, my heart stops as a flicker of movement catches my eye. And when I turn to look at the swinging door into the kitchen, I find a black-clothed figure standing there, dark eyes watching me through the gap of a ski mask.

Adrenaline floods my body as my fear spikes, and I freeze as I realize I'm in very real danger.

In that moment of hesitation, the intruder gains the upper hand, leaping into action as he closes the distance between us with frightening speed.

No time to think, no time to scream, I spin on my heel to flee.

Heart hammering in my chest, I race for the door. My fingers close around the handle, but my hands are still stiff from the burns, not functioning to their full capability, and before I can force the door open, he's on me.

Gripping a handful of my hair, the man jerks me backward, and I cry out as the maneuver snaps my head back and launches me toward the ground.

I fall hard, my butt landing on the carpeted floor as the impact jars through my body. But I'm not about to roll over and die.

As soon as I hit the ground, I roll away from my attacker, scrambling onto my hands and knees as I change directions to escape down the hallway and the emergency exit.

"Where do you think you're going?" the man asks, his calm, flat tone making him that much more frightening.

He's not angry. He's not emotional in any way. He's not even out of breath. He's taunting me. And his cool confidence chills me to the bone.

Still, I manage to scramble back to my feet and sprint with all my strength away from him.

Feet pound behind me, and I know he's too fast. I'll never get away. Grabbing chairs on my way, I fling them behind me, trying to hinder his pursuit. Lungs burning from exertion I shouldn't be putting them through so soon after their trauma, I gasp for air.

I don't dare take a second to look behind me, to see if my efforts are working. But I make it to the hall.

And then strong hands find my back, shoving me forward with such force that I plummet toward the ground. My knees hit the floor, and I cry out as my bandaged palms catch my fall before my face meets the carpet.

Then a strong hand wraps around my ankle and jerks me onto my back. Dragging me toward him, he effectively ends my escape attempt. Screaming bloody murder, I try to call attention to my plight. Maybe, just maybe, someone walking by the restaurant might hear me.

Pain tightens my throat, cutting my shriek short, and I'm sure I reinjured the raw flesh that was damaged from smoke inhalation. But my sense of self-preservation overcomes any other thought.

"Hold still," the man commands, like he thinks I might actually obey.

Then he flicks open a cruel-looking knife that sends a shiver down my spine.

"Please," I beg, trying to jerk my ankle from his grasp. "Please, I don't want to die," I sob.

"It's nothing personal, sweetheart," he promises. "You just made friends with the wrong family."

Heart stopping, I'm overcome with icy terror as I face my own death. I'm going to die here tonight. But what fills me with sheer panic is my inability to save my baby.

"No, no, no!" I scream, gripping his wrist to delay my last

moments. "Please, don't kill me. Please, please. I'll give you whatever you want. Just please don't hurt me. I'm pregnant. Please, please, don't hurt my baby!" I sob, looking up at my masked attacker as I try to find a sliver of empathy.

But I find none in his cold eyes.

"I'll make it quick," he assures me, like he's just ripping off a bandage. Then he wrenches my hand from his wrist and raises the knife.

The agonizing inability to save my child's life overwhelms me, and I curl into a fetal position, trying to protect my belly as my eyes squeeze shut. Bracing for the agonizing pain to follow, I tense.

But it doesn't come.

Instead, a sharp pain twists my wrist, and suddenly, I find myself free as I hear a heavy thump.

Opening my eyes in disbelief, I find my attacker on the ground, another figure wrestling violently with him for ownership of the knife.

I should run. I know I should, but I can't seem to tear my eyes from the frightening scene. The new, larger figure clearly has the upper hand, his surprise attack leaving my would-be killer at a disadvantage. But their fight isn't over in an instant. They tumble across the floor, crashing into a table and sending chairs down on top of them.

Then the knife trades hands, the larger man wrenching it from the masked man's fingers. He brings it down without hesitation, driving it into my attacker's side with practiced ease. My attacker's eyes open wide in shock, and a moment later, the knife flashes across his throat, opening a deep gash that leaves him choking blood.

His body jerks, convulsing as he fights for air, his fingers clawing at the second intruder's arm. And as the life slowly drains from his eyes, the man who won slowly rises. Chairs shifting around him as he stands, he slowly turns to face me, knife loosely gripped in his hands.

And my body goes numb at the murderous rage in his eyes.

38

Dimitri

Dialing the hospital yet again, I try to keep my emotions in check as I drum my fingers on my desk and look out the office window at the dark sky.

I've been tortured by guilt and regret at the way I left things with Camille. I never should have let my anger consume me like I did. But I'd been so overwhelmed by the sight of her fear and vulnerability that I couldn't express myself. I didn't want her to know that I'm the reason she's in pain. I'm the reason someone set Le Fleur on fire.

And before I could find the words to express my fury at the man who tried to take her from me, she lost it. I admit, I shouldn't have let her comment about the loan get under my skin. She was clearly distressed and probably confused by why I would be there when our last conversation ended in a blowout about the lien her boyfriend created.

But to suggest that all I wanted was her restaurant?

I couldn't stop my temper. Because after everything that's happened between us, how can she not know that I'm crazy about her? Why else would I keep coming back for more torture when she clearly doesn't want me?

I tried to go back in, to see Camille at the hospital after I regained control of my temper. But the staff refused to let me see her. They consider me a hindrance to her recovery, and clearly, she didn't want me there. So instead, I've been calling to check in on her several times a day.

The receptionists don't tell me much, but at least I know she's still alive and recovering by my frequent inquiries.

"St. Mary's, this is Joyce. How can I help you?"

"I'm calling to inquire about a patient, Camille Anderson."

"Camille Anderson?" the receptionist confirms, tapping issuing through the phone as she searches Camille's information. "Umm, it looks like she was discharged earlier this evening."

"What?" I demand, my pulse quickening. "No one said anything about it when I called this morning."

"I'm sorry, but we're not allowed to give out confidential information. We can only confirm if a patient is here or not."

Snarling in frustration, I hang up the phone. I know it's their job, but the hospital has made it impossible to keep an eye on Camille. With her attacker still on the loose, I wanted to be there the moment she was released—even if she didn't want to see me.

But I know where she'll go.

Snatching my suit jacket from the back of my chair, I don't even bother putting it on as I rush from the Federov Brothers Investments building.

I'm speeding toward Le Fleur minutes later, eager to see Camille is safe. And maybe we can finish the conversation we started. Only this time, I'm ready to tell her everything. As hard as it's going to be, I know it's necessary if I have a hope of reconciling with her.

Pulling up outside the empty building, my suspicions are confirmed as I see the lights on in the dining room. I put my Lamborghini in park and step out of my car, glancing up and down the street out of habit.

As my eyes land on a small black sedan parked almost a block behind me, I pause. The shiny new fender catches the streetlight's glow, contrasting starkly with the worn paint and rust stains that cover the hood and doors. My stomach drops as warning bells go off in my mind. It's the car that's been stalking her.

I glance back at the restaurant. This time when I look at Le Fleur, I'm searching for a sign of a disturbance, but aside from the lights being on, I find nothing. All is quiet. Maybe it's actually the owner of the black car inside, not Camille.

A wicked smile curls my lips at the thought. If he's in there, he's about to face the consequences of his actions.

I creep toward the front door, keeping low so no one will see me approach. And though the caution tape would indicate no one should enter the structure, when I twist the handle, it gives readily. The door's already unlocked.

A blood-curdling scream within turns my heart to ice as I crack the door open.

Camille.

All sense of caution abandons me as I push the door wide and duck beneath the tape in an instant, entering the restaurant without hesitation.

"Please, don't kill me," she sobs, her plea wrenching my heart, but I don't see her from where I stand. "Please, please. I'll give you whatever you want. Just please don't hurt me. I'm pregnant. Please, please, don't hurt my baby!"

Baby? I'm crossing the room in an instant, following the sound of her voice until I find the horrifying sight of a masked attacker looming over her, knife in hand.

My vision goes red with rage.

"I'll make it quick," he promises calmly, his voice apathetic to her terror.

Like hell, you will.

Consumed with violent fury, I dive forward, driving my shoulder beneath the guy's armpit and launching him off his feet as I stop him from harming Camille with his blade.

He's strong, clearly built for this line of work, but I'm stronger.

And he didn't see me coming. He was too focused on the victim in his grasp. By the time he twists to face me, I'm already on top of him.

Colliding with the base of a table, we wrestle for possession of the knife, and I bare my teeth, snarling silently with my determination to kill the man at any cost. Because he's responsible for the fire, for the car accident, for terrorizing Camille for weeks.

I want to kill him slowly, to make him suffer for what he's done. But more than that, I need Camille to be safe, and time is of the essence. So when I force the blade from his hand, I don't hesitate, driving the knife into the soft flesh of his belly. And as the pain incapacitates him, I end his life with one more violent slash across his throat.

The fight is over in the blink of an eye.

Breath heaving from my lungs, I rise slowly, refusing to take my gaze off him until I see the light leave his eyes, the last gasp of air escaping his lips. Adrenaline pounds through my veins as I turn slowly toward Camille. And my heart twists painfully.

She looks terrified, her wide eyes staring up at me like I'm a demon risen straight from hell. Realizing what a sight I must be, I toss the knife aside, intensely aware that my hands are spattered with bright, gruesome blood.

"Camille," I murmur, talking softly to try to ease her fear. Then I slowly kneel before her trembling figure, holding out my hands, palms up, to prove I mean her no harm.

For one excruciating moment, I think she might run. She looks deathly pale, her body shaking violently. Her eyes scan me with disbelief.

And then she throws her arms around my neck, sobbing uncontrollably as she tucks her face against my skin.

"Shhh," I soothe softly, pulling her close and reveling in the feel of her warm, soft, living body pressed against my chest. Sweet relief washes through me as I breathe deeply, overwhelmingly grateful that she's safe. "You're okay," I say out loud to reassure myself as much as her. "You're safe now."

Her tears slowly subside, and she pulls back slightly to look at me.

My hold constricts around her as I refuse to let her go. But she only shifts enough to bring our lips together. And then she's kissing me, her fingers curling in my hair, her mouth covering mine with desperate greed.

I kiss her back just as fiercely, all my feelings for her bursting to life inside my body. All I can think about is that she's safe. Her attacker is dead. And she feels so good in my arms.

Then, as if echoing back from a distant memory, her last words trickle into my head, *I'm pregnant. Please, don't hurt my baby.*

Separating our lips, I jerk back from her as the betrayal hits me like a punch to the gut. Camille looks shocked, her balance wobbling as I release her in an instant to put space between us.

"You're pregnant, and you never told me?" I demand, the hurt lacing my tone and making my voice gruff. "How? Why?"

It feels like every time I extend myself, every time I try to take care of Camille, whenever I do something to protect her or show her how I feel, it uncovers some new lie or secret she's kept from me. And this betrayal feels far worse than any before. *Was she planning on keeping my child from me? Could she possibly hate me that much?*

Camille's lips part, but no sound comes out as she stares at me, wide-eyed.

"Did you ever intend on talking to me about the baby?" I growl, my temper spiking as I wonder just how long she's known and not said a word.

Her face clouds over, her eyebrows pressing into an angry frown as she leans away from me. Crossing her arms over her body, she's immediately defensive. "Are you kidding me? You're the one who shut me out first," she snaps, her blue eyes igniting.

Sharp laughter bursts from me in disbelief. "That's rich," I scoff, "coming from the woman who pretended to want me, the woman who slept with me so she could avoid paying off a debt. I've never lied to you, Camille. But it seems you just can't stop lying to me."

"You're right, Dimitri. You don't lie. You just won't admit the truth," she fires back, her tone just as hard and hurt as mine. "Like how about the fact that you killed Roy when he couldn't pay off his debt in time?"

My jaw snaps shut at the sudden, blatant accusation that throws me entirely for a loop. Off balance, I try to catch up, my mind racing to recall this very familiar conversation. And then it hits me. She all but said as much the night she got in her car accident. The night she told me she loved me.

I'd completely forgotten she'd hinted about Roy's death. Between rushing to the hospital to help my mother and the fact that I wanted to talk about my relationship with Camille more than I did her dead boyfriend, that detail had slipped my mind.

But clearly, Camille's been holding onto it this whole time. Holding it against me, it would seem. Her face fills with conviction as she watches me flounder. And I can see her building a federal case every moment I fail to provide an explanation.

39

Camille

The range of emotion that flits across Dimitri's face reinforces my anger. I can't believe he's mad at me when he still won't admit to killing Roy, and from the way he flounders, I know he wasn't ready for me to state it so brazenly.

When he does speak, it's the last thing I expect him to say. "Why in God's name would I kill Roy Lochte for falling behind on payments?"

"Well... because... that's what you do," I insist, frowning in confusion as I'm thrown off by his question. *How am I supposed to understand the reasoning behind mafia violence?*

"That would be a stupid business plan if I went around killing anyone who fell behind on their payments," he points out, his anger softening as amusement tinges his tone. "Half the profit we make comes from interest."

Dimitri smiles softly as my jaw drops, ready to argue, to press him for the truth. But his logic is so sound, I don't know what to say.

"I didn't kill your boyfriend, Camille."

"Someone killed Roy," I insist vehemently.

I can feel it in my gut. His death was far too convenient, too contrived. *Why else would he be found in a house fire at the home of some random guy whose name I'd never heard before?* The police came asking questions for good reason, and I'm not about to believe an accidental fire caught Roy by surprise in the middle of the day. Not after my first-hand experience. No, he was dead before that house went up in flames.

"I know," Dimitri says calmly, and there it is again, that complete lack of shock or horror.

"How could you possibly know if you didn't put a hit out on him or something?" I demand, my temper rising. He's doing it again, jerking me around, tiptoeing around the truth so he won't have to admit the part he played in Roy's death.

Dimitri's humor falls away at my accusatory tone. "I sent men to follow Roy when he got behind on payments. They were supposed to rough him up, intimidate him, remind him why he needed to keep up on payments—maybe shake him down for extra interest. But Aleksandr Volkov got to him first. My men said that Aleksandr shot Roy because he got in too deep on a gambling debt at the Volkov casinos and pissed Aleksandr off. I assume that's where he blew the money from my loan, and he fell behind on payments when he couldn't win the money back. He must have placed some very bad bets."

My heart sinks as the truth is finally laid bare—the full extent of Roy's betrayal becoming clear. I believe Dimitri. *Why would he lie about it?* And his explanation makes far too much sense.

I knew Roy had a gambling problem. I knew he got pretty passionate about sports betting before he lost his job. It had always made me nervous, though he'd assured me he had it completely under control—that it was just for fun.

I never imagined he would have the audacity to take out a loan in my name to continue his obsession after he lost his income.

Slumping in shock, I gape at Dimitri, at a loss for words.

"How did you think I knew to approach you in the first place?" he points out.

Another fair point. I shake my head, dumbfounded, and frustration flashes across Dimitri's face. But the wave of relief that washes through me leaves me almost giddy. Dimitri didn't kill Roy. And while he is now officially a murderer—seeing as he killed my attacker—I don't think I've ever been so grateful in my life.

"You know what, this is completely beside the point," Dimitri growls, his irritation flashing white-hot in an instant. "Why are we even talking about your dead boyfriend? He used you and was a waste of air as far as I'm concerned. I think the bigger question that you're avoiding is how you could fail to tell me you're pregnant. Were you planning on getting an abortion? Did you think I'd try to stop you, so you just decided not to talk to me?"

My stomach plummets at the awful suggestion, but my temper roars back to life at the way he points the finger at me. "You're the one who made it clear you didn't want me or our baby," I shoot back, tears stinging my eyes once more.

Dimitri's head jerks back in apparent confusion. "What are you even talking about?"

"You. At the hospital. The doctor told me I was pregnant as soon as I woke up, and while I was still trying to wrap my head around the fact, you'd probably had hours to process the information—to work yourself up. When you came in, you couldn't even talk, you were so upset about it."

My voice cracks as the painful memory lances through me, the way he couldn't look me in the eye he was so mad. "I thought you might demand I get rid of it if I kept pressing you to talk about it. And I didn't want to give it up, so I decided I would have our baby with or without you."

Silence stretches between us as Dimitri watches me with unreadable eyes. My tears start to flow as I realize I must have hit the nail on the head. He doesn't want this baby, but now that we're having the discussion, he's realized he won't be able to convince me to abort it.

Drawing into myself, I feel a deep chasm opening in my chest, leaving me raw and devastatingly broken.

He doesn't want us.

I choke down a sob, trying not to show my pain, but the aching hollowness is so devastating I can't breathe.

And then strong hands pull me close as Dimitri's arms envelop me. "Is that really when you found out about the baby?" he breathes, his anger gone in an instant. "That's why you got so upset when I came back into the room?"

This time, I can't contain my sob, and I nod as I relive the painful memory in vivid detail. The anger radiated from him like he'd just been told I'd given him some kind of incurable disease. And then, after he stormed out, the utter silence he's shown me since.

"Oh, Camille," he sighs, stroking my back as he tucks my head beneath his chin. "The doctor wouldn't tell me anything because we aren't related or married. They only let me stay because I'm the one who brought you in. But then, after our fight, they wouldn't let me see you again. They wouldn't tell me anything, either, except that you'd been released tonight."

Confused, I frown as I pull back to look him in the eye, my breathing short and erratic as I try to calm my tears. "But then... why were you so mad?"

Dimitri releases a heavy sigh, that same resistance to speak locking in place as his jaw clenches, the tendons raising beneath the skin. But this time, he pushes through that reticence.

Silver gaze seeking mine, he looks deep into my soul, almost as if to search for forgiveness. And the intensity of his emotion makes my heart flutter.

"I came back in after speaking to my brothers. We received a message from someone taking credit for the fire. They set it intentionally, probably one of my enemies." His eyes flick toward the masked man lying dead on the floor.

My heart stops as the full implications of his words hit me. I could have died—multiple times over—because someone wants to hurt Dimitri.

"I was furious because I unwittingly put you in danger, and I could never forgive myself if you were killed because of me." His voice dips low, his eyes shifting back to mine, and I find that same raging inferno in their depths.

It fills me with relief to know he wasn't mad about the baby, that he isn't mad at me now. At least not about that. But it still doesn't fix the bigger problem in our relationship.

Because he left in the middle of our conversation about how we came together in the first place. About how I slept with him to find answers about Roy. And it doesn't matter if we can work through all the rest, if he can't forgive me for that, I don't see how we can move forward together.

"You didn't want to be responsible for my death," I confirm, my eyes falling to the floor as I read between the lines. "But that doesn't change the fact that you don't want to be with me," I murmur.

"Why would you say that?"

"Because I poured my heart out to you. I knew I'd made a terrible mistake, that I never should have tried to manipulate you because I'm in love with you. And you didn't say anything. You just... walked out the door," I state, trying to keep my tone factual, but the truth cuts me to the core. "Clearly, you don't love me. Maybe you felt something for me before. But it's over now, and I feel so stupid—especially after learning you didn't even kill Roy."

Sniffling, I wipe furiously at the tears that start to trickle down my cheeks once more.

And then he laughs.

The rich sound fills the empty room, making butterflies erupt in my stomach even as his laughter hurts.

"What's so funny?" I demand, glaring at him as he revels in my remorse.

"You have terrible logic," he observes, his smile radiant even as he tries to suppress it. "If I didn't want to be with you, why would I keep showing up to save you?"

It's a good point, one I don't readily have an answer for. "Because... you would feel guilty if I died?" I suggest, but that theory has holes in it.

Clearly, he feels no remorse for my attacker's death, so it's not that he's overburdened by being responsible for someone dying. Then another realization hits me.

"Wait, how have you known when to come save me? Both from the fire and when I was attacked just now, you came in just in time. Like you were just waiting for the right moment."

A crooked smile graces Dimitri's lips in a heartwarmingly sheepish expression, like he's about to confess an embarrassing weakness. "I feel very protective of you, a drive I seem to have no control over. It makes me lose my mind sometimes. After I learned about that black car that was watching you, I started to worry for your safety. And when you were in that crash, my instincts told me it wasn't a coincidence, that someone was trying to hurt you."

He shakes his head, looking at the floor. "I lost sight of it for a moment after our fight, and then my mom ended up in the hospital—"

"Wait, what?" My eyes grow round as my heart hammers in my chest. "When did this happen? Is she okay?"

Dimitri frowns. "Well, yes. She's out of the hospital now, but... Camille, you were there. Alexei—my brother—said it right there in front of you."

Quirking an eyebrow, I wonder if he could possibly be serious. "Dimitri, I don't speak Russian."

The light of understanding dawns in his gray eyes. "You didn't know..."

"From my perspective, you were so sweet and gentle after my accident, I thought maybe we were okay. And then we had insanely good sex, which made me think you'd forgiven me. But after, you stormed off, still mad at me about lying to you—which I get—but when I poured my heart out, asked for your forgiveness, and told you I love you, you had nothing to say. You just left with a random guy without a word of explanation. No reciprocation. Nothing."

The hollow ache in my chest returns in full force, my final words tapering off.

Cupping my cheeks with strong hands, Dimitri lifts my gaze, holding my face close to his. "I wanted to say I love you as soon as you told me how you felt. But then my brother showed up, and I couldn't do it after I found out my mom was in the hospital. The timing was all wrong, and I thought she might be dying... and it took days to get everything straightened out so she could return home safely. So, when I got back, you were gone."

"You expected me to wait around for *days*?" I demand, but I'm not really angry. My heart keeps doing somersaults because I'm pretty sure he just said he loves me.

Dimitri gives a low chuckle, catching the humor in my exasperation. "I knew you had better things to do than wait around for me. But then you went and sent me a check, and I just about lost my mind because I thought we were past all that."

"Yeah, I've never seen anyone get that mad about receiving money before," I tease breathily.

Warmth fills his silver gaze as Dimitri's thumb strokes my cheek tenderly, the soft smile that curves his lips filled with understanding.

"I love you, Camille. You're the best thing that's ever happened to me. And I'm overjoyed that you're pregnant. I want to be with you, to be a father to our child. If you'll still have me."

40

Camille

Deep joy fills me to the brim, and I'm suddenly crying happy tears. I've done so much crying lately, I can only hope it's because my hormones are kicking in.

Dimitri's face falls. "Oh God, please don't cry," he murmurs, looking genuinely distraught.

And though the tears keep falling, I start to laugh. "No, they're happy tears, I promise," I say, running my fingers into his hair and pulling his forehead against mine.

Releasing a breath of relief, Dimitri chuckles as he tips my chin to kiss me.

Bubbles of excitement explode in my belly, and I kiss him back with enthusiasm. The intensity of my happiness leaves me giddy and shaking as I cling to him, reveling in the feel of his strong arms around me.

I don't care that we're sitting on the floor of my smoke-damaged restaurant or that Dimitri's wearing the blood of a man who tried to kill me. All I need right now is to feel him close to me, to know that he loves me, and to tell him how I feel.

"I love you," I say vehemently between kisses. "I love you so much, and I want to have this baby with you."

Dimitri groans, his lips rewarding me with scintillating kisses, and when we finally break apart, we're both breathing heavily. His eyes turn down to my stomach as he places a warm palm over my abdomen.

"I can't believe I'm going to be a dad," he breathes, his voice filled with wonder.

I giggle, covering his hand with mine and kissing his temple.

Then his deep, emotion-filled eyes shift to meet mine. "I know it's sudden, and I promise I'll do this again the right way, but will you marry me?"

"What?" My eyes widen in shock at the entirely unexpected proposal.

"I've never felt for anyone the way I feel for you. You fill my days with joy and my life with excitement. I want to make a family with you and treat you like the goddess you are. So, Camille Anderson, will you marry me?"

Tears blur my vision as I nod, overwhelmed with happiness. "Yes," I gasp. "Yes, I'll marry you!"

And this time when he kisses me, it's like he's worshiping my very lips.

My mind's a blur of images and emotions as Dimitri sweeps me up and takes me home to his apartment. My legs are shaky enough from my near-death encounter that I'm grateful for his strength, and I love the way he holds me close.

His hand leaves mine on the drive home only to make a quick call that takes place entirely in Russian. And when I ask about it, all he says is that the dead man in my restaurant dining room is being taken care of.

I shiver from the brutal honesty of his statement, though it reveals to me a new intimacy in our relationship. No more secrets, no more lies. From today, we're a team, inseparable.

In the elevator up to Dimitri's penthouse, he holds me close, showering my face with soft kisses. And though they're tender gestures, they light my body on fire. I can hardly believe that after everything I've been through, I could possibly crave him like I do.

But after nearly a week without him, my body yearns to be with him, to reaffirm our scintillating connection.

"I should... take a shower," he says as we step inside the grand entry.

"I'll join you," I offer, biting my lip playfully.

Dimitri releases a snarl of anticipation. Clasping my hand, he leads me through the vaulted living room to his glass stairs. We climb them quickly, his enthusiasm matching my own. And when we reach the master bath, his hands are on me in an instant.

Giggling as he strips me of my open cardigan, I get to work on the buttons of his shirt. He helps me, shrugging out of the soiled top a moment later and throwing it in a corner. Then he gets to work on his pants as I pull my loose dress up over my head.

He turns on the water as I strip off my panties and bra, and he gets right in, grasping the soap to scrub his hands clean with vigor. I follow him inside the luxurious rock wall shower with its glass door.

Swinging the door closed, I trap the steam inside with us as the last of the pink suds swirl down the drain. Then I take the soap from him, ready to fully appreciate this moment.

Starting at his shoulders, I lather him with the spicy soap as the shower head pours water over his impressive form. I take my time rubbing the suds over his taut muscles, the beautiful flames of his tattoo.

"Thank you," I murmur as I work, glancing up at him through my lashes.

"For what?" His deep voice is alluring as his lips curl into a soft, amused smile. "You're the one bathing me," he points out. "I should be thanking you."

I shake my head as I return his gentle smile. "For saving my life." Pausing my cleansing ritual, I rest my bandaged palm over his heart and peer deep into his eyes. "You saved me twice without any concern for your own safety. You came to get me after the car accident, even when you were still mad at me. You saved me, Dimitri. In so many ways, and I can't tell you how grateful I am to have you in my life."

Humming appreciatively, Dimitri pulls me close, bringing me under the warm shower as he kisses me. "I would save you every day for the rest of my life if it means I get to keep you," he murmurs.

"I'll hold you to that," I promise. Rising onto my toes, I wrap my arms around his neck and kiss him deeply, stroking my tongue between his lips.

"God, you're sexy," he rasps, and slowly, he kneels before me, his hands resting lightly on my hips as he trails kisses down my chest and between my breasts to my belly. There he lingers, murmuring softly to our child growing. "You and I have a job to do. We have to keep your mom safe because she's something special you know. We're the two luckiest people in the world."

Overwhelming joy warms my body at the sweet, fatherly way he whispers to our child, sharing a secret with them, though he speaks just loudly enough to let me in on it. I comb my fingers through his hair, smiling down at him, and when he looks up to meet my gaze, I can see the overwhelming love there, the awe for the tiny life inside me, the depth of devotion he has for me.

Then his eyes flicker with mischief as one hand glides down my thigh to grip my knee.

"What are you...?" I start, my suspicion rising.

And then he hooks my leg over his shoulder, his strong hands holding me steady as he makes me balance on one foot. I gasp as his head dips forward to press a kiss to the peak of my thighs, his lips brushing my clit.

Oh, holy hell, it feels good.

Tongue dancing out to stroke my slit, Dimitri makes love to my pussy with his mouth, and I've never felt anything so tantalizingly euphoric. His fingers press gently into the flesh of my hips as he works, his shoulder muscles bunching as he leans forward to gain better access.

Gasping as he licks and kisses my sensitive folds, I tremble at the intense pleasure.

Hips rocking forward, I find myself lost in the tantalizing pleasure. My pussy throbs with sudden need, eager to have him inside me, to feel that relief that only Dimitri can bring.

"Mmm, Dimitri," I moan, my fingers knotting in his hair.

And his tongue presses more insistently between my folds, stroking upward until he flicks the tip across my clit. I shudder, my legs turning to jelly at the agonizing pleasure. I don't know how I'm supposed to stay standing while he's doing this, but somehow, that makes it all the more exciting.

Zinging euphoria crackles up my spine each time he repeats the motion, building my desire into a steady fire until I'm molten inside, my body tensing with the building climax.

His lips close around the sensitive bundle of nerves, and I cry out as tingling excitement washes through my body, bringing me right to the precipice. And when he sucks, pulling my clit into his mouth so he can roll it with his tongue, that's all it takes.

Gasping with the suddenness of my release, I brace against his strong shoulders, holding myself up as my knees buckle. His hands support my weight even as he continues to suck and lick my clit, forcing each blissful twitch from my body as my pussy clenches, craving his hard cock.

Chest heaving as I breathe deeply, my lungs burning from the exertion, I find I don't care. The intensity of my pleasure far outweighs the pain of my injuries.

Dimitri eases my foot back onto the floor, allowing me to stand evenly as he rises slowly. His hands never leave my hips, ensuring I don't fall. And then he's towering over me, his eyes liquid metal as he looks at me with a heat that sets my skin alight.

"You are the single best flavor in the world," he rasps, his lips covering mine as he pulls me firmly against his chest.

My palms find his pecs, my fingers spreading across his soft skin. Breaking our kiss, Dimitri looks down as his hands find mine, and he holds them gently, his face devastated as he takes in my bandages for the first time.

"You're getting them all wet," he observes, concerned.

"It's fine. I'll wash and re-bandage my hands when we're done," I assure him. "Now kiss me, fiancé," I command, and the word sends a giddy shiver racing up my spine.

The carnal desire in Dimitri's gaze takes my breath away. And then he reclaims my lips, his tongue stroking between my teeth to share the tang of my juices that linger there. Moaning with appreciation, I kiss him fiercely.

Strong hands guide me to turn around, though his lips continue to hold mine captive, and Dimitri presses me against the rough stone wall of the shower. The fresh scent of wet rock fills my nose, and I gasp as my nipples find the cool, coarse surface.

Pressing his cock adamantly between my ass cheeks, Dimitri shows me just how excited he is, and it makes my stomach quiver with anticipation. His foot finds the inside of mine and pushes outward, guiding my legs apart.

I obey willingly, arching my back to give him better access. And as his silken cockhead finds my slick folds, my fingers comb into his hair, deepening our kiss as I show him just how eager I am for him to fill me.

He presses inside me with agonizing tenderness, his hard cock stretching my tight walls as his fingers grip my hips, slowly guiding me back as he rocks forward. And a sultry groan escapes me at the intense satisfaction of being whole once more.

"God, I love you," Dimitri breathes against my lips, and my pussy clenches with excitement.

Air hisses between his teeth on a sharp intake of breath, and his cock twitches inside me. He slides back out several inches before pressing home again, and as we start to move together, I can feel myself quickly climbing to a second orgasm.

I never knew making love could be so earth-shattering. When we did it the first time, I was so freaked out by my feelings that I couldn't fully enjoy the moment. But now, I'm struck by how intense and powerful it is to have him showing me in the most intimate way just what I mean to him.

One hand gripping my hip firmly, Dimitri reaches around with the other, his fingers finding my clit to stimulate me and intensify my pleasure.

"Oh yes," I moan as he circles the tiny nub, his cock sliding in and out of me at the same tantalizing rhythm.

"You like that, *kotenok*?" he purrs by my ear, his low voice making my stomach flutter.

"Yes!" I gasp, my clit twitching as my walls tighten around his shaft.

Dimitri groans, his thrusts growing steadily more adamant, each penetration deep and fulfilling.

"What do you want, Camille?" he asks, his voice hoarse with the intensity of his need. And my name on his lips fills me with a deep, consuming satisfaction.

"I want you to make love to me all night," I plead. "Oh God, I want you to come inside me."

He hums appreciatively, his fingers circling more quickly as he increases the pressure on my clit. I shiver violently, as fiery lust devours my body.

"I'll fill you so full of cum you're dripping," he promises, his voice dark and enticing.

"Oh God, please, please, please," I beg, my clit throbbing as my arousal spikes.

"Say my name, *kotenok*," he commands, making me whimper with anticipation.

"Please, Dimitri," I plead.

One arm wrapping firmly around my waist, he holds me close as he drives into my G-spot and circles my clit adamantly. The soft scrape of rock across my hard nipples stimulates me further, and when his teeth close gently on the lobe of my ear, I'm a goner.

Crying out, I shove forcefully back onto his cock as I come hard, my walls gripping euphorically, my clit spasming with the intensity of my release. And I shudder as I feel hot cum burst deep inside my depths as Dimitri comes with me.

Giddy excitement washes through me, knowing this is the kind of pleasure I get to experience for the rest of my life. The intense satisfaction of having a man who makes me come, and finds his own release by giving me such intense ecstasy.

The depth of our connection overwhelms me, the way he understands my body without even trying. Dimitri is a man in full; a lover I can hardly believe I get to claim as my own.

And it fills me with bone-deep contentment that he and I are going to make a family together. As we both come down from the high of our simultaneous climax, he eases out of me, and I turn to face him.

"I hope you're ready for a big family because I love making babies with you," I murmur looking up at him playfully.

"We can have as many as you want," he promises, his eyes lighting with a loving warmth.

And as he pulls me close against his chest, his lips finding mine in a passionate kiss, I'm overjoyed that this is my forever. The road to happiness might have been a twisting, turning one with an abundance of peril in our path. But with Dimitri by my side, nothing feels unachievable.

With him, I think happily ever after might be more than just a fairy tale.

EPILOGUE

Dimitri

"I now pronounce you man and wife. You may kiss your bride," the officiant says, and before the word *bride* has left his mouth, my arms are around Camille as I lean her back to give her a deep and passionate kiss.

She squeals, her hands gripping my arms like a vise, and I know I'll get a scolding later for startling her when the baby's due to come any day now. It was a risk to put the wedding so close to when the baby might come, but Camille really wanted to be married before our little girl arrived.

I'm more than happy to call her my wife and the quiet ceremony wasn't too challenging to put together in less than nine months. But the venue Camille wanted, the Conservatory of Flowers in Golden Gate Park, only had a few dates available on such short notice—especially considering the need to hold the March wedding inside.

Boisterous cheers come from the hundred or so guests who fill the pavilion, and Camille melts against me, her arms wrapping around my neck as she embraces the flirtatious kiss.

And when I bring her back onto her feet, breaking our kiss, her eyes are sparkling, her breath-taking smile so big it reveals all her pearly-white teeth.

"It's my pleasure to introduce to you for the very first time, Mr. and Mrs. Dimitri Federov!" our officiant says, his voice jubilant as we turn to face our gathered family and friends.

Camille's restaurant family whoops and hollers, her friend Hannah beaming from the front row, representing the closest of her living family.

On my side of the aisle, my mom beams at me, her eyes glistening with unshed tears. Next to her, Alexei sticks his fingers in his mouth to release an ear-splitting wolf whistle, and Maksim throws him a dirty look as Camille breaks into giddy laughter.

Raising our hands in the air, I give the gathered witnesses one last chance to cheer before I walk Camille back down the aisle toward the pavilion doors.

"In case anyone didn't get the memo, the reception will be starting in an hour at Le Fleur's new location on Pier 39," our receptionist adds as we make our exit.

I guide Camille to my Lamborghini sitting out front, the words *Just Married* spray-painted on the back window and decorative cans tied to my poor car's bumper.

"Alexei?" she guesses, taking in the sight.

"How'd you guess?" I growl.

"I think I like his sense of humor," she says and giggles as I give her a thunderous scowl.

But it only lasts a moment because this day is too special to let anything bring me down. I'm a husband and a soon-to-be father with two of the most precious girls a man could ask for.

I can't wait to meet little Hailey, and in the meantime, I plan on spending a very wonderful wedding night with her mother.

Helping Camille into the passenger seat, I wait until she's settled before I close the door for her and make my way around to the driver's side.

I'm rather excited about the reception because this will also be the first time Camille sees the finished product of Le Fleur. It's not set to open for another three months—when she's ready to go back to work.

But rather than rebuilding in the tiny spot she occupied because that was where she could afford, I chose to supplement her insurance payout so she could have her restaurant in her dream location, right along Fisherman's Wharf.

To top it off, I had her pick out all the decor while I managed the contractors—so while she knows what Le Fleur is supposed to look like, she hasn't seen it since the old floor plan got gutted to make way for her vision.

"You ready?" I ask as I park in front of the pier.

"Yes." She smiles at me, radiant in her happiness, and I lean across the console to steal a kiss.

Then I climb out and come around the car to help her out. She's so adorably round in her pregnancy that it takes effort to guide her safely from the low seat, and I think I might have to change out my sporty car for something that will suit a family better. Not that Camille has complained a single time.

Her flowing white gown is simple and elegant, the cap sleeves and sweetheart neckline showing off her mouth-watering breasts in gauzy beaded fabric. But the skirt is made of soft material that hugs her baby bump, calling attention to her pregnancy rather than trying to hide it but still allowing her to be comfortable.

I think relinquishing her heels for a pair of bedazzled tennis shoes was Camille's only hard loss, but with the pregnancy, it became a necessity. And I'm grateful she has good shoes as I lead her around the front building to the sky-blue one with a floral sign and the cursive script marking it Le Fleur.

Eyes tearing as she takes in the sign for the first time, Camille looks up at her dream restaurant in wonder. "I love it," she breathes.

"Just wait until you get inside," I urge, pressing a kiss to her temple.

With shaking fingers, she accepts the key I hold out to her and unlocks the frosted glass doors. I pull one open as she does the other, stepping into the atrium that will limit the amount of cold air that might enter the restaurant.

Unlocking the second set of solid wood doors, Camille throws them wide and gasps at the restaurant's interior. Adorned with extravagant, curling chandeliers that look like lace dripping with diamonds, the exposed-beam room glimmers with romantic yellow light.

Matching sconces occupy the walls over each booth, and curving staircases lead up to the second floor, where an open balcony looks out across the lower dining room. The rustic wood chairs and tables are reminiscent of a French countryside cottage, and the green vines that wind around the solid wood beams give the space an almost fairy-tale forest atmosphere.

It's already set for the reception, the tables decked out with fine silver and delicate china.

The kitchen, which runs along the length of the back, is exposed to the dining room with a half wall showcasing the stainless steel appliances. The caterers already bustle in the space, putting the final touches on the dinner for our wedding guests.

A lone sweetheart table sits next to the half wall, keeping us slightly separate from our guests.

"Oh, Dimitri, it's perfect. I don't think I've ever seen anything so magical," Camille breathes, her eyes scanning slowly around the open space to take in its grandeur.

"I'm glad you like it. It's all yours, though. This is your vision, your business, your dream. I only hired out the manual labor," I say, giving her a wink.

"I love you," she breathes, turning to wrap her arms around my neck and kiss me.

"I love you too," I murmur, pressing my forehead to hers.

"Get a room" Alexei teases, bursting through the door with verve.

Camille laughs, giving me another quick peck before she turns to accept his congratulatory hug. And moments later, our guests trickle in, each giving us warm congratulations before they make their way to the tables.

At last, everyone is seated and the serving staff is more than on top of it as our guests are each supplied with a glass of champagne. Camille and I make our way to the sweetheart table, where I raise a glass as she finds sparkling cider in hers.

"To my incredible wife," I say, "and to all the family and friends who could celebrate our union today. I never knew I was missing part of my soul until I found Camille, and now I can't imagine how I lived without her."

"*Za zdaróvye!*" my brothers call in unison, and the rest of our guests follow suit, attempting the Russian toast with verve.

As we settle in at the table, the food starts to come from the kitchen, beginning with salad as the servers rush to distribute the first course.

"I think this is officially the happiest day of my life," Camille says warmly, her smile contagious. "I only wish my dad could see me today."

A hint of sadness tinges her tone, and I take her hand in mine, bringing her knuckles to my lips.

"I wish I could have met the man who raised someone as special as you."

Tears shimmer in Camille's eyes, but she releases a soft laugh. "You know, that's the first place you ever kissed me," she observes.

Repeating the action, I chuckle with her. "That's how I won your heart, right?"

"You certainly got my attention," she concedes.

Then she gasps, her eyes flying wide in shock, like she's only just remembered something.

"What?" I ask, amused.

"Dimitri, I... I think my water just broke," she breathes, her cheeks flushing.

"What, now?" I ask, my eyebrows raising.

"Yes, like right now."

Excitement jolts through me as that means the baby's on its way. "Okay, well then, let's get you to the hospital."

Camille pales, and her fingers tighten around mine as her free hand splays on the table, her eyes growing wide.

"What's wrong?"

"Whoa, God, yes definitely going into labor," she confirms, her voice tense with what I can only assume is her first contraction.

And in an instant, my cool is gone. Rising from my chair, I come around to help her out of hers.

"Is it time?" Hannah asks, by my side an instant later.

"Uh-huh." Camille nods jerkily.

"I'll get your go bag and meet you at the hospital?" she suggests.

"Agreed." Raising my voice as we make our way through the sea of tables, I say, "Sorry, everyone. Enjoy the dinner and dancing. We're off to have a baby."

Cheers follow us as Hannah and I give Camille a double-door exit, and then I'm rushing her to the car as Camille's friend makes a beeline in the other direction. Leaning heavily on my arms, Camille grips me with fright, her breathing erratic.

"Slow, steady breaths, remember?" I coach.

"Right," she agrees, nearly hyperventilating.

"You'll be okay. I'm right here," I promise, wrapping an arm around her as I help her into the car.

"Mmmm," she moans, biting her lips as another contraction hits her.

"Breathe, love," I command, cupping her cheek and stroking it gently.

This time, she does as I say, breathing in through her nose and releasing the air through her lips. She does it a second time, and her shoulders begin to relax as her eyes find me with relief.

"Better?"

She nods, and I give her chin a light pinch before I step back and close her door.

This is it. I can't believe it's happening. My heart pounds with excitement as I race around the car to the driver's seat. Once I put the car in gear, my eyes intent on the road as I head toward the hospital, Camille's delicate hand finds mine.

I grasp her fingers reassuringly and press them to my lips once more.

And when our eyes meet for a moment, I can see the same elation I feel reflected in her blue gaze. This is the first day of our grand adventure together.

And I can't wait.

EXTENDED EPILOGUE

Alexei

I hate ballet—or so I thought—but I endure it because my mother loves it so much, and it's a sin for Russians not to like something so deeply rooted in our traditions.

But the principal ballerina of tonight's performance has me spellbound. I've never seen someone move with such otherworldly grace. Her perfect body seemed to float across the stage, capturing my attention and ripping me from my typical state of boredom.

It's agony as she takes a final fluid bow and the curtain falls, stealing her from my view.

"That was simply breathtaking," my mother says, her voice warbling on the brink of tears from the moving performance.

"Yeah," I breathe, my eyes lingering on the stage as my muscles tense.

"You look like you're about to be sick there, brother," Maksim observes dryly from his seat next to mine.

He and his fiancée, Symphony, joined us at the ballet tonight. But not Dimitri and Camille. With a new baby at home, they haven't had much time or energy to come out for a performance like this. Though

I would have preferred it if Camille could have come rather than my older brother's fiancée. She puts my teeth on edge.

"You know what? Maybe I am," I state distractedly, rising from my chair to push past my brother and his fiancée without another word of explanation.

But I'm on a mission to find her.

The ballerina.

Making my way toward the back of the house, I know I'm going to have to get by security. But I don't care. I have to meet her. To learn her name.

"Sorry, no audience members backstage," a burly security guard confirms, holding up a hand as I reach the ramp leading to the dressing rooms.

"Right, of course. But I'm not an audience member," I bluff quickly. "I'm actually part of the security team."

"Really?" he asks, his eyebrows raising in surprise. But when he scans my broad shoulders and fit physique, he seems more inclined to believe my story.

"Oh yeah, I—"

"Alexei?" Sergei, one of my new recruits, steps out from a door just down the hall and approaches.

"You know this guy, Serg?" the other security guard asks, turning to him.

"Oh yeah. He runs one of the top security firms in San Fran. You here on business?" he asks, turning back to me.

"Of a sort. I need to speak with the prima…"

"Yeah, of course. Her dressing room's down at the end of the hall. On the left."

The other security guard throws him a sharp look but says nothing.

Poor Sergei. I know I'm taking advantage of our working relationship, but nothing's going to stop me from meeting this girl. And it's enough to get me past the guard who otherwise would have made my life impossible.

Stepping sideways between them, I head straight for the end of the hall and find the title *Principal* marking the dressing room door. Reining in my impulsive urge to burst into her dressing room, I take a deep breath and knock.

"Come in," comes the muffled reply, her Russian-accented voice authoritative.

I do so, stepping through the door and closing it behind me a moment later.

"You can just leave them on the—" The raven-haired beauty cuts herself off with a gasp as she spots me in the mirror, and she whirls.

Still in full makeup, she wears her hair in a high and tight bun that accentuates her prominent cheekbones. She's already started to undress, and my body responds eagerly to the sight of her bare shoulders and the cleavage that forms between her breasts as she pulls her costume up to cover herself.

She looks livid in an instant. Her silver-and-black face paint, which mimics the eyes of a swan, makes her emerald eyes look all the more fierce as they spark. "What are you doing in here? I thought you were one of the girls delivering flowers. You're not supposed to be here. Get out!" she barks.

"I'm sorry, but I can't do that. Not until I know your name."

"You think you can just barge into my dressing room, demanding my name, and expect me to give it to you?" She tips her sharp chin defiantly, holding it high with impressive dignity, though she's clearly infuriated by my presumption.

"Actually, I was hoping you might say yes to a date," I press, taking a slow step toward her.

She doesn't miss a thing, her eyes shifting to my feet to watch their movement before flashing back up to my face. "I don't date strange men who enter my dressing room unannounced," she says, her voice icy.

"Alexei Federov," I offer casually, flashing her a winning smile. "And you are...?"

"Nadia... Lukyan," she says coldly after a moment's hesitation. Her sharp eyes remain watchful.

How very Russian. "See? Now we're no longer strangers," I quip.

And to my delight, she laughs. The sound is soft and melodic, a stark contradiction to her hard, abrupt demeanor. Her thin yet athletic shoulders drop as she relaxes, signaling that I'm winning her over in spite of her attitude.

"Now that we're properly acquainted, will you let me take you on a date?" I take another tentative step forward.

"No," she says, rejecting me a second time, though this time, a smile plays at the corner of her full, heart-shaped lips.

"You know, most girls would sell their souls for a date with me," I point out, wearing her down with persistence as I slowly close the distance between us.

"Well, I'm not like most girls," she says defiantly, adjusting her arms over her breasts as she keeps them masterfully covered.

"I can see that," I acknowledge appreciatively, openly admiring her perfection.

She bristles slightly, her lips pursing, but I can see the glint of satisfaction in her proud gaze. "Well, perhaps if you want a yes, you should go try one of those other girls because my answer is still no."

"What will it take to get you to go out with me?" I stop my approach just a few feet from her, lingering on the edge of her personal space.

Nadia stands her ground, not a sliver of fear in her bearing, though my proximity forces her to look up at my face. She narrows her eyes in a silent warning. "A lot more than the effort you've put in," she states, and though her voice is sharp, I can see the glint of laughter in her eyes.

She's enjoying the banter.

She might be telling me no, but her resistance is flirtatious enough that I sense a game forming between us. One in which I'll have to break down her defenses if I want to reap my reward. When I hook a finger under her chin and bring my lips within inches of hers, electric tension crackles between us.

But the fiery girl doesn't even flinch.

"Very well, Nadia Lukyan," I murmur, peering deep into her

striking green eyes. "I accept your challenge. But I promise you'll give in to me eventually."

"In your dreams," she breathes, her voice low and sensual, her smug smile daring me to do my worst.

Continue reading Nadia and Alexei's story here.

BOSS DADDIES (PREVIEW)

DESCRIPTION

It was meant to be a swimwear modeling job.... But now my three bosses have me on my knees asking for more.

One of them is my baby's daddy... and *he has no idea.*

What was I thinking, accepting a modeling job in a freaking bikini? I *used* to be a model, but my life is so different now... I'm a single mom trying to make ends meet when they hire me.

There's **Harper**, the tall, tattooed, serious and gorgeous billionaire who wants to change the world.

Player **Desi** is the confident, handsome stylist on set, teasing me relentlessly and making me want more...

And there's also quiet **Silver**, the irresistible shy photographer for the shoot.

I may be wrong... but I think they all want *me*.

I know not to mix business with pleasure. My main worry is making enough to pay for my daughter, but my money worries are soon erased as the three fashionable billionaires shower me and my little girl with expensive gifts.

Temptations arise at every opportunity and I succumb to my irresistible bosses... but soon, the fire between us sparks hotter, and I end up with a baby in my belly...

And no idea whose it is.

1

LUNA

"I'm sorry but I just don't believe you."

The words washed over me like the first burst of a cold shower on a hot summer's day. It took all of my self-restraint to keep the smile on my face as the growing warmth from the cup in my hand teetered towards painful.

"I can assure you," I replied as sweetly as I could manage, "I definitely used oat milk."

"I was watching you," the customer replied, "and I didn't see you use that oat carton at *all*." The lilt in her voice matched the sharp way she pointed a manicured blue-tipped finger at me. The tart disbelief in her tone was abundant and as we stared each other down, I knew I didn't have a chance in hell of winning this argument. I could have made this drink right in front of her salmon-spectacle-clad eyes and it wouldn't have been good enough. Judging by the purse of her lips and the blonde bob of her hair, I was pretty sure she was simply spoiling for an argument.

"Ma'am, as you can see, we're really busy today and I'm having to make multiple drinks at the same time—"

"That's not my problem!" She cut in with such glee that I had to fight the reflexive urge to toss the cup at her and storm away.

"I understand that, I'm just trying to explain that you've seen me making other drinks—"

"I don't care," she interrupted again. Her raised voice caused several seated patrons to glance up from their various drinks and meals to check out the commotion. Fuck. The muscles in my face were already aching from my forced smile and keeping that up with an audience was even harder.

"I *want* another coffee. Made correctly this time." Her beady eyes narrowed behind her glasses, and for a few seconds, I entertained the rather abrupt intrusive thought of dragging her over the counter and giving her a close-up view of the difference between our milk cartons.

That fantasy would be my only retribution today.

"Right away, ma'am."

I didn't miss the victorious smirk that curved across her lips as I turned away, and the image burned into my mind as I discarded the oat latte—and it *was* oat, we may be busy but I made that drink correctly—and started on another. Unsatisfied groans about the extended wait rose up from the queue that had formed behind Mrs. Oat Milk during her little rant. The sound sent a wave of burning, embarrassed heat across the back of my neck and down my spine.

Spending every available hour working my fingers to the bone serving coffee and cake to Chicago's business elite was not how I wanted to spend my days, but it was a job. A job I'd poured my heart and soul into for the past five years just to make ends meet. Yet, every time I came face-to-face with someone like Mrs. Oat Milk—someone who took pleasure in making the jobs of service workers that much more difficult for their own twisted pleasure—I contemplated my survival rate if I just quit and lived on instant noodles until the end of my days.

A sweet, selfish fantasy that didn't take into account my adorable daughter, Hazel, and her hatred of noodles. The desire for something better burned hotter with each passing day.

Coffee remade, I turned back to the customer and offered her the drink with the same fake service smile fixed upon my face. She sniffed and opened her sleek black purse. That thing likely cost more than my entire month's wages.

"You could learn a thing or two from this," she said stiffly. "If you'd done the job correctly the first time then we all wouldn't have had to stand around waiting for you to fix your mistake. It's coffee, how hard can it be?" A tinkling laugh followed her words, a sweet sound that was so detached from the smarminess of her words.

I cast a quick eye down the queue with as much apology as I could muster in my eyes, but there wasn't a sympathetic gaze to be found. Of course not, these people were all the same. Running around the world with their fancy jobs, fancy clothes, and not even five minutes to spare standing in a queue.

"You ought to be more careful," the woman continued and the embarrassed heat from earlier was slowly morphing into anger mixed with tension in my chest. "I'm doing you a favor, coming to drink here instead of at the office. Without people like us, dinky little coffee places like this would go out of business. And you think it's okay to try and poison me with *dairy*?"

She tossed a few coins onto the counter so hard that one bounced against the hard surface before it rolled off the edge and clattered somewhere on the floor.

"Well, I'm not picking that up." Her beady eyes narrowed at me once more and the building anger within my chest snapped. My smile vanished.

"Without people like *you*—"

"Luna!" A warm, cheery voice tinged with the slightest hint of a French accent cut right through the wick of my explosive response and a warm hand landed on my shoulder.

I turned to see Cerise, my best friend and suffering co-worker by my side. Before I could react, she had taken the coffee from my hand and set it on the counter.

"Here's your drink, have a lovely day!" she called cheerily as her hand hooked around my elbow and dragged me a few feet away from the service counter.

"Cerise..." I began and my chest clenched like the snap of a rubber band as the anger I almost released on that awful woman stalled with nowhere to go.

"Luna," Cerise warned softly, "I know. Awful people with awful requests, but if you had yelled at her, there's no way Dickie would still let you off early. I swear, your temper runs as hot as your hair!"

Just like that, a small laugh bubbled in my chest and broke through the tension of frustration. Cerise was, of course, referring to my flaming auburn hair. At the mention of Dickie, I sought out the clock on the wall and groaned.

"Shit..." Cerise was right. It had taken me days to sweet talk my boss, Dickie, into letting me off early today to coincide with my daughter getting an early release from pre-school. If I was late and my mother found out, I'd never hear the end of it.

"Take five minutes. I'll handle this." Cerise patted my elbow and swept past me before I could even respond. Her cheery voice filled the cafe as she began apologizing for the wait and rapidly taking orders from the disgruntled queue. I took my leave and darted through the gray double doors into the back of the cafe.

Cerise always had my back, ever since she'd stumbled upon me sobbing amongst the garbage cans not two weeks after I'd started working here. She'd been so kind as I'd poured my heart out about not knowing how I was going to afford diapers after Dickie had shot me down about an advance on my wages. The next day, I'd come into work and she had left a baby care package outside my locker with all the essentials. I'd never been more grateful for such a kind act, and from then on we were best friends.

I stumbled into the toilet, locked the door behind me, and sank down onto the chilled toilet seat with a groan. Already my heart was beginning to slow without the crowded bustle of the cafe. I took a few deep breaths and the tension that burned like static in my chest started to ease.

Fuck.

I had almost lost my cool and something like that could easily have cost me my job. Losing this would turn the blogging site I freelanced for into my sole income and that was definitely not enough to live on.

"Come on Luna," I sighed, "keep it together."

It was just a shitty customer. Another hour and I would be out of here. I dug around in my apron and pulled out my phone. If I had any chance of making it to the school on time, I would need to call an Uber, an expense I was loath to create but in the interest of getting to Hazel before school finished, it was essential. I flicked through to the Uber app, added my details and request, then tapped on my emails to wait for the booking confirmation. Upon opening my inbox, however, something new caught my eye.

New Leaf

A pulse of confusion shot through my gut as I opened the email.

Dear Miss Luna Quinn,

I hope this email reaches you well. Please forgive my forwardness but I am writing to you in regard to a modeling opportunity that I believe will be extremely lucrative for us both. I came across your account on Instagram and I was blown away by your pictures.

If you haven't heard of us, my name is Harper Saunders. I am the Lead Designer and co-owner of New Leaf. We are a luxury fashion brand that specializes in lingerie, swimwear, and more for those needing a little boost to their confidence after physical alterations. Each year we put together several calendars for charity. These calendars showcase each of the designs of that year. If you haven't seen us around in stores, I've included a few links in this email for you to take a look at.

I understand that this may seem rather presumptuous but I think your style and confidence would really enhance the New Leaf brand. If you are interested, I would like to offer you an interview at our downtown office to discuss this opportunity more.

The opportunity includes a three-week all-expenses paid trip to one of our beachside shooting locations as well as compensation for any disruption this may have to your regular life. Childcare is included and you will be paid a total of $1,000,000 upon completion of the calendar.

I've included my details below and I very much look forward to hearing from you.

Best wishes,
Harper Saunders
CEO, New Leaf

A million dollars?! This was a joke, right? I read the email several times, unable to comprehend what I was reading. Harper Saunders, *the* Harper Saunders had emailed me? The billionaire CEO of one of the most famous fashion brands in the entire *world* had emailed me? No. No way. This had to be fake.

Despite my doubts, I quickly checked the email and all the attached information against what was on the New Leaf company website and it matched. It was *real*?

I had been following New Leaf on all their socials ever since I stumbled upon one of their charity showcases not long after Hazel had been born. I was drawn to them immediately as they had been showcasing lingerie and underwear for mothers who no longer felt sexy after going through such a powerful change to their bodies. A few of their photographs had even become the inspiration for some of my own designs.

Before Hazel, amateur modeling was my passion but pregnancy had definitely hindered those plans. I had been working to rebuild that confidence on my Instagram. With a modest following, I couldn't complain, but the thought of those pictures catching the eye of Harper Saunders?

"No fucking way," I breathed out and returned to the email, reading it over again and again. The amount glared back out at me.

One million dollars.

An email like that direct from a billionaire CEO... there had to be a catch. Men as rich as him surely had assistants for this sort of thing, right?

However, no matter how many times I checked, the information remained the same and everything provided looked legit.

Was I dreaming? I had to be. This was too good to be true.

"Luna!" A sharp rap of knuckles against the bathroom door made me jump, dragging me back down to reality, and yet even as my boss's dull tones drifted through the door, the email remained on my phone staring up at me.

"Luna! You've been pissing for ten minutes, get the fuck back to work!"

Suddenly, the prospect of going back out there to face my overly handsy boss and a cafe full of people much richer than me was exhausting and I glanced back down at the email. The temptation was rising.

"Luna!" My manager knocked rapidly on the door again.

"I'm coming!" I called back as sweetly as I could. I still needed him on my side in order to get out of here early. As I flushed the toilet, I shoved my phone back into my pocket but the email was crystal clear in my mind's eye.

It was just an interview, right?

I opened the toilet door and came face-to-face with my boss and his stubbled jowls broke into a toothy smile when he caught my eye.

"About damn time, I don't pay you women to fuss about in there."

"Sorry, Dickie." I gave him my sweetest smile and slipped past him, narrowly avoiding the usual pat on the ass he liked to give anything with a skirt.

It was just an interview... and the prospect of anything that wasn't this place was *exciting* despite my disbelief.

If I said yes... what was the worst that could happen?

2

LUNA

"An' Mrs. Walker said, she said I wasn't allowed in the sand pit but—but Adrian was in the sand pit and I wanted to be too!" The grumpy way my daughter stamped her feet next to me as she talked made it difficult to hide my smile, even as she turned her bright face up at me complete with a furrowed brow and pursed lips.

"I'm sorry honey," I replied, keeping the amusement out of my voice. "That doesn't sound very fair at all."

"Yup!" Hazel stated matter-of-factly. "But it's okay 'cause I went on the swings with Hailey and we didn't let Adrian on." Just like that, the pout changed into a devilish grin and Hazel burst out laughing as if she had just revealed to me the intricate details of some diabolical plan. It was impossible to hold in my own laughter then and I squeezed her hand lightly. I certainly wasn't going to get involved in the playground disputes of five-year-olds, but knowing Hazel had enough of a spark to defend herself definitely brought me comfort.

The warm afternoon air made the walk home pleasant, and I happily listened to Hazel as she recounted the wild and exciting things that happened that day. Maisie's water bottle exploded at break time and *another* marker was missing from the bucket but

Hazel didn't care because it wasn't the blue one she loved so much. All these little details were things I was soaking up as we strolled, and it was difficult to imagine how my life could have been anything other than this.

Six years ago, I was a single, struggling college student and I had the world at my feet to make all the bad choices and crazy mistakes people are supposed to make at twenty-one. Now I had a five-year-old and the opportunities at my feet were vastly different... and limited. I wouldn't change it for the world though, not with how much light and life Hazel has brought to me. But because of my limited options, the offer from New Leaf looked all the more tantalizing.

I kept an ear on Hazel and her story as we turned the corner towards the park and our apartment building came into view, while the other half of my mind replayed Harper's email over and over. *One million dollars.* What a mind-blowing amount of money. It would more than pay for everything I needed, and that kind of cash would open up a world of prospects to Hazel that I wouldn't be able to offer her on my own. That was the main attraction here and the moment I realized that, the harder it was to try and wave the offer from my mind.

Three weeks posing for a calendar and we would be set. No more shitty jobs, no more pervy bosses, and getting yelled at by obnoxious know-it-all customers. Hazel could have all the markers in the world and then some, and I could give her everything I never had. At the end of my shift, I had sent off a quick reply stating my interest and asking when he would like the interview. To my surprise, Harper had replied almost instantly stating that he was happy to accommodate me and my schedule, but that it would need to be before the end of the weekend as he was only in the city for a few more days.

Knowing my schedule, I had only *one* window of free time and that was Saturday afternoon. The only problem was, I couldn't bring Hazel to the interview which meant I would need to find a babysitter.

Only one person I knew would be free and it was the one person I didn't want to ask.

My own mother.

"Mommy!" Hazel's demanding tones pulled me from my thoughts, and I glanced down to see her beaming up to me.

"Yes, sweetie?"

"Look!" Hazel thrust her free hand, curled into a small fist, right towards me and I paused to lean down.

"What is it?"

Hazel opened her fist and to my horror, revealed a small spider she had snatched from the passing hedge. I recoiled immediately with a yelp and Hazel fell into peals of giggles.

"Hazel!"

"It's just a spider Mommy, you're so silly." Hazel gave her new friend all her attention as we resumed walking, and I fought the curl of repulsion that shot through my gut. Ever since a wildlife expert had dropped by her pre-school to teach the children about animals and insects in the wild, Hazel had become obsessed with anything with 8 legs. God, what I wouldn't give for this obsession to pass swiftly.

"Well, make sure you drop her off before we get home," I said stiffly, clearing my throat and keeping a keen eye on the spider.

"I wanna keep her!" Hazel exclaimed, and when she lifted her face to meet mine, that stubborn pout was back.

"You can't keep her. She probably has lots of babies that need her, you learned about that right? She has lots of little spiders to take care of so it wouldn't be fair to take her all the way home." I had no idea if that was true, but it seemed to work as Hazel gave a slow, knowing nod.

"Of course," she said seriously, and I had to contain my smile as she crouched down on the ground and let the spider scuttle away from her palm. "Goodbye."

The rest of the walk home was spider free, thankfully, and it didn't take long to get Hazel situated and settled as I started to make lunch. The fridge was a little light, so I settled on whipping up a chicken salad while Hazel sat at the counter with her activity book and several coloring pencils spread out before her.

"What did you do today, Mommy?" Hazel asked. Her voice was

slightly muffled by how far she had hunched over her book to color a particularly vibrant elephant. The question made me smile though, warmth settling in my heart as I chopped up the lettuce. I had been working hard at making sure we communicated our days with each other so I could keep track of how Hazel was feeling and progressing. As a result, she started asking the same of me and I would respond in kind.

"Well, I worked really hard, and it was really busy," I explained, giving her an abridged version of my day. "I did have to face down a really grumpy witch though."

Hazel's head snapped up, her eyes wide. "A witch?!"

"Oh yes," I nodded seriously, tossing the lettuce into a bowl. "She was very grumpy and in need of some very specific potions."

"Did she have warts?" Hazel asked, her eyes still saucers.

"Yup. And only one tooth."

"Ewww!"

"It was very scary," I continued, "but I was saved by Auntie Cerise, and we were able to send that witch on her way."

"Wow," Hazel breathed out, then she quickly returned to her drawing. "I'm happy Cerise was there."

"Me too," I murmured, casting a warm eye over Hazel. The salad was completed with some chopped-up cucumber and tomatoes, as well as some slices from a somewhat sad-looking yellow pepper, but before I could tend to the chicken, the tune of my phone ringing filled the kitchen. I glanced over my shoulder at the screen and my heart immediately sank into my stomach as 'Maggie Quinn' blinked back at me.

Of course, she would answer my text with a phone call.

My relationship with my mother was strained at best. She had me at sixteen, and I did occasionally feel pulses of sympathy as to how scary that must have been for her. That sympathy was usually quickly drowned out by the memories of her absences in my life growing up, or the multiple men that visited like a constant revolving door. I had planned to cut her out of my life, not that she had much of a presence to begin with, but she had flourished with enthusiasm when Hazel was born as if she saw Hazel as *her* chance to do things right a second time.

I glanced at Hazel to check on her, then I answered the call and stepped a few feet away.

"Maggie."

"What exactly are you planning on getting up to on Saturday that you can't spend time with your own daughter?" My mother's dry, demanding voice filled me with dread each time I heard it, and this was no different.

"No, 'Hi, hello, how was your day?'" I asked.

"Don't give me that," she snorted. "I haven't heard from you in weeks and now you need me to babysit?"

The urge to hang up on her rose like vomit, but unfortunately, she was my only hope as Cerise had been taking all the weekend shifts to allow me time at home with Hazel. I had to play it nice.

"Well, if you must know, I have an important job interview and it's an amazing opportunity. It's too good for me to pass up, but it came up on short notice so I thought you would like to spend some time with your granddaughter," I explained carefully.

"A job interview, on a Saturday?" My mother's three-pack-a-day habit had added a huskiness to her tone that grated against my very soul. "Don't be ridiculous. What are you really up to? Why do you need another job interview, did you get fired? I'm not surprised."

"No, I didn't get fired," I snapped back. Out of the corner of my eye, I caught Hazel lifting her head and quickly reined in my frustration. "If I get this new job though, I would be able to quit the cafe. It would mean more regular hours too and better pay, both of which are good for Hazel don't you think?"

"If you moved back home with me and accepted that job at the library like I *told* you to do, you wouldn't need to be running around willy-nilly to interviews, and Hazel would be cared for. When was the last time you even bought her some new clothes?" Maggie replied shortly.

"There isn't enough money in the world that could persuade me to move back in with you," I grumbled. Not even a million dollars. As

Maggie's voice hitched up in anger, I moved the phone away from my ear and called loudly to Hazel, loud enough that my mother would still hear me at least.

"Hazel! Do you want to spend Saturday with Grandma? You haven't seen her in *ages* have you?"

"Grandma!" Hazel yelled, and she clapped her hands together. "Yay!" As much dislike as I had for my own mother, she had always doted on Hazel, and I was not going to be the one that ruined that. Maggie would ruin it in her own way, I was sure.

"See?" I pressed the phone back to my ear, having missed whatever tirade my mother had sent my way. "Hazel is excited to see you, and you wouldn't want to disappoint her, would you?"

Maggie muttered under her breath, words I couldn't decipher but didn't really care.

"Fine," she replied. "I'll see you on Saturday but if you think—"

I hung up before I could hear any more. As much as I could hold my ground against her, she still made me feel sick to my stomach even after all these years. A childhood of neglect and absence did that.

I turned back to the chicken and tried to shake the sickly, anxious feeling that had settled in my gut as Hazel broke out into a rough rendition of the wheels on the bus. It was a nice distraction as I set the chicken down on the pan, then quickly sent an email off to Harper asking if Saturday afternoon would be good for an interview.

It was only after I sent it that I realized I should have confirmed with him *before* making plans with my mother, but it was too late now.

No sooner had I set my phone down than it pinged with an immediate response, and my heart jumped slightly in my chest. I tapped with one hand as I flipped the chicken with the other.

Dear Luna,

Saturday afternoon is perfect. I'm eager to get into discussions with you as I think you will find this to be a very exciting opportunity. I have included the address and directions below; but if you need travel assistance, please let me know, and I can send a driver.

See you then.
Best wishes,
Harper Saunders
CEO, New Leaf

He would send a *car?* To be expected of billionaires I suppose, but the prospect still excited me a fraction, soothing the remaining anxieties from talking to my mother. The chicken sizzled softly, Hazel sang louder, and my heart skipped a beat.

Stuff like this didn't happen to people like me but I couldn't help but feel that if I played my cards right, maybe this could be the start of something *amazing*.

End of preview. Continue reading this sizzling hot, reverse harem romance here.

Printed in Great Britain
by Amazon